W9-CJF-236

FOX GIRL

VIKING

FOX GIRL

NORA OKJA KELLER

VIKING

Published by the Penguin Group

Penguin Putnam Inc., 375 Hudson Street, New York, New York 10014, U.S.A.

Penguin Books Ltd, 80 Strand, London WC2R 0RL, England

Penguin Books Australia Ltd, 250 Camberwell Road, Camberwell, Victoria 3124,
    Australia

Penguin Books Canada Ltd, 10 Alcorn Avenue,
    Toronto, Ontario, Canada M4V 3B2

Penguin Books (N.Z.) Ltd, Cnr Rosedale and Airborne Roads, Albany,
    Auckland, New Zealand

Penguin Books Ltd, Registered Offices:
Harmondsworth, Middlesex, England

First published in 2002 by Viking Penguin, a member of Penguin Putnam Inc.

10   9   8   7   6   5   4   3   2   1

PUBLISHER'S NOTE

This is a work of fiction. Names, characters, places, and incidents either are the product of the author's imagination or are used fictitiously, and any resemblance to actual persons, living or dead, business establishments, events, or locales is entirely coincidental.

LIBRARY OF CONGRESS CATALOGING IN PUBLICATION DATA

Keller, Nora Okja.
    Fox girl / by Nora Okja Keller.
        p.   cm.
    ISBN 0-670-03073-2
        1. Korea—Fiction. I. Title.
    PS3561.E38574 F68 2002
    813'.54—dc21   2001046803

This book is printed on acid-free paper. ∞

Printed in the United States of America
Set in Bembo, with Sundance and InfoOffice display, and Europa Arabesque ornaments
Designed by Carla Bolte

For Tae Kathleen and Sunhi Willa

I love you both higher than the sky,
more than the stars upon stars
in the universe

My deepest thanks to the following people:

My sisters Myung Ja Dawn, Lisa, and Lynn and brother Keum Sik for the stories and memories that form our childhoods and friendships we've built as adults.

My mother, Tae Im Beane, for nurturing her grandchildren, feeding their minds with Korean ghost stories and their bellies with mandoo and musubis. Your help made it easier for me to finish this one.

My father, Robert Cobb, who taught me to love the written word.

Diane Lee and Grace Yoon Kyung Lee for "Camp Arirang," J. T. Takagi and Hye Jung Park for "The Women Outside," and Kathy Moon for their extensive research of American camp-towns in Korea. Like shamans, you see the invisible.

Jeff Johnson, Pete Thompson, and Katherine Loo for allowing me to pester them with questions about immigration history, law, and loopholes. I owe you all another lunch, or ten.

Judge Patrick O'Connor and Sergeant Robert Rawlins and Officer Jesse Victorino of the Honolulu Police Department for answering my nitty-gritty legal questions and escorting me through booking and into the jail cell. The ending has changed, but I'm confident that what I learned will one day find its way into another story.

The National Endowment for the Arts for its generous and timely support.

Susan Bergholz for her faith in the story and for her vision of its possibilities.

The Bamboo Ridge Study Group for their patience and enduring belief that there would be an ending, even when I had given up hope. I kept writing because you all asked, "What's next?"

Lois Ann Yamanaka for being an auntie to my girls, for reminding me to find the light, for a karaoke party with several glasses of merlot when I most needed a night out.

Leslie Bow and Elena Creef, my Santa Cruz sisters, for your intense readings and insightful criticism, but most of all for your friendship through the years.

And Jim, you are my rock. I love you.

FOX GIRL

I dream of her still.

It's been years since I've seen her, my oldest friend and truest enemy, but she drifts through my sleep almost nightly. Though her face is usually hidden, my heart recognizes her. "Sookie," I call out, voiceless as if underwater. She turns and all I can see are her teeth gleaming white in the blackness. Her mouth stretches wide, smiling, as if she is happy to see me. But even in my dream, it doesn't seem right, her joy doesn't fit. And then I notice how pointy her teeth are, how they are fangs, really, and how through the slightly open mouth, they are glistening, as if about to take a bite.

When I wake, I try to envision her face, but her features melt into one another; I see a smudge of black hair, dark eyes, a smear of mouth as if through churning waves. Or as if through several layers of photographic negatives: Sookie at eight when we fought Lobetto in the ditch behind her apartment; at fourteen, peeking out from under the paper bag she had put on her head when we went to Dr. Pak's VD clinic; at seventeen when, with her mother's makeup smeared over her face, she taught me about "honeymooning" in the backbooths of the GI clubs; at twenty when she pushed a wet and wailing Myu Myu into my arms and told me, "She's your daughter now." In every memory I have of her, I can hear her words, see her gestures, but her face remains a fragmented blur.

I've written to her—postcards, a line or two on the back of photos of Myu Myu, who wants to be called Maya now. I indulge the child to make up for the beginning of her life, watching her carefully for signs of developmental delays, erratic behavior, eccentricities that could be blamed on me. I am the only mother Maya knows, but for me, in the shadows, there will always be another. These letters are my guilt payment, I suppose, and one day I will send them, these years' worth of notes, to her, care of Club Foxa Hawai'i.

One day, when it is safe, I would like to see Sookie again, once more, face-to-face, so that I can reconcile her in my memory and banish her from my dreams. Maybe after enough time has passed, I could see her clearly, without money or love or other people's vision clouding my eyes.

‑‑

1

When we were children, everyone in Chollak thought Sookie was ugly; this is what I loved most about her. Her ugliness— bulbous eyed and dark skinned—was greater than mine and shielded me to some degree. *"Gundong-hi, ssang-dong-i,"* the neighborhood boys teased as we walked the path from school. "The Butt Twins," they called us. Sookie covered her ears— bony elbows sticking out like a kite—and I tucked the stained side of my face into my shoulder. Reasoning that they couldn't call me ugly if they didn't see the birthmark, I turned my good side toward the taunting and let the teasing fall on my friend.

"Blackie, black dog," they shouted at her. Sookie, hands still over her ears, would recite the alphabet.

"Your father must be a U.S. darkie!" the boys spat at us. Even Lobetto, whose father *was* a black GI and whose skin was darker than Sookie's, teased her since at least he had a father.

"Eh, *chokka!*" I screamed, stooping to pick up a broken piece of concrete from the sidewalk. "I'm gonna kick your penis!"

Young Sik and Chung Woo swiveled their hips and "ooohooohed" us. Lobetto yelled back, "I doubt you'd even know where to find it, you pile-of-shit-face! What did your mama do to make you born so ugly? Eh. *Hyung* Jin?" He pronounced the first part of my name with a hard "g" at the end, changing its meaning from *wise truth* to *scarred truth*.

"At least we're pure Korean, not like you, half-half." I jutted out my hip and shook the chunk of concrete at him. Back then, I was the bolder one, secure in my family's station, our relative wealth. I thought we were rich because we never had to worry about rice and once a week we ate meat. Chicken, pork, even beef sometimes.

My mother's family, who had lived in Chollak generations before the start of World War II, owned the sweet shop we worked and lived in. We had an actual house—two rooms with an inside kitchen—not like the *piramin* shacks that the northerners or the GI girls from America Town lived in. Not like the dump Sookie and her mother had lived in before they found an "uncle" from the base.

"You are pure Korean, hah, Sookie?" I asked under my breath, testing the heft of stone in my palm. I was pretty sure if she wasn't, I would have been forbidden to play with her, just as

I had been forbidden to play with Lobetto and Chosopine, before her father had taken her but not her mother to America.

"Ka na da ra!" Sookie continued to sing the alphabet, still holding her hands over her ears. I could see the muscles in her thin arms quivering.

"Hana, dul, set," I growled, and on "three" I whirled and let the concrete fly. Since I never bothered to aim, but threw blindly at the group of boys, I didn't think I'd hit anyone. That day, though, I hit Lobetto in the face, opening a gash across his forehead. "Aaah, good luck!" I cried as I grabbed Sookie's arm to run.

"No, bad luck!" Sookie gasped as the boys, leaving a dazed Lobetto sitting in the middle of the street, swarmed after us. "If Lobetto tells his daddy, my mother will have a hard time getting on the base. Then I might have to be hungry again!"

We cut through the narrow winding alleys toward America Town, jumping over piles of chili peppers laid out on mats to dry, dodging an old *halmoni* who carried her colicky grandson on her bent back. "Excuse me, Tong Su's Grandma," I called over my shoulder before she began yelling about ill-mannered children racing through the streets like criminals. With luck, the boys would crash into the grandmother and be taken inside to be punished with a lecture and some ear pulling. We bolted into my father's store before Lobetto and his gang turned the corner.

Since our store sat just outside the entrance to America Town, near the point where the GIs divided the streets into white section and black section, we had both pale *miguks* and dark *gomshis* stop in to check our merchandise. But our best customers were the kids who liked to come by after school to look at the Juicy Fruit or Coca-Cola, then buy *yot* or wax lips for something sweet. Only the Americans and their whores could afford the *miguk* gum and soda.

My father had a big red and white refrigerator especially for the Coca-Cola. When the *miguk* gave it to us, we tried to put it inside the store, but once it was in, we couldn't open the door and there was no place to put the table of candy. Now the refrigerator sits in front and people call our store Coka, even when all we have in the cooler is kimchee.

The one time the American who installed the cooler came for a maintenance check, he asked my father, "Where Coca-Cola? This only Coca-Cola." He held his fist to his mouth and *glug-glugged* smacking his lips.

My father pretended not to understand his Korean, pointed to two dusty bottles of Coke we kept on the counter for display, and said, "Three thousand won."

Years later, I understood that the Coca-Cola refrigerator came through Sookie's mother, a gift because of my friendship with Sookie, and because of the promises her mother and my father had made to one another before we were born.

"Appah!" I called out when Sookie and I burst through the door and scuttled under the candy table. I tugged the tablecloth down a few inches, trying to create a shield without tumbling the trays of sweets off the counter. Pulled as far as I dared, the cloth barely covered my face. I scooted toward the shadows against the wall. Sookie squeezed her shoulders between the legs of the stool; with her arms splayed out in front of her and her dark hair hanging in front of her panting face, I thought Lobetto was right: she did look like a black dog.

My father came through the beaded curtain which separated the store from our living space. "What, did I hear my daughter's voice?" he teased, talking to the air above us, pretending not to see us. "Or was that a ghost? A faceless fox spirit that will steal my heart when I sleep?"

"Shh, Daddy," I scolded. "We are hiding from the boys."

Appah laughed. "That is no way to catch a husband, girls. At least let me see what they want." My father strode to the door. When he flung it open, he caught the boys huddled in front, debating whether or not to hunt us in our own territory. "Sirs, come in. Come in."

The boys shuffled in, bare feet tracking in the dust from the streets.

"Would you gentlemen like a piece of *yot?* Some juice? Mother of Hyun Jin made some fresh plum juice this morning." My father talked to them formally, as if they were paying customers.

Sookie pinched me. "Tell your daddy to throw them out. Tell your daddy to scold them for teasing us. Tell your daddy they called us the Butt Twins," she hissed.

I bit my lip, hating that my father acted so kind to them, yet reluctant to remind him of my ugliness. Wavering, I did nothing.

The boys circled the candy table, kicking under the hem of the tablecloth with probing toes. I scratched at the blackest ones and heard a yelp. Ducking my head to peek out, I saw Young Sik hopping on one foot. I stuck out my tongue at him.

"You decide what you want?" my father asked, stepping in front of the table. I scrambled back, shuffling around his legs for another viewpoint. Pressing my face against the floor, I could crane my head enough to see up the nose of the closest boy.

"Three wax lips," Lobetto grumbled and swatted at a fly circling lazily around the cut above his eye; the blood had gelled so that it was almost the same color and consistency as the cherry-flavored wax lips. Lobetto was the only one with money and had to buy something with my father waiting on him. Swaggering past my father, he thunked his won onto the counter.

Startled, I flinched and pressed closer to Sookie. Above Sookie's breath in my ear, I could hear the boys slurping the juice inside the wax. Imagining them grinning at one another with the fat red wax wedged over their teeth, I rolled my eyes at Sookie. She giggled.

"So, boys." My father clapped his hands over her laughter. "Which one of you has come to propose a match with my daughter?"

One of them choked, spitting his lips onto the floor. The boys stammered, stepping on each other's feet, their bodies bumping together. Lobetto kicked at Young Sik who kicked Chung Woo. Chung Woo bent down to pick up his candy, shooting a look under the table where we crouched. He lifted his real lips toward his nose, like a snarling dog, and narrowed his eyes. Then, slipping the wax lips into his mouth, he flashed us a candied grin before standing.

After the boys left, *Appah* pulled us out from under the table. "My girl is so popular, the boys follow her home from school." He was joking, but still I preened, thrusting my bony chest out and holding my head high, knowing that he loved me, that he, at least, did not consider me deformed.

While my mother often poked at me to straighten my spine, to braid my hair, to stop looking so cross-eyed—which was difficult since I was also told to cock my head to hide the birthmark—my father pampered me with treats and stories. He told me tales of bears turning into women fit to marry the king of heaven, of beautiful princesses trapped for three hundred years in the form of centipedes, of girls haunting the earth as nine-tailed foxes. Always, they were stories of transformation, of ugliness turning into beauty. Sometimes as he talked, I thought he looked at my birthmark with remorse, but when I would turn sharply to confront him, his eyes were filled not with guilt or shame but with bright laughter. Despite what I looked like, I was still his only child; I worked hard to be perfect in other ways.

"I am still Class Leader," I said, lifting my head. "I'm number one, Sookie's number two." I side-eyed Sookie to see if she minded my boasting, but she smiled big enough to show her teeth.

I always tried to be number one in school, the leader of the class—the one who led the line to the yard, the one who could call on rivals when I knew they would give a wrong answer. When Esteemed Teacher called on the rows to recite the countries and capitals of the world, I made sure my voice was loudest, unfaltering.

During tests when the teacher knew I knew all the answers, I was chosen to patrol the rest of the children. If they looked numb with chanting, I'd slap them on the head to wake them up. If they mumbled wrong answers, I'd mark down their names. I stood with my ear against their faces to make sure they were not just mouthing the words. I'd point at the map of the world taped on the front wall and, cunning as a fox, cull out by instinct the most vulnerable: "Lobetto, what is the capital of Germany?" "Kyung Hu, who is the prime minister of Canada? Speak up!" "Young Sik, who are the Republic of Korea's giant allies? If you do not answer by the count of three, I will make you stand in the corner to answer harder and harder questions!" By the time we graduated from primary school, Sookie was my only friend.

I grabbed a handful of *yot* from the table and when my father tapped my hand, I raised my eyebrows. "We need energy for homework," I said.

"Is that so?" My father laughed and picked up more of the sticky candy. He gestured to Sookie and laid three more pieces in her palm. "Then I expect you both to do extra well today." We went into the back room, rolled up our shirts and lay bare-belly on the cool stone floor to do homework.

I pushed my tablet to Sookie. "Ho Sook," I wheedled, using her formal name to show respect, "same deal?"

Sookie pinched her lips together, but nodded. She was better at art than I was, so I had convinced her to draw my homework as well as hers. I couldn't stand it when her pictures—dogs that looked like dogs, people that looked like people—received praise over my smudged circles and stick figures. In return, I would correct her English assignment. Of course, I left a few mistakes, so she would receive only an 80 or 85 percent. Only one of us should have a 100 percent. Only one of us could be class leader.

That day, we were to draw self-portraits. As I skimmed over Sookie's English paper, she stared intently at me. I tried to turn away, but she cupped my chin in her hand. The pads of her fingers flickered along the line of my jaw, my cheek, my nose, across my eyes. Then, gently—so softly I barely felt her touch—she outlined with her caresses the continent of blue-black skin that stretched from my temple to my chin. And as she touched me, she drew, as if to memorize me with each stroke of her pen.

When Sookie handed the paper back to me, I saw that she had drawn a perfect me, a me without the birthmark. Through her eyes, with her touch, I was transformed; I saw that, with the darkness erased, I had what the old ladies would call *bok-saram*, a face as lucky as the full moon.

After we finished our homework, I walked Sookie home. I liked to visit her apartment, especially when her mother was on base or at the club. Then we had the afternoon and the apartment to ourselves. I liked to wander through the rooms, discovering the new American knickknacks that her mother smuggled home. Once we found a small, big-eyed doll with a curled helmet of yellow hair. Another time we found a slim, green bottle called "Youth Dew"; when we pressed the button, a mist that smelled like bug spray wafted over our faces. Sometimes we'd open up a drawer and find strange things to eat, like Ho Hos. The first time I tried that chocolate roll, I spit out the cake with its too-sweet lining of sugar cream. I couldn't believe that Americans, who could have anything in the world, would eat that. I thought Sookie had played a joke on me, handing me that shiny wrapped present and telling me it was *U.S.A.* so I would expect something delicious.

"You're mean!" I cried, scraping my tongue with my fingernails. "That tastes like dirt!"

"No, no," Sookie laughed, tearing open another silver pouch. "It's a delicacy; you have to learn to like it. Really, really, it's American so you know it's good." She and I ate our way through the box before I decided I liked it. I saved the wrappers from those Ho Hos for a long while after that day, pasting them on my bedroom wall with chewed-up bits of rice. I liked the way the shiny paper caught and flung the afternoon light around the room. My mother, who called anything from America "whore's rubbish," threw them out while I was at school.

Sometimes Sookie and I would hit the jackpot and find not just snacks, but makeup: Touch and Glow base foundation, Beach Peach and Swinging Pink lipsticks, Coty puff powder. "Your mother gets a lot of presents from the GIs," I said.

"I guess," she said. "You know how the Joe-sans are."

I nodded, though I really didn't.

Once we walked into the apartment when her mother was at the PX and found a darkie GI sleeping in the bed. Sidling up to the bed, we bent over to study him. Sookie poked at him with the corner of her writing tablet.

"Is he dead?" I asked. I didn't bother to whisper, thinking that even if he wasn't dead, he was American and couldn't hear Korean anyway. Up close he smelled like tobacco, stale and smoky. His chest, covered with coarse kinky hair, looked dark—like the underbelly of the black pig our family once raised. I watched his belly for movement so didn't notice when he opened his eyes. Sookie screamed and when I jerked my head up, I saw his white-white eyes blinking open then shut then open. And I saw his white-white teeth mouthing "*Anyang haseyo,* baby-sans" like a trained monkey saying a very polite "How do you do?" before it bites. I screamed, too, I think, and pushed past Sookie to run away. Even from outside the door, we could hear him laughing.

This time I made Sookie check the apartment before I entered. "Okay, come in," she whispered. "Darkie's not here today."

"How come your mother goes with the ugly, black dogs?" I grumbled.

Sookie shrugged and turned to the desk decorated with makeup containers and beer bottles. I reached over her to touch the most elegant bottle I had ever seen: pasted over the dark brown glass was a picture of a smiling yellow-haired woman holding up a bouquet of foaming mugs.

"Try some candy," Sookie said, unwrapping a bar. "It's called Hersheys." She broke off a piece and popped it into my mouth. Sweet explosion, dark and bitter as blood, erupted in my mouth. Delicious. American. "My mother said darkies are the kindest," said Sookie, her teeth glistening with strings of chocolate. "The most grateful. They go with anybody who is lighter than them. Even the ugly ones." She gulped the last of the Hersheys. "I could get a darkie," she said, licking her teeth. "Even you could, maybe."

We looked at our faces in the mirror, cataloging our ugliness. My birthmark gleamed, an ebony light, black as Africa. Sookie held up a white jar. "Pond-su cream," she said to my face in the mirror. "Made in the U.S.A."

"*Pansu?*" I repeated. "Reflection cream?"

"Uh-huh." Sookie twisted open the jar and scooped the cream onto her fingers. She sniffed at it. "First time I found this, I thought it smelled so good, I ate it." She giggled, then poked the tip of her tongue into the mass. "Even knowing how horrible it tastes, I still can't resist."

Sookie rubbed the Pond-su over my birthmark. "To lighten and soften your skin."

I held my breath and as she rubbed, I thought I could see my stained skin dissolving under the layer of white cream.

"Look," Sookie breathed. "You are almost beautiful."

Our eyes met in the glass. We looked from my face to Sookie's. Sookie lifted her arms. "I don't think there is enough Pond-su cream in this jar to cover my whole body," she said, trying to joke away her ugliness.

"Mmmm," I said, "then you just have to go to America where you can buy all you want."

Sookie's reflection lowered its arms, stopped smiling. "Yes," the mouth said. "That's what I am going to do."

It turned out that Sookie did not need Pond's Cold Cream to cover up her ugliness. Her ugliness turned into beauty without her having to do a thing. She didn't grow into beauty with womanhood—her boyishness developing into lush curves. Her body stayed long and thin, what the old grandmothers still call unlucky. Her skin didn't lighten with age; her face did not grow into her overly large eyes. In fact, she looked much the same as an adult as she had in childhood. There were times when we were grown that I saw her as I did when I was younger, and was shocked into remembering that she was as ugly as she always was. And I would be reminded that what had changed was not so much how we looked, but how we looked out of our own eyes, our perceptions of beauty and of ourselves.

When the Americans first ventured off the base and into our neighborhoods, we though that they—with their high noses, round eyes, and skin either too white or too dark—were ugly. *"Kojingi,"* we would squeal, shielding our faces from the Big Noses. Or, holding our own noses as we ran away from soldiers who smelled like decaying boots, we sang out, *"Shi-che nemsei!"*

Slowly, though, we began to view their features as desirable, developing a taste for large noses, double lids, and cow eyes just as we had learned to crave the chocolate candy and cakes we had once thought sweet as dirt.

2

On Thursdays, after her tests at Dr. Pak's Love Clinic No. 5, after she had washed and hung the sheets which snapped and murmured like giant gossiping tongues on the line outside her apartment, Sookie's mother taught us ways to protect ourselves.

"Never depend on a man," Duk Hee said one Thursday, drinking and watching us eat *jajie* dogs she had placed on the Western-style table. Sookie's mother had set up the table and chairs for her boyfriends; their bodies could not fold under normal tables. I liked eating American-style, my back pushed straight against the backboard, even though my legs sometimes fell asleep as they dangled above the floor. I had to shake them as I chewed.

"Use one of these," she said, holding a thin packet that could have been candy in front of her. She tore the square open with her teeth, reached in with two fingers and plucked out what looked like a large plastic coin. "*Kondom.*" Duk Hee flicked "the reliable choice" onto the table in front of Sookie, then poured more *maek-ju* into her glass. She swirled her fingers in the beer, then, after sucking them dry, lifted her glass against ours. This was our cue to shout out, "Cheezu!" and "Down-da hat-chi!" in English.

I was the only one to toast that round. Sookie refused to lift her cup—which was just water anyway. She only drank beer if her mother brought home an American brand from the PX. I took a sip of my drink, choking as I worked through my second cup. The fumes from the alcohol made my head ache with its stink.

Sookie poked at the translucent disk her mother had tossed across the table. Grimacing, she nudged it away from her with the nail of her index finger.

I leaned over, squinting at it. "Use it for what?" I asked.

Duk Hee laughed and I knew she was feeling good. This had been a profitable month for her; she had three boyfriends who loved her so much she had almost paid off what she owed her bar mama. Sookie's mother reached for the last fried hot dog. She pointed it at her daughter, where it wobbled and bobbed like a swollen, accusatory finger. Sookie's mother concentrated on squinting at it, then announced: "This is about the size of it. They don't call them penis dogs for no reason."

I wanted to hear more, but Sookie scolded: "You're drinking too much, *Omoni*. Maybe you should eat that instead of waving it around like a flag."

Sookie's mother pretended to shudder. "No thanks. I eat enough of them at work."

I remember thinking how lucky that sounded, to work in a place where you could eat as many hot dogs as you wanted. I hadn't tasted anything so good, except for maybe American burga-fries and Spam—which I assumed Sookie's mother could also have whenever she wanted.

Sookie glared at her *omoni*. "Then why don't you go to bed? Hyun Jin and I have to study for school."

"You're a good girl." Sookie's mother, attempting to reach out and pat her daughter on the shoulder, lurched forward and fell against her. The hot dog hit Sookie in the head, splattering her hair with animal fat.

Sookie scowled, but I burst out laughing. The laughter pushed bubbles up into my throat; I burped and laughed some more. Sookie narrowed her eyes at me and her mother as she began to stack plates to carry to the kitchen.

Sookie's mother and I looked at each other, her eyes focused only on my good side, and smiled. She scratched at her kinky head. She'd just had her hair permed, to be more like the darkies at the clubs where she worked, and her head still itched from the chemicals. As she scratched with her free hand, the hot dog, like the hind leg of a real dog, quivered in sympathy. It was the last one and I wanted it, but could not ask someone older to hand over such a prize.

"Yeah, my Sookie is a good girl," Duk Hee muttered. She looked at me and her gaze sharpened. "Have you gotten your period yet? It should come soon."

"Ah, ah," I gaped, my tongue too thick with beer and embarrassment to answer. I had started bleeding the year before. Too afraid and ashamed to approach my mother, I had turned to Sookie for help. "You're not a baby anymore," is what she told me. "Now you have to be careful."

"Of what?" I had asked.

"Of everything," Sookie answered.

With the onset of blood, the world seemed a more menacing place.

"Just be careful," Duk Hee said, echoing my memory of Sookie's warning. "Blood changes everything." She turned to face the doorway to the kitchen. We heard Sookie drop the plates into the plastic washtub, heard the water from the hose hit the side of the tub like the fast-beating drum in a shaman dance. Then, when it stopped, we heard the rush of water hit the floor and the squeak of Sookie's rubber slippers pushing the lingering puddles into the floor drain.

"When I was little," Sookie's mother announced, "I always dreamed of water." Her voice, loud and sudden, broke the stupor I had fallen into with the rhythmic squeaking of Sookie's slippers.

"Ugnnh," I grunted and nodded my head. I forced my eyes to open wider.

Duk Hee closed her eyes. "Always water. Rain. Rivers. Puddles, cloudy and full of tadpoles. Waterfalls. The hot springs at Tongnae-gu that bubble with the smells of yellow." Her eyes snapped open and she grinned. "I wet my bed until I was almost your age! Drove my mother crazy until the dreams finally stopped.

"Then when I became pregnant with Ho Sook, I started dreaming about water again. But this time, it was always the same body of water: Chonji." She frowned at me. "You know Chonji? The Lake of Heaven at Paekdu-san?"

I nodded, unsure. "The Paekdu Mountain in the north?" My father had told me that Paekdu Mountain was the place where the Prince of Heaven was lured to earth by the bear woman; they mated on the slopes overlooking the lake and their children became the people of Korea.

Sookie's mother picked up the soggy hot dog and tapped me on the hand like a good student. "Good!" she said. "When I first started dreaming my Chonji dreams, I had to hike the steep cliffs of Paekdu-san. I traveled paths where I had to hug the mountain's white face, my feet shuffling bit by bit along icy narrow ledges. Only after falling to my death once, twice, three times was I able to look down and see—between the forest trees and mist—the Lake of Heaven below me.

"Each dream brought me closer and closer to the lake, till finally one night I stood at the edge, its waves lapping at my toes. When I looked into the water, I saw, just under my own reflection, a flash—a small movement made by a water spirit. I jumped in after her and as soon as the water closed over my head, I awoke to my own rush of water: my water bag had burst.

"First I thought I was a girl again, that I had once more messed my bed in the night. But before I could call out to my mother in shame, waves of pain hit and I knew I was giving birth to the water spirit in my dreams."

Sookie returned with a bowl full of peeled and sliced apples and pears, her face looking blank. I could tell she didn't want to hear anything else from her mother, but her mother added: "That is why I named her Ho Sook, Clear Lake. When I held her in my arms, I could see my own reflection just under her skin." Duk Hee grabbed at Sookie's hands, jostling the fruit bowl, but Sookie snorted and dodged away.

I cleared my throat and asked, "What's going to happen to that last *jajie* dog?"

"This?" Duk Hee waved the hot dog at me. I tried not to drool. "I want to teach you something." She waited until Sookie settled into her chair at the table, then held her empty hand to me. "Pass me the *kondom*," she said.

Wrinkling my nose, I pinched the slimy ring and dropped it in her palm. The tips of my fingers felt greasy where I had touched the rubber so I rinsed my fingers in my beer as I had seen Sookie's mother do.

"I learned this at the clinic when I was about your age," she said. She frowned, looking first at the hot dog, then at the *kondom* as if trying to puzzle out a knot. Then, drawing her knees to her chest, she gripped the *jajie* dog between her knees. With a grin, she flourished the rubber disk as if about to perform a magic trick and placed it on top of the hot dog. "Pinch the end," she instructed. "And smooth it down." The *kondom* slipped over the meat like the pantyhose she wore to the clubs. "There," she said, dropping her knees and holding the covered hot dog vertically on the table. "Protection."

It looked like a small red soldier standing at attention in his coat and hat. I tried to hide a giggle behind my hand, but when Sookie raised her eyebrows at me, I laughed with mouth open wide. "It looks like it's going to war," I sputtered.

Sookie's mother chuckled. "It is a war," she said, wiggling the tube of meat like a marching soldier.

I clutched my stomach in laughter and fell off my chair.

"Stop it," Sookie growled.

"I'm trying," I panted, but when I rolled onto my back and

peeked a look at my friend, I realized she had been talking to her mother. I pulled myself back into my seat. "What's your problem, Sookie? Your mother is just teasing us."

"It's no joke," Sookie said, staring at her mother.

Duk Hee's lips stretched open in what should have been a smile, but wasn't. She gazed at her daughter with red-rimmed eyes and said, her voice so soft I almost didn't hear: "No, it isn't, is it?"

The hot dog lay on the table between Sookie and me. I poked it and it rolled unevenly toward Sookie. "Uh, anyone want this?" I asked.

Startled, Sookie looked down at the table, then pushed the penis dog back to me. She shuddered and reached for a sliver of apple.

"I'll have it then," I said, grasping the uncovered tip of meat. I rolled the thin plastic back up the soldier's body, and when he was naked, bit the head off.

I almost spit it out, the taste and smell of new rubber coating my mouth.

"Don't eat it!" Sookie shouted.

Meat smashed in my teeth, I smiled, then swallowed and took another bite, in part because Sookie told me not to, in part because it was American and I didn't want it to go to waste.

Weeks later, exploring the apartment when Duk Hee was at the clubs, we found a drawerful of those protection packets. She hadn't seemed to have used any. Sookie and I both took one. I figured we could use all the protection we could get from Lobetto and his gang.

Thinking the *kondoms* were like the talismans the shaman *mudangs* gave out to protect the wearer from bad luck and evil ghosts, I punched a needle through one corner of mine, widening the hole with a pencil until string could struggle through, and wore it around my neck, under my school uniform. During tests, I would touch my chest and feel the packet crinkle against my skin.

I don't know what Sookie did with hers.

I started walking Sookie home every day, not just every Thursday. Sometimes, in the place where sheets hung to dry, a row of lacy underclothes waved to each other and to passersby. When we saw this, we knew we would be welcome inside. Sookie's mother would not wash clothes if a boyfriend was home with her.

I liked when wash days stretched into weeks, even if that meant Sookie's mother could only offer rice and sour kimchee stew for lunch. Duk Hee always sat the table with us, drinking and urging us to eat, and talking like we were her girlfriends at the clubs. Even though this irritated Sookie, she tolerated her mother's advice because I loved it.

"If you ever catch an American man to marry," Duk Hee would say, "you need to learn their secrets. The more you know about them, the more power you will have. Remember, it is war." Then I'd laugh, picturing the *jajie* dog soldier marching across the table.

She'd drink a little, thinking of something bizarre about American Joes she could tell us, something that would test our credulity. "When hair stops growing on top their heads, it will find a new path, sprouting out of their ears and on their knuckles," Sookie's mother offered.

Even Sookie laughed at that, but she shook her head and said: "Strange, yes, but Frog-Face Ota from Okinawa has no hair on his head and still has hairy arms."

"And ears," I added.

"And nose." Both Sookie and I squealed.

"Okay, how about this." Sookie's mother tapped the table for attention and tried again. "The *miguk* GIs grow so tall, that their heads hit the ceiling on buses and they have to walk like apes to get in the door of people's houses."

I pretended to consider this, not wanting her to know we had seen one of her darkie boyfriends draped in her bed, his legs hanging off the mattress. He easily could have been that tall. "Heard that already," I finally said.

Sookie's mother tried to think of something stranger, something that would stump us. "*Miguks* can't see us," she said. "Korean faces blind them."

"Aha!" said Sookie. "That can't be true."

I thought about it for a moment. It could be true Americans didn't see like Koreans did; they had overly large, odd-colored ball-eyes. "What do you mean?" I asked.

"Just that it's possible to be invisible to them." Sookie's mother pushed away from the table and held her hands out to us. "Come," she said, "I'll show you what I mean."

Duk Hee led us to the back room where she and sometimes her boyfriends slept. Sookie and I perched on the edge of the bare mattress while she searched through her drawers of makeup. When we saw her filling her cosmetics bag, looking over her shoulder once in a while to consider our faces, we started wriggling like market dogs for sale.

"For some reason," she explained, "American Joes cannot see our faces clearly. Especially when we use the eye shadows, lipsticks, powder, blush-i they give us, we confuse them."

I pointed to the bottle of foundation. "What's that?" I asked, pretending I didn't know. The last time we had played with her mother's cosmetics, Sookie and I had used up so much foundation we needed to make up the noticeable difference with water.

Sookie's mother poured the liquid skin on her hands and rubbed it over my face. "Magic," she breathed.

When she came to my birthmark, she hesitated and frowned, then dabbed more foundation into the creases and darkened pits. Again and again her fingers rubbed my cheek. I closed my eyes as she touched my face. Only she and Sookie had ever acknowledged my defect; not even my own mother would caress me there.

"You know Grandmother of Chung Woo, right?" Duk Hee asked. When I nodded, she gripped my chin to still my head. "Let me put some blue eyeliner on you, then I'll line Ho Sook's eyes in black." I felt the brush lick around my lashes like a small snake. "Well, Grandmother of Chung Woo has to work in the clubs when her good-for-nothing son spends all his money on his *chop*. I tell you, he cannot even support the family he has and he is off trying to make a new one with his mistress." She snorted in disgust. "I heard that was against the law in America— that's a good country for women, I think."

I opened my eyes when I felt the makeup crust around them. Duk Hee turned to rim Sookie's eyes with a thin paintbrush dipped in black ink.

"Anyway, when Grandmother of Chung Woo does this to her face," she continued, "she can get any man at the clubs, even one young enough to be her son. Imagine, they cannot even tell how old she is." Sookie's mother clucked and shook her head as she sketched an extra line above her daughter's eyes, then licked her smallest finger to erase a smudge. Then she blew on Sookie's face. When she was done, Sookie opened her eyes.

"You look like the king of raccoons," Sookie said, teasing me.

"Don't bother looking in the mirror," I retorted. "You look like a ghost." Secretly, though, I thought I looked glamorous.

"Shup!" scolded Sookie's mother. "Let me work on your mouths. I'll tell you what I think. I think that this makeup is magic—a disguise that lets us move through their world safely."

I tried not to smile as Duk Hee brushed a fluorescent pink on my lips.

"Ooooh, Hyun Jin!" Sookie squinted and raised her hands in front of her, groping air. "Where are you? I can't see you anymore; your mouth is blinding!"

Duk Hee knocked her daughter's hands down, ignoring her giggling. "It's like the story of the fox who wraps herself in the skin of a dead girl," she explained. "Somehow, in real life, we have to become like the fox girl."

I didn't like the story of the fox girl. In the version my father told me, a big fox visits a country school. It is late at night and the students have decided to sleep in the schoolroom because it is too dark to walk home. All but one of the hundred students have fallen asleep when the one awake hears a soft guttural voice counting pairs of shoes outside—*hana, dul, set, net*—all the way to one hundred.

Through the window, the boy sees the snout of a fox, but as it crawls through the window, it takes the shape of a beautiful young woman. The boy thinks he must be dreaming and rubs his eyes. He strains to see in the darkness and notices: the dirt from a newly dug grave lodged under her nails; the blood like lipstick staining her mouth; the glittering of a hunter's eyes in the night.

The boy crawls away, hiding in a far corner of the room. He watches the fox girl count the students with a kiss that steals their breaths. With each kiss, a boy stops breathing and dies in middream.

When she approaches the corner where the youngest boy is hiding, he creeps back to his sleeping place. Sick with fear, he lies down among the dead bodies of his friends. When the girl reaches the end of the row of students, she growls. "Only ninety-nine! There is one missing. How can that be?"

She rushes outside to recount the pairs of shoes. One hundred. She counts again, to be absolutely certain, and all the while the boy inside tries not to move, tries not to breathe. After again finding exactly one hundred pairs of shoes, the fox girl turns toward the door to recount the boys. Just then, a cock crows. The demon drops to all fours and scampers into the nearby woods. The clever boy is saved, the only one out of a hundred to live.

"I don't want to be a fox girl," I told Sookie's mother. "They are evil creatures."

Sookie's mother shrugged. "I suppose it depends on who tells the story," she said, choosing a deep red lipstick, like blood from a fox's mouth, for her daughter. I smacked my own lips, which felt heavy and thick. The smell of the lipstick reminded me a little of the taste of rubber and hot dog.

"The fox girl was only trying to regain what those boys stole from her," Sookie explained, making an effort to keep her mouth open and still.

I frowned, and Sookie's mother finished the story. "The fox was once the keeper of the jewel of knowledge. She kept it safe, hidden under her tongue. One day, a young scholar hunted her down, begging her to teach him a little of the world. He seemed a nice boy, sincere and eager.

"The fox allowed him to kiss her, so he could have a taste of knowledge. But he became greedy and swallowed the jewel, planning to look up at the sky, then down at the ground before it could dissolve, knowing that if he did so he would possess all the wisdom of heaven and earth.

"But the fox pulled at his chin to try to get her jewel back, and he was forced to look only at the earth. That's why men only know about things on earth. And that's why the fox borrows a human form, forever searching each man for that lost jewel."

I stared at Sookie's mouth—her teeth looked sharp and white in that red, red mouth. "I never heard that ending before," I said.

Sookie laughed. "Maybe my mother made it up then."

"Both of you, close your mouths and your eyes." Sookie's mother ordered. She dusted powder across our faces, and when the cloud evaporated, settling on the oils of our skin, I began to understand how makeup could be worn as a disguise. It felt like one, a shield over tender skin. And the face I saw across from mine was Sookie's but not Sookie's. It was instead an ageless mask, cool and deadly, capable of swallowing the jewel of a man's soul.

One Thursday, no sheets were hanging in the yard. Thinking Duk Hee must have snuck in a boyfriend, Sookie and I waited in the ditch, kicking away a pile of rotting lettuce leaves and fish bones to set up a game of seesaw in the dust. We pried a board loose from the shed Crazy Lady Li slept in at night and balanced it across a brick. We jumped for a while in the hot sun, until we were too thirsty to continue. Dragging our feet through the gray dirt to Sookie's apartment, we peered through the kitchen window, but couldn't see much through the boards; it was too dark. We stomped around the building, shouting at each other—"We're home from school now!" and "It must be past dinnertime!" hoping Sookie's mother or her Joe would at least throw down some won for us to leave.

When one of Sookie's neighbors—a *yong sekshi* who had just started working at the same bar as Sookie's mother—opened her window and threw water on us, I called her a fat hippo whore.

The GI girl waggled her butt at us. "See me, see yourself," she sneered and slammed her window shut.

I wanted to pound on that girl's door, then on her face when she opened it, but Sookie stopped me from marching over there. "Stop fooling around," she scolded. "Something's wrong."

Sookie hit the door of her own apartment with the brick we had used to balance the seesaw and splintered the frame by the doorknob. After pushing our way in, we were forced to realize the room was empty. *"Omoni,"* Sookie called out in the darkness. *"Omoni!"*

We lit a lamp. Our faces looked sharp and ghostly. "I have to go home," I whispered.

Sookie nodded. I didn't move.

"Go on, Hyun Jin," she said, lifting her chin toward the broken door. "It's okay."

"One of her boyfriends probably asked for her at the club," I offered. "And she had to go, right?"

We both knew she wouldn't have worked at the clubs on the day she checked in at the clinic. It was against official policy. But Sookie said, "Right, She'll be home soon or in the morning, like always."

"I'll meet you here before school," I said, though I didn't need to remind her of our established routine.

Sookie turned away from me, leaving me in the dark room.

I wanted to ask her to come home with me, to eat with me at my house. But I knew and she knew my mother didn't like to feed her. "Stray cats will keep coming back if you feed them," my mother always said about Sookie, though not in front of my father. My father had a soft spot for my friend. But I knew he wouldn't stand up for her against my mother. My mother was the head of the house and the kitchen; she was the boss of the food.

When I stopped at her house the next day for school, the door was wide open. Sookie lay sleeping in the middle of the floor, the lamp still burning dimly by her head. She hadn't bothered to lay out her blankets and the *ondol* floor was cold. She hadn't even bothered to fire up the heater before curling in on herself like a wounded animal.

"Sookie," I whispered. Clearing my throat of its scratchy worry, I tried again, louder: "Sookie, time for school." I shook her shoulder, tickled her toes. She kicked out at me, then growled. "Shushushu," I crooned. I sat cross-legged behind her and stroked her hair. I thought I heard her whimper. I hugged her, trying to pull her into my lap. We were the same size, but she made herself as small as possible to fit across my legs. I stroked her, humming softly. "It's okay, it's okay," I crooned even though I was afraid, too. I kept thinking what her mother had told us: that we were in the midst of a war, and that anybody—even a fox in disguise—could get bitten.

I gathered Sookie closer and let words tumble out of my mouth. "Your mother is a fox, she can take care of herself. She's smart and she's beautiful. She'll be home soon."

I sang on and on until Sookie lay quiet across my lap. "Your *omoni* knows you're waiting for her, Sookie, and she's looking for a jewel to bring home to you."

3

When I was about six or so, I found a basket of grapes my mother had bought to make candies. I knew they weren't for me; treats were for paying customers. I eyed the nestling grapes, bunched into tight family clusters. They were perfect in their roundness, the dusky purple ready to burst their waxy skins. I rubbed their small bodies between my fingers, enjoying the firmness of their flesh.

I knew my mother would beat me if I ate them, but I couldn't resist a taste. Looking for a small baby grape, one that wouldn't be missed, I plucked it from its family and into my mouth. I loved the sudden pop of sweet juice, but it seemed to me I had swallowed faster than I could taste. The next grape I decided to roll around my tongue, savoring the anticipation.

Before I knew it I had devoured not only all the baby grapes, but the mother-father and ancestor grapes as well. In fact the entire village of grapes that existed in that basket had been wiped out. Shocked, I stared at the skeletons of stems and withered rejects, then rushed to bury the evidence.

My mother found me outside the house, patting the earth. I don't know how long she had been watching me, but when she spoke—making me jump out of my skin—I realized that I had been sitting in her shadow.

"Hyun Jin, have you seen the basket of grapes I bought at the market?" she asked, staring at my mouth.

"Grapes?" I gulped, rubbing a hand across my lips. I tasted dirt.

My mother sneered, not bothering to hide her contempt. "You know, the little round fruits that grow in bunches on the vine?"

I ducked my head, thinking I was going to get slapped. I closed my eyes and waited. But instead of hitting me, she asked if I would like to walk with her to Grape Auntie's farm, which was far, far outside of the village.

"Why?" I croaked, blinking up at her.

"Because I seem to have lost the grapes I bought and the next farmers' market is five days away." She narrowed her eyes at me. "And I need to start the new batch of candies today."

I should have said no. Or at least been suspicious. My mother never wanted me to accompany her anywhere. But I thought that her asking meant that she didn't know I ate her grapes, and also, maybe, that she loved me. I wanted her to love me, so I nodded. My stomach gurgled a sudden warning. I felt a little sick, my belly as full and taut as the grapes I had eaten.

My mother walked quickly, her back straight and mean. I tried to match my legs with hers, leaping to meet her strides. She sped up and I fell behind. When I began to jog, I felt like throwing up. "*Omoni,*" I panted. "I don't feel so good."

"Stop whining," my mother scolded without looking down. "You sound like the squealing pig you are."

The grapes burned my throat, threatening to come up. I swallowed, then gagged. "I'm sick. My stomach." Knives stabbed me from the inside and I had to stop running. I rubbed my stomach, pressing under the ribs and—in a sudden rush—I vomited. I didn't even have time to bend over. Chunks of purple flesh and a watery stench gushed down the front of my clothes, tinging my *hanbok* lavender.

"*Ohma!*" I screamed at her retreating back. "Mama!" I tried to run after her, but my dress stuck uncomfortably to my chest and I stank. I gave up, sat in the middle of the road and cried.

I wasn't sure she would, but my mother stopped walking. She stood with her back to me for a short while, then turned. She marched back, as if ready for battle. The closer she loomed, the more I shrunk into myself, swallowing my cries and turning them into hiccupping sobs.

My mother grabbed my upper arm and jerked me into the air. "Next time, think before you eat what's not yours."

She dragged me the rest of the way to the grape farm, my feet tripping, flailing for traction. And with each step, she scolded: "Pig. Dirty pig. Fat pig. Selfish pig. Black pig."

We stalked through the staked rows of fruit, searching for

Grape Auntie. When we saw her, her large frame bent over the delicate vines, my mother dropped my arm. It had gone numb, but when she let go, pain flooded through it. I felt the throbbing where her fingers indented my flesh. Later it would turn blue, then yellow, but then it was just a red shadow of her hand. For the longest time, I imagined I could feel her fingerprints on my bone.

Omoni handed me a square of cloth. "Spit," she ordered, and when I did, told me, "At least clean your face. You're disgusting." When I fumbled it around my chin, she grabbed it back and scrubbed at my cheeks, then at the front of my dress.

"Don't embarrass me any more than you already have," she warned.

I whimpered and would have started crying again, but Grape Auntie was upon us. She plucked me like a piece of ripe fruit and swung me through the air before putting me down. I remember wondering how a woman could be so strong, that maybe she was really an uncle because her arms were so thick.

"You big girl, don't tell me you're tired from that little walk out of town!" Grape Auntie clucked. My lip quivered, but Grape Auntie tweaked it and laughed. "Go, eat as many grapes as you want, until you feel better."

"No," I groaned.

My mother placed her hands at the back of my neck and squeezed. "Say thank you," she said, her words grinding out between her clenched smile. To Grape Auntie she said, her voice sugar sweet and overripe, "Hyun Jin loves grapes. Can't eat enough of them."

My mother pushed me and I wandered through the field. But instead of eating, I crawled into one of the furrows and fell asleep, the thick scent of fermenting fruit making me dizzy.

I woke in the shadow of a dying sun, my face sticky with sweat, my dress crackling with dried vomit. I sat up, getting tangled in vines. *"Omoni, Omoni!"* I screeched. "Monsters, monsters!" I clawed at the talons gripping my hair, pulling at my neck. Sweat trickled down my spine like fingers and I knew the fox ghost was sniffing at the back of my neck.

I screamed when she grabbed me.

"Hush," the fox spirit said, her voice rumbling into my ear. "You're a big girl, no need to cry."

I turned into the warm, fleshy arms of Grape Auntie. "Mama-ma," I hiccupped.

Grape Auntie nestled me against her chest, pulled leaves and stems from my hair, patted my back. "Shu, Shu," she murmured until I quieted. "I thought you left with your *omoni,* but here you are, hiding. You shouldn't hide away like that. Your mama probably thought you had run home ahead of her."

I pressed against her warmth, not wanting to tell her my mother left me on purpose. I knew, but didn't say, that she wanted to teach me a lesson. "Maybe I should stay here with you," I said.

Grape Auntie chuckled, her body jiggling. "Wouldn't that be fun? But I'm sure your parents would miss you too much. They are probably crying for you now—hoo, hoo." She wailed as if in mourning and pressed her fists against her eyes.

I laughed.

"That's better," Grape Auntie said. She took my hand and together we marched toward the road. "You come visit me on my farm anytime you want, but right now, let's get you home where you belong."

Though she was a big woman, with long, muscled legs that strained against her skirt, she walked with mincing child steps. When I caught a pebble in my shoe, she scooped me up and propped me on her back as if I were a baby. I entered America

Town like a pampered princess, perched on the shoulders of a striding giant.

The last time I saw Grape Auntie was not at the farm, but at the weekly farmers' market where she pulled her wagon, piled high with bunches of black grapes. I was with Sookie, holding her hand as we cut through the market on our way to Dr. Pak's Love Clinic No. 5 in search of Duk Hee. Though I had never been there before, like everyone else in America Town, I knew where VD Road was and the fastest ways to get there.

"Hyun Jin! My favorite customer! I'm still waiting for you to come back to help me harvest my grape farm!" Grape Auntie greeted me as we passed her wagon. Years had passed, yet she never failed to tease me about the one time I had visited her. "Tell your mother I'll give her a good price this week!" she added. Then she looked over at Sookie and her face stilled.

"Tweggi." Eyes narrowed, she spat the word at Sookie. To me she said, "Little Jin-Jin, how can you be out with this trash animal?" she asked.

My mouth gaped open in shock.

"Does your mama know what kind of people you spend time with?" Grape Auntie, whom I had once loved for cradling me in her giant arms, sneered at my best and only friend.

Sookie looked down, cowered, and tried to back away. Her backward shuffling made me bristle. I thrust out my chest. "You cow!" I yelled. "Mind your own business!"

"Hyun Jin!" Grape Auntie gasped. "I'm looking out for you, can't you see? I know your mother would never approve of . . . of . . . She flicked her hand at Sookie, and even the meat of her upper arm quivered in disgust.

"Say anything to my mother," I growled, "and I'll make sure she never buys from you again."

Grape Auntie hissed, as if I had poked a hole in her belly and let the air out. "Your mother would never listen to you," she said, but her face dropped, deflating.

I shrugged, shoulders stiff and tight, unyielding as stone. I felt heavy with anger, but also with sadness because I remembered her kindness to me when I was little and lost.

When I turned to walk away, I realized Sookie had stepped back, blending into the crowd a few vendors away. Her eyes followed me as I jogged up to her, but she didn't say anything when I reached her side. I had expected her to curse Grape Auntie for shaming her and to thank me for defending her. She did neither.

"Come here, come here, young ladies!" Merchants called to us as they waved from their makeshift tents stocked ground to ceiling with their specialties: flat sheets of dried squid, bulbs of garlic, cooking pots. "Buy this! You won't find a better price anywhere."

I looked in the purse I carried about my neck, pretending to count money. "Hah," I joked backed, hoping to cheer up Sookie, who was still sulking, "too expensive. We're not *miguk* that can afford such prices! Give us the real, Korean price." And I laughed, knowing that Americans would never wander into this neighborhood market. Joe-sans only wanted the fanciest merchandise, from eel-skinned wallets to high-heeled girls.

That week Grandma of Chung Woo was at the market with her dog's newly weaned puppies. "Let's say hello," I told Sookie.

"Hyun Jin," Sookie complained. "I don't want to. I need to find my mother."

I dragged her by the elbow. "Stop being selfish," I told her. "I want to have fun on the way."

Chung Woo's grandmother squatted next to the wire cage

where fat puppy bodies wiggled against each other. Feces stuck to their nubby brown fur.

Bending over them—not close enough for the fleas to jump on me—I teased her: "*Halmoni*, who's going to buy these dirty runts?" Pushing a finger into the cage, I prodded the ribs of one mongrel. "This one won't even make a mouthful."

The grandmother flicked her fly fan at us. "These are not runts," she grumbled. "They're young and tender enough that even their bones can be eaten. They have more meat on them than you two!" She waved the fan over her face. "And they smell cleaner, too."

She laughed as I frowned at the undersides of my arms. Black worms of sweat-softened dirt nested in the crease of my elbows. I spit on my arm and rubbed until small tendrils of dirt flaked and fell to the ground. "Not anymore," I sniffed, but I was trying to remember when we had last gone to the bathhouse.

"Ho Sook and I have an appointment to go to the *mokyok-tang*," I lied. I grinned at Sookie, willing her to play along, but she stood like a post, eyes drifting into space, her face blank, as dumb as the half-breed animal Grape Auntie had accused her of being.

Chung Woo's grandmother cackled. "Oh ho, so that's how it is! Since when do such grubby monkeys need appointments to scrub under the showers. Just go to the bathhouse with your mamas! Wash each other's backs."

I wrinkled my nose at her. In fact, my mother had been trying to pull me into the bathhouse for the past month, but I was still afraid. I had been having nightmares about the steaming pools after the baby of an older girl had drowned there.

Sookie pulled my sleeve. "Can we go now?"

I sighed, irritated at her determination not to enjoy the day. "Go, go, rude girls." Grandmother Chung waved us away. "Why you still stinking up my space?"

When we turned, I saw Frog-Face Ota squinting at us over his peanut cart. "Hey, hey," he croaked. "Why you girls not in school? Kong Hyun Jin, I know who your father is!" I stuck my tongue at him like I was catching flies, then ran through the snaking dirt path toward the main road.

Skipping into a narrow alley between high brick walls, we rounded the corner where one of the walls was split by an iron gate. Though the gate gaped open, we stopped, hesitating at the entrance of VD Road. I touched the rusted dragon-head handle for luck. We shuffled along the dirt path, not looking at each other but at the signs posted in English and Korean above the doorways we passed. We found Dr. Oh's No. 1 clinic, Mr. Lee's No. 3, and others marked with only numbers—No. 6, No. 7, No. 11. At the time, I imagined that the GI girls gathered in front of the clinics stared at us as we passed them, that I could feel their eyes on my back. Now, in hindsight, I realize they had too much on their minds to pay much attention to a couple of young schoolgirls.

Thinking we must have overlooked clinic No. 5, we turned back toward the gate, determined to search more carefully. I reasoned it had to be a smaller clinic hidden behind the No. 3 or No. 6. Only after walking the road a second time, circling each building, did we realize that the numbers were in no particular order. We trudged on until, wedged against a chain-link fence between clinics No. 13 and No. 2, we found Dr. Pak's Love Clinic No. 5.

The clinic, an old-fashioned village house hidden amid modern wood and brick buildings, looked small and somehow vulnerable with its straw roof and dirt walls patched with the *Il Bon*

News. I imagined that if I kicked through the newspaper bandages, into the building's intimate wounds, I could bring the whole clinic down.

Sookie grabbed my elbow and edged us into the cluster of women hanging around the clinic's entrance. "Act like we belong here," Sookie hissed into my ear. As we approached them, I wished we had thought to put on makeup; the women, lounging against the wall, squatting on the steps, smoking cigarettes, and talking about men and America, seemed confident and sophisticated.

"We come here once a week, fine," a woman seated on the bottom step said, talking to a woman with her back to us. "But I don't see why we got to miss a whole day's work."

"It's not the day's work I mind missing," another woman snickered. "It's the night's."

The woman facing away from us rubbed her lower back. "Well, I'm glad to have a day off."

"Mi Ok, sit." The lady on the step frowned as she scooted to the higher step, pushing someone else closer to the doorway. The woman who was pushed looked up from her knitting and scowled.

"Sorry, sorry," Pushy Lady said. "But let's make some room for the one with the condition."

Knitting Lady looked at the one called Mi Ok and then cleared more room by pulling her knees up. "How far are you?"

As Mi Ok turned to sit, I saw the soft bulge of her stomach between the stretch of her T-shirt and her unbuttoned jeans. "Four, maybe five months," Mi Ok answered. "I'm getting it fixed today."

Pushy Lady nodded. "Good. Any longer, it'll be more painful for you. You cannot work for a long time."

Knitting Lady picked up her needles and began to click a

row of yellow. "Me," she said, "I've had two so far. Next one I think I'm going to keep. Three's a lucky number."

Another woman snorted just before someone from inside the clinic shouted "One-one-seven!" The numbers were carried like a wave, echoed by several women looking at the tickets in their hands.

The snorter was the one who saw us first. "What are you girls doing here?"

Knitting Lady squinted up at us. "You're too young to be here, you guys don't even have any *chi-chis* yet!"

Pushy Lady laughed. "Some men like that!" she said. "Did you see the styles in the American magazines? *Cosumo, Vo-gu,* all have that Twiggy girl who looks like a boy."

"*Tweggi?*" I asked, shocked. "Her mother is Korean? She is a half-half girl?"

The women erupted into laughter. "Are you really that stupid," Pushy Lady taunted, "or are you just faking it?"

Knitting Lady made a big show of wiping tears of laughter from her eyes. "In American language," she gasped, wheezing out an explanation as she caught her breath, "Twiggy means *changaji.* So this girl is skinny as a stick from a tree."

I could feel the flare of heat in my cheeks. "I knew that," I retorted. I side-eyed Sookie so I wouldn't have to look at the women's smirking faces, and for the first time realized that Americans might see Sookie's dark angularity as appealing.

"That girl's funny." Pushy Lady pointed at me.

"What she is is scary," Snorting Lady said. She cleared her throat and spat on the dirt near me. "What's wrong with your face? How'd you get that scar?"

"It's not a scar," I said, but I looked down, hoping enough of my hair would fall over the birthmark.

"Sure it is," Snorting Lady cackled. "From the evils of a past life."

"Stop teasing," Pushy Lady said. "That's only superstition. And GIs, they go for any *yong sekshi*—doesn't matter the face so much."

Mi Ok rubbed her stomach. "Shouldn't they be in school now?" she asked no one in particular.

Snorting Lady guffawed. "Maybe they are bringing kids here for field trips nowadays? That'd be a different sort of education!"

Mi Ok, her face without makeup and her hair cut short below her ears, looked like a schoolgirl not much older than Sookie and me. She tugged at her shirt, a splash of colors that strained to cover her midriff, then folded her hands across her belly.

"I'm looking for my mother," Sookie announced.

"It's not me!" Snorting Lady joked.

"Why don't you go home to wait for her?" Mi Ok said. She sounded kind, but tired.

"I waited, but she never came home," Sookie said, her voice small as a rabbit's.

Snorting Lady sneered. "She probably owed the club too much money and ran away to Cheju Do—the Korean Hawai'i!"

"She did not!" Sookie shouted. I think only I heard the fear laced between the words, because I knew that it was true her mother owed money.

"Really, Hae Cha!" Mi Ok scolded. "What mother would leave her babies behind?"

"Mine did," Snorting Lady said. She turned away from us and walked into the clinic.

"Oh her," Pushy Lady said. "She's always stomping off for

some reason or another." She fumbled through her purse and pulled out a square of white paper which she waved at us. "Here, you might as well take my number. I'll tell that witch at the front desk I lost mine and need another. I don't have anything else to do today, so I might as well hang out here and socialize." She grinned and when Sookie reached for the ticket, Pushy Lady added, "When one-two-nine gets called, go in and ask the doctor about your mother. He might know."

"One-one-eight!" I jumped each time a number was called. Knitting Lady and Mi Ok both entered before us. Knitting Lady came out quickly, shuffling a sheaf of papers as she walked out. "More papers, another office to visit. Like rats in a maze," she grumbled as she passed us. When number one-two-nine was called, Sookie and I hooked elbows and, leaning against each other, entered the dark doorway.

Dazed by the sudden change in light, I had to blink before I could see. We stumbled into a narrow front room lined with more women waiting to visit the doctor. I spotted Snorting Lady squatting in the corner smoking a cigarette, but she didn't look at us. A white-capped nurse stationed behind a large Western-style desk blocked the entrance to the inner room.

Holding the ticket in front of us like a talisman, we approached the nurse. "Our number was called," I whispered.

The nurse pursed her thin lips like she was eating unripe persimmon. "Where's your ID tag?" she spit out the soured words.

"T-tag?" I stuttered. Sookie and I swiveled to look at the other women in the room and noticed for the first time the plastic cards around their necks.

"Are you new?" The nurse shoved two sheets of paper at us. "If you're new, you each need to fill out a form before you see the doctor." I scanned the papers as Sookie tried to explain to the nurse that we only wanted to ask the doctor a few questions, not receive the exam or shots.

"Not allowed," the nurse sniffed. "The doctor is here only to give clearance examinations for women working as patriots of the Republic of Korea."

I pulled Sookie away from the desk, telling the nurse, "Just give us a minute to fill out the forms."

"One-three-zero!" the nurse shouted.

Borrowing a pen from a woman near us, Sookie and I scanned the questions. After filling in Sookie's name and address, we invented the rest: identification number, club name, club owner, date of last VD clearance, date of last menses. At the bottom of the sheet was the question, "Did you attend the American etiquette education class?" I scribbled "yes" on mine, assuming etiquette—identified as American—was a good thing.

I handed the papers to the nurse, feeling like I was turning in a school assignment. The nurse frowned, as if we had a wrong answer—which we probably did—but jerked her head toward the door. "Wait!" she grabbed me as we edged around her. "One at a time."

"But—" Sookie stammered, trying to convince her we must go together, just this once. The nurse looked away from us, as if she couldn't hear our voices.

"Oh, Sookie," I said, trying to pry her off me. "Just go. I'll wait out here."

"No, don't leave me!" Sookie cried and continued to beg the nurse. "I need my friend to come with me," she said, her voice breaking. "She's my sister—just like—to me. Please, Auntie, please, let us go together just this once."

The nurse grumbled, "You'll go to hell together, too, I suppose." But she let go of my arm. When she sat down behind the desk and turned her attention to another woman, another number, Sookie and I hurried past.

The inner office looked modern: tiled floors, metal chair in one corner, metal table in the center, an installed sink and faucet, a glass cabinet next to the sink filled with materials—cotton balls, wooden sticks, needles. The doctor, in a white knee-length coat instead of an old-fashioned black hat and suit, seemed modern as well. I remember wondering how often his maid had to wash his coat to keep the white that clean, and if the government paid him enough to wear a fresh coat each day of the week.

The doctor started when he saw us at the doorway, his eyebrows arching toward his hairline. I supposed he was surprised at seeing two girls instead of one. Then his eyebrows slammed downward. He paced away from us and muttered to himself, just as my father did when he was angry at something my mother did.

"Too young," he said under his breath. "Shouldn't be on the streets or in clubs. Their own mothers will put them to work right out of primary school if the money's right. 'Personal goodwill ambassadors,' my ass." Later, on the walk home, Sookie and I argued over whether or not the doctor had said "my ass." Sookie insisted that I made that up, along with the rest of his tirade. We couldn't hear him clearly, she claimed; he mumbled and his back was toward us.

We had tried to inch closer to hear better, but the doctor suddenly whirled and marched back to us. This time his face sagged as he looked over our heads. "One of you sit on the chair. Wait." He jerked his head in the direction of the metal chair as he spoke. "The other one, take off your clothes, even your undergarments. Lay down on the table." He stomped to the sink to wash his hands.

Sookie and I didn't move. We didn't even look at one another, too embarrassed to imagine ourselves doing what the doctor had ordered. I wondered if Sookie was also embarrassed to know that her mother did this each week.

"I don't have all day!" the doctor stormed when he turned around to find us still dressed, slack-jawed and big-eyed. "Don't you know how many of you I have to see in one day?"

I wanted to run out, but Sookie found a voice, weak as it was, that came out in a choppy rush between gulps of air: "Sorry, but. I but. We. Are looking. For my mother she came here last. Week and hasn't. Come home yet we thought you. Might. Know where. She. Is."

The doctor left the room. Sookie's panting sounded loud and harsh in the empty room. Without meaning to, I started to match her breaths. When I began thinking I should sit down before I fainted, the doctor came back into the room. "Here," he said, handing Sookie a brown paper bag. "Put it over your head and try to breathe slowly."

"Now you." The doctor touched my shoulder, bending toward my face. "Tell me what you need."

I chanced a glance at his face, then looked quickly down so as not to be disrespectful. But that quick look into his eyes helped me not to be afraid. I saw not only that he wasn't angry anymore, but that in some ways—the greased style of his black-pepper hair, the brown fullness of his cheeks, the sweet-tea warmth of his eyes—he reminded me of my father.

"We're looking for her mother," I said. "She never came home from here."

From the corner of my eye, I saw Sookie nod her paper bag head.

The doctor straightened, rubbing his eyes. "I'm sorry, girls. I wouldn't know who your mother is. I see so many women a day, I can't remember the person behind the number."

Sookie grunted under her bag.

"She said her mother's name is Cho Duk Hee," I translated.

The doctor shook his head and started to speak. "Like I said." Then he looked at the bag squared on Sookie's shoulders, saw the darkened dampness where her wet lips pushed at the paper with each breath. "But, if she checked in here and failed the exam, she'd have been taken to the Monkey House."

Pushy Lady was still on the steps when we walked out. She had brought lunch with her and now ate under the strip of shade provided by the roof's thatched overhang. "Find your mother?" she asked, her mouth full of *kimbap*.

Sookie looked at the dirt in her toes.

"They sent her to the zoo," I stomped my foot, answering for her. "She's not an animal."

Pushy Lady chewed slowly, puzzled, then suddenly choked on the rice ball she was eating. Grains of rice and seaweed shot out of her mouth as she laughed. "The zoo! That's a good one! You are so funny!" She shook her head, dabbing at her mouth for the rice she lost. "I'm guessing you mean the Monkey House?"

When I nodded, angry at her for laughing at me again, Pushy Lady said, "Oh don't be so serious. It's no big deal, really. I been there before. Lots of us have and most of us come home quickly. In fact, Mi Ok has to go there to get herself fixed up."

I thought about it, then asked, "The Monkey House is like a hospital?"

"You could say that," Pushy Lady chuckled. "For certain kinds of sicknesses."

"How can we get there?" Sookie asked.

"Easy," Pushy Lady joked. "They'll take you up to the front gate in a truck if you fail the exam. And really, who can pass it all the time—not every Joe-san is going to agree to wear protection."

"How can we get there if we don't ride the government truck?" I said, irritated with Pushy Lady not only for laughing at me, not only for not telling us what we needed to know, but also for not offering us any of her food. That was rude, and I was hungry.

Pushy Lady took another bite of the *kimbap* before she answered. "The train to Seoul passes near the Monkey House. Get off at Pusanjin-gu and walk toward mountains. You still have to do a bit of walking to get there." She picked at a bit of seaweed lodged in her teeth. "Really, I think you girls should just go home and wait. Your *omoni* will be home soon as she can."

"Thank you, Auntie," Sookie said, but I turned away without saying anything to Pushy Lady.

"Let's go, Sookie," I sniffed as I took her hand. "Come to my house for lunch. Maybe we can make our own *kimbap.*"

Once again Pushy Lady found me hilarious. I could hear her big-mouth, ear-cracking cackles as we stomped away, but at that point I cared more about my stomach than my pride. When I think about how hungry I thought I was that day, after having missed just one meal, I feel ashamed. Because I never once worried about the hunger Sookie must have felt when—day after day, week after week—her mother failed to return.

4

While her mother was in the Monkey House, I still saw Sookie every day, but somehow I learned *not* to see her as well. It was difficult, at first, to pretend that things were normal for her. Then, perhaps because pretending so relentlessly begins to blur the distinction between invention and reality, it became easy to believe things were normal. Practice formed a new pattern, a new way of seeing.

In avoiding her mother's absence, I became adept at ignoring the obvious regarding Sookie. I stopped noticing how pale and gaunt she became, how circles blackened her eyes, how her hair—wild and uncombed—inched past the approved school length. I forgot what she was supposed to look like.

It became normal for me to bring her her breakfast before school. A ball of rice wrapped in seaweed. Shreds of dried squid. Half a pig's foot. A handful of nuts or grapes. A few pieces of *yot*. Little things that I could hide in my book bag. "Here," I would tell her each morning as I handed her my left-over dinner, "now give me my homework." And Sookie would dutifully pass me the art or history assignments she had completed for me in trade.

My father, who prepared breakfast before opening the store, began serving me the largest portions of rice to eat with the previous night's leftovers. Sometimes he'd boil two eggs, telling me to eat one at the table and the other on the way to school. "She's growing," he'd say in response to my mother's glare. He knew, I now think, that I smuggled food to Sookie.

Looking back, I have to believe my mother also knew, but said nothing. The day Sookie and I returned from Clinic No. 5, I had asked my parents if she could stay with us until her mother returned from the Monkey House.

My mother slapped my face. "Don't ever let me hear you speak of that place again."

"Stop, *anae*." My father grabbed my mother's hand. When she tried to slap him with her free hand, he pinned her arms against her sides. I had never seen my parents embrace before. Without glancing at me my father said, "Leave, Hyun Jin. Your mother and I need to speak privately."

I ran outside, scurrying around the back of the house, where I squatted underneath the window of the rear sleeping room.

Though they tried not to raise their voices, I caught fragments of what they said:

My father's rumbling voice: "I promised . . ." countered by the sharp whip of my mother's: "She is no better than she has to be."

Their alternating voices, the low and the high, crisscrossed:

"I knew her as a girl—" my father began.

"That's the problem," interrupted my mother.

"She wasn't always—" my father started again.

"Yes, she was," my mother insisted. "It's in the blood. Everyone's life is mapped from the moment of birth."

My father's voice dropped, but I thought he said something about parents and choices, to which my mother—inexplicably to me at the time—said: "That's why you have to be strong with Hyun Jin."

Hearing my name, I jumped away from the window. I thought that somehow my mother knew I was eavesdropping, that her anger had eyes that could see my heart. I almost begged for forgiveness, but when I realized that she was still speaking with my father, I ran away instead. I was too relieved to wonder why my mother mentioned me in the first place.

What I didn't have to wonder about, what was clear from what I had heard, was that Sookie would not be allowed to stay with my family. My father had no power against my mother. And though she did not expressly forbid me from playing with her, I knew my mother never approved of my friendship with Sookie. Whenever I mentioned Sookie—what she said in school, how she had laughed when we played seesaw or *salgunori,* what American treat she had given me—my mother, her face pinched, would spit out, "It's in the blood." Then she would turn on me.

Eventually, I learned not to speak about Sookie because

when I did, nothing I did pleased my mother. The fruit I sliced for the *yot* was too thick, she would complain, pushing my hand away as she grabbed for the knife to rechop what I had already done. In tempo with the downward strokes, she muttered, "Like this, like this, like this! How easy!" louder and louder, the knife slashing—quick and violent—killing the fruit, splattering its meat across the floor.

Or the *mandoo* I folded looked like a closed fist instead of a half-moon with edges pinched into delicate dimples. Or the way I swept was unlucky, scaring up clouds of dust demons. Once when I had tried appeasing her by fixing my hair like hers and saying, "I hope I look like you when I grow up, *Omoni,*" she slapped me on my stained cheek as if to emphasize my imperfection. Because of my deformity, that slap said, I could never hope to be anything but ugly.

"You will never look like me," she spat as I cringed under her open hand. "Blood will always tell."

In a way, though, Sookie did move in with us. Something like her shadow breathed through the empty spaces of our home. Her presence was felt in the absence of small foodstuffs, in the secrets and suspicions left unsaid, in the guilt that caused my father to boil eggs two at a time.

At night the shadow of Sookie entered my dreams. Sometimes I dreamed Sookie was far ahead of me on a deserted wooded path. Dark-leaved trees bent toward me with gnarled, flexing fingers. Embedded in their trunks, faces grimaced, carving the air with wooden howls. "Sookie!" I would shriek. "Wait!"

She'd stop, her back to me, until I was just a few feet behind her. Then I'd hear her panting, and it was the panting of a fox.

Her shoulders heaved, bucking with the force of her gasps and I knew that if I touched her, she'd turn, and her face would be the face of a green-eyed fox girl with bloody, pointed teeth ready to take a bite. In my dream I stood frozen, poised just behind her, unable to touch her, unable to run away, riveted by the sound of her breathing.

Sometimes her breathing became the gasps I heard the day Sookie had hyperventilated at Dr. Pak's Love Clinic No. 5. With each inhalation, the space around us grew smaller. Like the fox who drains the blood of her victims, Sookie sucked and sucked, stealing the air from my body. Her wheezing grew louder, the forest darker, the air thicker yet more fragile in my own lungs. I fought the fox girl for each breath, struggling in my sleep until I woke to the sound of my own harsh choking.

One morning, alarmed by my struggles to breathe, my mother decided to take me to her *hanyak-chesa,* reasoning that the herbalist would be able to pinpoint the reason for my weakening system. Gripping my elbow, she propelled me through America Town, down the winding alleys in the direction of the bay. Just visible in the hills behind us, nesting like open-beaked birds, loomed the shadowy outlines of the pointy-roofed, double-story houses where the *miguk* officers kept their families.

We marched past several GIs with their club girlfriends, their big meaty arms flung over the women's shoulders, hairy hands cupped around breasts. "Don't watch," my mother hissed, slapping my jaw.

Obedient, I turned my head away and looked in the other direction. Other GI girls, their loose hair mussed, leaned out of their apartment windows and yelled to the men leaving their rooms. "Hey, Saxy! You be back to see me?" They pursed their reddened lips, blowing kisses into the wind.

My mother walked without taking her eyes off the ground.

"I would kill myself before I let the big nose *miguks* touch me."
She shuddered, sidestepping potholes and groping couples as she would piles of dog dung. "Dirty animals."
I wasn't sure if she was talking about the GIs or the women.

Lobetto and Chung Woo, who often crossed Chinatown to play at the train tracks along the pier, would tell stories about our Chinese neighbors, who seemed just as foreign to me as the *miguk* and *gomshi* soldiers. "You can't trust them," Lobetto once hissed. "The *Chinke* are really bandits who smuggle opium in the linings of their raggedy clothes and pointed hats."

"*Ye, ye,*" Chung Woo added, "and they eat the raw livers of their enemies."

Lobetto, who always seemed to have something in his mouth, spit his gum at my feet. "You can't make eye contact with them," he growled, " 'cause you never can tell what they're thinking. They might think you're the enemy and slice you up."

When my mother led me past the first bakery with almond cookies, fried dough stuffed with black bean, sticky *gau gee* cake sprinkled with sesame, I knew we had entered Chinatown. I looked for the bandits and opium addicts. To my disappointment, the only remotely mysterious person I spotted was an old woman who wore silver and jade in Buddha-long earlobes. Baskets hooked over her arms, she tottered in and out of the shops that sold firecrackers and beads, dried roots and sugared fruits. Everyone else I saw along the streets and through the shop windows looked ordinary. Korean.

Though my mother visited Chinatown often for ginseng, snake wine, and iris root to bolster what she called the softening of my father's vigor, I could remember, dimly, visiting only once before.

I remember reaching up to hold on to my father's hand,

skipping to match his pace, as we wandered past shop windows stocked with the fantastic: jars as tall as I was, filled with what looked like clusters of little white people, limbs entwined, suspended in amber; blood red pigs' heads perched on pointed sticks, their mouths gaping open in silent laughter at some secret porcine joke; snakes hanging by their silvery tails, their fangs open and ready to swallow my eyeballs.

My father and I had entered the store that seemed the most magical of all; its window was a vision from an enchanted forest. Strings of dried-mushroom stars danced across the top of the frame, and from behind a tangle of disembodied antlers that looked like a network of tree branches, a buck stared at me, transfixed. I stared back, and in his liquid eyes, I could also see myself. I knew then, in a moment more of looking, I would become the deer and the deer me.

My father, having finished his business with the herbalist, pulled me away before the transformation could take place. We walked into one of the alleys and up a set of wood stairs that groaned at the weight of our steps. At the top, we pushed open a door decorated with a small painting of one of the little people I saw dancing in a jar of amber water. Tendrils of cigarette smoke spiced with the pungent smells of hot cinnamon and ginger wrapped around us, pulled at our legs like lost and tricky spirits as we waded toward an empty booth.

My father ordered *chat juk* for me and a serving of fruits steeped in wine for himself. After tasting, then spitting out a potent slice of tangerine from my father's bowl, I settled down to sip my sweet rice and pine nut porridge. Before I was through with my treat, a woman emerged from the mist, pulling a girl taller but skinnier than me behind her. The lady stopped by our table, but instead of sliding into the booth with us, she knelt before my father. My father nodded briskly at her bowed head, then pushed an envelope toward her. "This is all I can get right now," he said.

The little girl stared at me as I licked each bit of rice gruel off my spoon. Her eyes were black in the dim light of the teahouse. I stuck my tongue out at her, but she didn't smile or frown. Mysterious, I thought, as I waited for those dark eyes to blink, mysterious as a *Chinke*.

My mother stopped at the shop with the deer in the window. Not as glamorous as I remembered, its coat was mangy and moth-eaten. And its eye—years older, I could see that it was only a glass marble, black and empty of life and magic. The herbalist, who had a growth the size of my fist bubbling up from the side of his neck, pushed his fingers into my throat. After taking my pulse at points along the meridians of my body—throat, temple, elbow, wrist—to see where my energy faltered, he rendered his verdict. "An overdose of *um*," he announced. Too much wetness and darkness had seeped into my lungs. I was slowly drowning.

"How come you can't cure your own self," I gurgled, eyeing his neck.

My mother flicked the back of my head with her fingers, and the herbalist clucked his tongue. "Very dark," he said, and he and my mother nodded in agreement over my head.

The *hanyak-chesa* then shuffled to the display in the window. He broke off a finger of the deer's antler and threw it into a bowl where he ground it into powder. When my mother turned away, the herbalist narrowed his eyes at me and plucked one of the long hairs sprouting from his neck growth. He blew on it, then mashed it in with the deer horn.

"Hey," I shouted. My mother flicked me again harder, and the herbalist continued to pound with his pestle. After adding pinches and spoonfuls of various black and brown powders from the jars behind the counter, he poured the mixture into a bag and handed it to my mother.

"Two things," he instructed. "One, make tea for her before she sleeps each night. Second, make a paste and put it over her birthmark. Slowly, it will fight the darkness coming from within her."

I presented Sookie with the bag of herb dust after a week of choking it down and rubbing it into my skin.

"What's this?" she asked, looking into the bag.

Feeling mean with power, I shrugged. "Breakfast."

"Not funny," she said flatly. "I'm hungry."

"So eat it," I teased. "It's good for you."

"Give, Hyun Jin," Sookie said. "I finished the map of the world for you." She lifted a scroll from her book bag and carefully unrolled it. "See? I colored it in special."

Frowning at her, I didn't bother to glance at the map. "I didn't get a perfect score on the last assignment."

Sookie looked down, rubbing one foot over the other. "No?" she said.

"No. But I saw you did."

Sookie bit her lip. "It was a mistake. I didn't mean to."

"Hah, I'm on to your tricks," I said. "I'm the one who taught them to you." I grabbed the map from her and studied the mosaic of neatly labeled countries and continents vibrantly bordered by ocean blue. It was better than what I could have done, and this irritated me.

Sookie's stomach rumbled. "Didn't you bring me real food?"

Her whining made me feel meaner, because in truth I had forgotten about bringing her anything to eat. I had just wanted to show her what, in my mind, I had to endure for her. I wanted to tell her stories about Chinatown, about the herbalist who stored poison in his neck. But instead I told her: "Take it or leave it."

She weighed the bag in her palm for a moment, then threw it to the ground. "I'm not so desperate I would eat your dirt."

"Fine," I said, shrugging. "See you at school then." I walked away from her. I thought she would catch up with me, give me a thump on the head for my crankiness. But when, without slowing, I glanced back, I saw her kneeling on the ground, sniffing the bag of herbs.

The next morning, I came to her front door bearing two boiled eggs. Feeling guilty, I had sacrificed my own breakfast as a peace offering. "No thanks," Sookie said airily, waving away my offer. "I just drank my breakfast. The herbs filled me up quite nicely."

She marched down her steps, pushing me slightly as she went by. I held the eggs tighter in my fists. One of them cracked. I wrestled with my book bag, shoving the eggs into one of the side pockets, and followed her.

"Ho Sook, wait!" I commanded, my neck prickling at the echo of my dream as I ran to catch up.

Just like in my dream, Sookie waited without turning to look at me. But unlike in the dream, the real Sookie spoke. "The colors are so bright today, aren't they?" she said. Her voice sounded far away, as if we were living her dream, not mine. She spread her arms, embracing the sky. "That blue fills me," she said, squinting at the clouds. "It hurts my eyes." She started to cry.

"Sookie," I said. I touched her shoulder.

Wrapping her arms around herself, she said: "The colors are tearing me apart." She lay down on her back, her chest arching upward over the hump of her book bag. Her head lolled back, the top of it touching the ground, her chin angled toward the sky.

"Don't look anymore." My voice sounded harsh because I was so worried.

"Yes, we're not supposed to look at the sky, at the sun. It's too bright. It's too full of color. But look around, Hyun Jin—at the dust we kick up as we walk. Look how it sparkles as it floats through the air, like little diamonds. Like tiny suns full of light and color. That's me now, Hyun Jin. I'm a tiny dust sun, exploding with colors, and soon I will be blown away. Breathe a part of me in, okay?"

"Please, Sookie, get up." I pulled her arms. She was limp as a doll. "School's starting. I hate to be late." I tried a threat: "If I leave you lying here, Lobetto and his gang will find you, and then what? They'd probably stomp on you; he still has to pay me back for the time I cut his eye. It scarred, you know," I said, fingering my own face. "He probably hates us more now."

She allowed me to pull her up and together we hobbled to school. Sookie didn't say anything else, but her head swiveled all the way there as she tried to watch each speck of dust smote by a shaft of light.

I got her into her seat before the teacher arrived, but when we were asked to stand for our lesson, Sookie fell back down. She crashed into two desks on her right, knocking them onto their sides. Her head smacked the corner of one of the desks, so that as she lay on the floor a bump the size of a baby's fist rose from her forehead. One of the girls whose desk was overturned screamed, "Sookie's dying!"

The teacher rushed to Sookie's side and poked at the bump with his long fingers. "Nothing seems cracked," he murmured. He pushed harder. "Does feel squishy, though."

"Ow," Sookie croaked.

The teacher looked into her eyes. "Do. You. Know. Who. I. Am?" he asked.

"Ow," Sookie said again. "Your voice is very loud." She closed her eyes for a breath and when she opened them, told the teacher, "You are a sun," and closed her eyes again.

The teacher looked up and frowned. At me. "Kong Hyun Jin, come forward!"

I panicked when he used his reprimand voice. The only thought in my mind was a defensive refrain: I didn't do it I didn't do it. "Yes, Respected Teacher," I answered.

"Take Cho Ho Sook home. Stay with her. Make sure she doesn't sleep. If she becomes sick, or if she falls asleep and you cannot wake her, run to the doctor."

On the walk home, Sookie explained her fall this way: "The colors rushed into my head, like the rockets Americans shoot into the sky the night before their new year. I had no choice but to fall down and enjoy the show."

"I think we better keep walking," I told her. Instead of heading straight to her apartment, I turned to follow the inside wall that surrounded America Town. I figured by the time we walked around the perimeter of America Town, it would be all right to let Sookie sleep. Teacher didn't tell me how long she should stay awake. Sookie leaned against me, and I leaned against the wall as we shuffled along.

We passed the building where two missionary women had set up a school for the throwaway children of the neighborhood. We passed the open window and heard the children roaring their answers to each of the teacher's questions:

"What are you?"

"American!"

"Why?"

"Our fathers are American!"

"Which is better: Korea or America?"

"America!"

"Where do you want to go?"

"America!"

I looked in at the group of chanting children and saw Lobetto staring out the window at us. Our Respected Teacher had suggested Lobetto change schools after Lobetto's father left for the United States. When Lobetto saw us looking, he pointed to Sookie and, holding a hand like a cup, tilted his head back like he was drinking a beer.

I shook my head and mouthed, No.

Lobetto made a rude gesture by poking his index finger in and out of the cup of his other hand.

As I gasped, he shuffled his fingers so only one finger stuck up.

I pointed a finger back at him.

"Wrong finger," Sookie commented. I thought her eyes had been closed while we walked, but she had been watching me.

"What?" I grumbled, looking at my index finger.

Sookie laughed, a quiet laugh. Through the window I could also see Lobetto holding his sides in laughter as well. "Doesn't matter," she mumbled. "Can we go home now? I'm tired and I want to eat."

Guiltily, I realized Sookie hadn't eaten that morning, and I didn't know if she had had dinner the night before either. Or, for that matter, when she had last eaten at all. I thought of the two eggs in my bag. "It's your own fault for skipping breakfast," I grumbled. Though I was hungry now too, I still planned to give her both eggs. She could eat them at her apartment, then rest. But if she looked like she would fall asleep, I would make her get up and walk again.

We cut through the courtyard between two apartments, ducking under a line of sheets hanging to dry. On clinic day, lines of laundry zigzagged throughout America Town: large flags of men's shorts, tiny butterfly wings of black and red lace, and diaphanous wraps and gowns—peach and pink ghosts— flapped and quivered in the wind.

On the wall of the apartment next to Sookie's someone had scrawled: "GOMSHI. SIR NIGGER, GO HOME." And under that, as if in response, another someone had scribbled in English, "FOK YOU. I AM." I thought that it could have been Lobetto; at his new school, he had learned to write English swear words better than anybody.

At her place, Sookie fumbled for the key around her neck. Pulling the chain out of her shirt, she leaned over and stretched it to jiggle the key in the lock. "I'm stuck," she croaked.

With Sookie's head bumping against the door, I twisted the key and the knob. The door opened with a quick jerk, yanking Sookie—still attached at the neck—over the threshold and onto her knees.

"Sookie!" I pulled on the key, trying not to jostle her further. "Are you all right?" The lock finally released the key with a scraping sigh while Sookie, kneeling on the ground with one hand cradling her head and the other her neck, groaned in short, hiccuppy bursts.

When I ran to hold her, I saw that she was laughing, not cry-ing. She dropped her hands, and I saw her lump was now ac-companied by a long rash on her neck. "Let me take a look," I scolded. Gingerly, I held her head in my hands and peered at her wounds while she tried not to laugh in my face. "You're messed up," I announced.

We both started laughing.

When we were exhausted, sides sore from struggling to draw a clear breath free of laughter, we clambered to our feet. "Come on," I said, taking her elbow to lead her to the kitchen. I lifted the book bag from her shoulder and pushed her into a chair. "Sit. Time to eat."

Swinging my bag onto the table, I sprawled into the chair next to hers and sifted through worksheets and notebooks for the eggs. I fingered the shattered shells, testing their rubbery bodies, then plucked them out. "See what I have for you?" I presented them to Sookie with a flourish, as if they were jewels.

She didn't smile. She stared at the eggs and, hands shaking, accepted my gift. Bringing them to her nose, she sniffed at the eggs, then placed one on the table. The other, she cupped in both palms and began to peel, rubbing her thumbs against the bits of shell that fell onto the table. When the egg looked clean and naked as a newborn, she held her palm up, offering it back to me.

I shook my head. "No, you eat it," I told her. "I'm not hungry."

"Liar," she said. "I heard your stomach rumble."

"Really, eat it," I said. "I brought them both for you."

"Thank you." She smiled, not at me but at the shivering egg, and bit. She ate the white first, exposing with each nibble the heart, until she held the marble of yolk between her fingers. After examining its perfection, she popped the yolk into her mouth. She sucked on it like it was candy, closing her eyes to savor the richness.

My stomach grumbled again. As I watched her peel the second egg, I decided that if she offered this one, I would eat it. She didn't. I couldn't watch her eat the last egg. Instead, I went to the kitchen for water. When I opened the cabinet for a cup, I found an American package. Blue with a picture of some kind of spotted biscuits and the words *Chips Ahoy.* I shook the bag, heard the rattle of a few biscuits left.

Without dropping the package, I opened the other cabinet and found more things American: an empty carton decorated with pictures of oranges; two tins with pictures of miniature hot dogs; a small, yellow-checkered bottle with no picture so I didn't know what it was; thick white envelopes that contained what felt like ground herbs. American herbs, I thought, were surely much better than the Koran weeds I had been forced to drink.

Clutching the secret stash against my chest, I confronted Sookie, who was still sucking on the last of my egg. I threw the food onto the table, screeching, "What's this?"

Her mouth opened, revealing a creamy mash of pale yellow.

Anger rolled over me, exploded in my head like Sookie's colors. "All this time I been feeding you with food out of my own mouth! I've been starving and you've been feasting on American treats!"

Sookie swallowed, quickly licking the last of the yolk from her teeth. "I'm not, I haven't—"

"You've kept it secret." I glared at her until she looked away.

"I was trying to save them until my mother got home," she said. Her voice quivered.

I shook the biscuit bag in her face. "It doesn't seem like you saved very much."

"I got hungry," she said, pushing her bottom lip out.

"But I've been feeding you every day!" I said, indignant. At that moment, I conveniently forgot the days I had neglected to bring her anything to eat. "You should have shared these with me like I've been sharing with you." I ripped open the blue bag. Reaching to the bottom, I pulled out a small, broken cookie flecked with chocolate. "In fact, you're going to share with me now." I gobbled up the cookie, then reached into the bag for a handful of crumbs to stuff into my mouth.

Sookie watched me with solemn, mournful eyes. *"Chipusa-Hoi ku-ki,"* she announced.

"Wha?" I mumbled, trying to work my tongue around the mass in my mouth.

"That's the name of that cookie," she explained. Sookie lined up the rest of the American goods on the table, naming them as I sampled each one: *"Be-enna sa-sa-gi. Pow-da mil-ku. Cheezu Wheezu."*

"They were supposed to be for my mother," she said after I had devoured everything. I was so angry that I couldn't taste what I had eaten, and that made me angrier.

"Don't try to make me feel guilty," I said, glowering.

"Her darkie boyfriend brought them one day," Sookie said, rolling the empty Vienna sausage can around the table. I didn't remember eating those, but I must have; I could still taste the juice it was packed in. "He came by a couple weeks ago looking for her. He had gone to the club where she worked and they told her she was sick at home. So he came here. 'You Duckie's sister-san?' he asked me.

"Do you know, Hyun Jin," Sookie asked, "what I thought of when he asked if I was my mother's sister? Remember what my mother told us, the secret about *miguk* eyes?"

"That fairy tale that Americans cannot see who we are?" I scoffed.

"I didn't believe her, either," Sookie said, "But when her boyfriend asked me that, I began to wonder if what my mother told us was true."

"What did you tell the guy?" My chest felt tight, as if I were the boy trapped by the fox girl's spell.

Sookie shrugged. "I told him, 'No I am not, you blind, fat-nosed American.'" She grinned. "Then I told him in English: 'No. No sister-sans. Me baby-san. Duk Hee mama-san.'"

I was impressed. I didn't know her English was so good. "Then the darkie left?" I asked, still wondering how she got the food.

"Well, the darkie didn't leave right away," Sookie said. "First he just stood at the door shaking his head, looking like a confused cow. 'Mama-san?' he repeated: 'Duckie mama-san, you baby-san? Old, how muchie?'

"I told him again, slow so he could understand: 'Duk Hee. Is. Not. Home. She's at the hos-pi-tal.' And I closed the door on his face."

"No!" I said. "You should have been nice to him. He's your mother's boyfriend."

"Well," Sookie shot back, "I could barely understand a word he was saying. Besides, I figured my mother could always get another boyfriend."

I shook my head. She knew her mother had been working that Joe for a while. Most of her boyfriends were *good-timu boizu*. But that one, she was hoping would get serious enough to ask her to marry him. Americans were different from Koreans that way; an American man would marry a "young sexy" if he thought he loved her enough.

Sookie held up her hands. "Hyun Jin, wait. Wait until I finish the story before you say anything. Listen:

"After I closed the door on his nose, I was thinking the same things you're probably thinking. That I ruined my mother's chances, right?

"But you know what, Hyun Jin? That darkie came back! The next night. And with a bag of food—American food that I never saw before." She held up the packages in front of her. "This and this and this. And more." She looked at the table and sighed. "Which is now all gone."

"He just gave you the food? All of this? For nothing?" I asked. I couldn't believe it. It would have taken all the money my father made in a year at the store to buy all that food.

"I told you to let me finish the story," Sookie snapped, suddenly angry. "When he gave me the food, he told me, 'You hungry, you find me. Chazu. Club Foxa.'"

"Why would he give you all that for nothing in return?" I stopped to think. "I bet he was in love with your mother! I bet he was coming to take her with him. I bet he saw you, and thought, 'Oh, no! she has a child from another man,' And that was it. I bet—"

"Stop!" Sookie sobbed. She pressed her hands to her ears. "I know I ruined my mother's chance!"

I jumped up and grabbed her hands in mine. "I'm sorry, Sookie," I said. "I was just talking, just making up stories, really. Don't listen to what I said."

"It's just that he came with all this food. My mother wasn't here. I was hungry. I—"

"It doesn't matter," I interrupted, afraid of what I might hear. "Who knows why GIs do anything? He probably didn't know why he did it himself." Feeling stiff and awkward, I patted her on the back, then sat back down.

Sniffing, Sookie rubbed at her eyes. "Well," she said, giving me a weak smile. "Why don't we finish this feast?"

She shook a packet of what she said was *pow-da* milk, then ripped a strip off the top with her teeth. A cloud of white dust rose into the air. Squeezing the sides so it opened like a cup, she tilted the packet toward me.

I looked inside. "It's dust. Reminds me of my dirt medicine," I said.

Giggling, she dipped her finger into the envelope and licked. "No," she said, "this is good."

I poked my finger—up to the line that marked the amount of water used to cook a pot of rice—into the packet, then licked the coating off. Back and forth, we dipped our fingers into the milk, until we scraped the clumped grains clean from the side of the packet. When it was empty, Sookie turned the envelope inside out, exposing the silver lining. Only then did I notice that the wall behind her reflected the light from the glittering skins of other milk packets and candy bars. "Next time," she said when she saw me staring at the decorated wall, "I'll save a little rice to paste this up, too."

"I'll bring you some rice tomorrow," I promised. "And some *chige,* too," I added, though I wondered about how to smuggle extra soup out of the house. I supposed I would have to request it for lunch and give it to Sookie instead.

"Don't bother, Hyun Jin," she said. She continued to look at her silver wall. "I never want to depend on anyone to feed me again."

A lump formed in the pit of my stomach. Waiting for her to turn toward me, I watched her in the shadowed evening. The only light, reflecting off the silver wall, flickered weak and uncertain around the kitchen, turning a room where I had spent so much time into a place suddenly and completely unfamiliar.

5

They came when the sky was at its darkest, without light from the rising sun or setting moon, the hour of ambivalence when nothing is as it should be. When they pulled her up from the sleeping mat, Sookie had been dreaming of flying. In the dream, she and her mother rode on the back of a gigantic flying pig. At first, Sookie had been afraid to board the bristle-backed hog, but her mother had laughed and pulled her up. As Sookie gripped the pig's long, sparse quills, it shrugged its dark wings and pranced into the air. Perched on the pig's back, her ears full of her mother's laughter, Sookie looked down as America Town turned into a set of children's blocks. Above her the sun burned unrelenting and ferocious, so bright she could not bear to look up.

Not quite awake when they jerked her to her knees, Sookie imagined she had fallen off the flying pig and her mother had grabbed her elbows to keep her from spiraling into the sun. But the hands on her were rough, and spoke with loud, harsh voices.

"Get up!" Claws pulled Sookie into a circle of light, the sun of her dream. Behind the light, Sookie was able to discern the shadows, like ghosts from the underworld, of a man and a woman. Squinting toward the edge of the flashlight, Sookie saw, in hyperrelief, sharp purple nails and the edge of a woman's long-sleeved *najang* dress. Sookie's mother told her once that rich gentlewomen wore these thin, loose-fitting silk dresses only inside the home, like nightclothes.

"She must be drunk," the woman hissed. "Who can sleep this hard?"

"Cho Ho Sook," the man intoned. "Where is your license?"

"I told you she doesn't have one!" the woman scolded. She kneed Sookie's shoulder. "You are a cheater!"

Tongue thick in her mouth, Sookie tried to answer: "No, no, I ah—" she croaked.

"Mrs. Kim, please. This is official business. Cho Ho Sook, is it true you have been working without a license? I warn you to answer truthfully; we have documentation."

Sookie pulled away from Mrs. Kim and turned to the man. She wrapped the blanket around her body. "I don't understand," she whimpered. "I don't work. I go to school."

"See!" Mrs. Kim crowed. "She's lying!" She raised her hand

as if to strike. Sookie flinched, closing her eyes, but when no blow landed, she opened them to see the woman release a handful of paper. Silver winged paper flashed in the light, fluttering about her shoulders, down to her feet.

"So I suppose these goodies were free?" the woman challenged. "Cigarettes. Biscuits. Milk. Chocolate."

She jerked the flashlight around the room; the erratic beam of light sliced her home to pieces. Sookie could see that the man and woman had gone through her cabinets, torn the wrapping off her carefully decorated wall. She hated to see the bare boards.

The man cleared his throat. "As I said, Miss Cho. We have evidence of your working. Clinic papers filled out and signed with your name. Witnesses who've seen men visiting this apartment recently. I want to know if you are working legally. That is my only concern."

"She's stealing my customers," Mrs. Kim whined. "And keeping the money her family owes to me." Her flashlight wavered between Sookie's face and the man's chest. "Respected Mr. Li, I need to eat, too. How can I run my hospitality club if the girls think they don't have to follow the rules? I want you to do something about that."

Mr. Li opened his hands in an attempt to soothe the woman. "Mrs. Kim, there are proper channels—"

"I paid you to fix this now!" Mrs. Kim snarled.

Before Mr. Li pushed the flashlight back into Sookie's face— blinding her—she caught a glimpse of his irritation at Mrs. Kim: he wrinkled his nose as if he smelled something rotten. "As a governing official of America Town," Mr. Li intoned, his voice placid, "I must see that things are done a certain way. There is the matter of license fee, health clearance, management and rental fees."

"My mother . . ." Sookie offered, lifting her hand to shield her face.

"Your mother hasn't been around for almost a month!" Mrs. Kim spat. "She probably ran off with some Joe and left you here to pay off her mess."

"No, that's not true," Sookie whispered.

"Who cares?" The light jerked toward the ceiling as Mrs. Kim shrugged. "She's not here."

"I will require that you address these certain matters," said Mr. Li, breaking into the conversation, "or you must leave this apartment."

"That'll teach you to steal customers out of my place." Mrs. Kim again bumped Sookie's shoulder. "If you want to work, work *for* me, not *against* me."

When they left her apartment, Sookie gathered the papers from the floor and piled them onto her sleeping mat. Making a nest for herself amid the torn labels and tattered wrappers, she thought about her mother flying away on the back of a pig. She thought about where to get money. She thought about me. And she waited for morning.

At least this is what she told me when I found her the next day. The apartment gaped open, the door swinging on its hinges like a broken tooth. "Sookie?" I called before entering. From the doorway, the room looked chewed up, half-digested. Beyond the upturned kitchen table and toppled chairs, Sookie sat calm as the Buddha in a sea of garbage.

Months later, Lobetto would tell me a story that would make me question what Sookie told me that morning. But then, I believed in her enough to want to help her. After brushing the silver foil from her—some of which stuck to her head—I stood her up. I braided her hair and wiped the sleep from her face, just as her own mother would have done. I righted the table and chairs and sat her down. Scanning the floors, I found a packet of unopened milk and poured it into a cup. I added water, mixing with my finger, until it resembled the sweet *chat juk* my father had once bought for me in Chinatown, and placed it in front of her.

Sookie drank without expression. Only her throat moved with each swallow as she held the cup to her lips. When she put the milk down, a ribbon of white lined her lips; the rest of the milk stuck like clumps of clay to the bottom of the cup. Sookie sat like a doll, her body stiff, her eyes fixed and unblinking as I gathered bits of rubbish from the floor, trying to corral them into neat piles, and folded her blankets into the bedroom chest for the day.

"If I were you, I would sleep on the bed while your mother is away," I said. I sat on the edge of the bed, then fell back against the pillow. The mattress was not as soft as I thought it would be, and the pillow was too soft. It also smelled musky and feral, like an animal. I sat up again, holding my nose. "Maybe not," I said, then waited for her to speak.

As I debated whether or not to leave for school without her, she said, "I have to find my mother."

"I don't want to be late for school," I said. If I was late the teacher would find someone else to be leader for the day, and whoever it was would certainly call on me, as payback, to answer the most difficult questions.

"Please, Hyun Jin," Sookie begged. "I have a plan."

"Ummm," I grunted, edging toward the door. "Why not just wait for her to come back?"

Sookie grabbed my hand. "I told you what they said to me.

Don't you understand? Don't you believe me? I can't just sit here waiting—no food, no money!"

I pulled my hand back. "Okay, okay. You can tell me your plan on the way to school."

"Wait, Hyun Jin!" Sookie scrambled through her book bag for a pencil and paper. "Let me write a note to our teacher. I'll say I'm still sick and that you need to take me to the doctor. Then you could come with me."

I frowned at her. "Where? Why can't we go after school?"

"I don't have time." Sookie started scribbling on the paper. Without looking at me she said, "And speaking of time, you're already late as it is—"

I wanted to grab that pencil away from her and stomp on it for spoiling my flawless attendance record. Instead I tapped my foot. "I'm not waiting for you much longer," I grumbled.

"If you're this late, isn't it better not to go?" Sookie asked. When I shrugged, she talked fast. "We can get Lobetto to deliver the message for us, and then we can go find my mother."

I pulled on my lip, pretending to consider. I had already made up my mind to go with her when she had said that it was better to miss school than to arrive after the start of lessons. Sookie, who knew how I thought, smiled at the paper as she finished writing the letter.

Lobetto hustled goods and information throughout Chollak, crisscrossing America Town, Harariya Base, and Chinatown for the GIs, their *yong sekshis,* and the black marketeers. This early in the morning, however, he'd be done with work and heading home.

"No," Lobetto grumbled. "Why should I do anything for you?" He squatted outside of his doorway, squinting up at us.

"What do you mean?" I scolded. "It's your job to deliver messages."

Lobetto continued to look up at us, his curls corkscrewing into his eyes. He yawned. Then he spat at our feet. "A job means money."

Spittle flecked the top of my right foot. Grimacing, I pushed my toes into the dirt to dry them off. Then I peeked over at Sookie. Money was the weak part of her plan.

She stepped forward. "We're going to pay you," she started.

Lobetto laughed. "With what? Everyone knows your mother left you with nothing! And you—" he said, glaring at me. "You going to get money from your mother to help Sookie? Everyone knows how your mother feels about her."

"What do you mean?" I asked.

Lobetto opened his mouth to shoot out his answer, but Sookie spoke first. "We're getting money from Duk Hee."

Lobetto stood, his knees crackling as he stretched upward. He pushed his nose into Sookie's face. "How? She's at the Monkey House."

"So?" Sookie shrugged like it was no big deal. "That's where we're going."

Biting his thumbnail, which was already torn past the quick, Lobetto frowned at Sookie through his bushy hair.

"You should cut your hair," I told him.

He sneered at me, his lip flipping up over his teeth, but as he turned to address Sookie, he wrapped his bangs around his ears. A faint scar snaked above his eyebrow. "You know how to get to the Monkey House?" he asked.

Again, she shrugged. "No, but I know people who know."

"Who?" Lobetto challenged.

"Mi Ok," said Sookie quickly, naming the pregnant girl we had met at Dr. Pak's Love Clinic.

Lobetto folded his arms across his chest and leaned against the wall. "That girl's already an inmate there."

Sookie looked at me. I shrugged. "There are others we can ask," she answered, though she sounded unsure.

Lobetto grinned. "You'll never find it on your own."

Sookie grabbed my arm. "Forget it," she said to him as we turned to leave.

"Yeah, we don't need him for anything," I said, though I was worried that without the note, the teacher would inform my parents that I had skipped school.

Lobetto jumped in front of us. "So what are you going to do?" he asked.

"Never mind," said Sookie.

"I'll deliver your note," said Lobetto, too quickly, I thought. "And I'll take you to the Monkey House. I need to drop some cigarettes there anyway."

Sookie nodded, but I asked, "What do you get out of it?"

Lobetto smiled. "Sookie's mama carries her purse with her, right? With all the money she made from the GIs?"

Sookie said nothing, knowing he already knew the answer. Everyone, especially Lobetto, knew the *yong sekshis* never went anywhere without their money.

"For one-half of the purse," Lobetto continued, "I'll deliver your note and take you to the Monkey House."

"Half?" I shouted. "That leaves Sookie and me with only a quarter each."

"What?" Sookie gasped. "I have to pay you, too?"

I folded my arms across my chest. "I am missing school for you. Or," I sighed, "I could always go to class late."

Sookie's eyes flickered quickly at my face. "One-third," she grumbled. "I'll give one-third to you, Hyun Jin, and one-third to Lobetto."

When Lobetto nodded, I pouted. "I don't trust him," I said.
"What?" said Lobetto. "I'm the one who's got to trust you.
You don't pay me till after we get to the Monkey House."

I pulled Sookie to my side. "It could be a trick," I whispered.
"He could jump us afterward and take everything." To Lobetto
I growled, "Maybe you want to get back at me for beating you
up when we were small."

"You never beat me up," he said. "And this is not a trick. I
swear it in blood and spit."

From his back pocket Lobetto pulled out a Swiss army knife,
a prize from his father, and sliced the palm of his hand. He spit
into the cut, closed his fist and waited for us to present our
hands.

Sookie and I glanced at each other, then down at our hands.
I almost told him that linking our littlest fingers together would
be promise enough for me, but Sookie gave Lobetto her hand.
I had to follow.

"I don't usually do this for girls," Lobetto mumbled. "But I
guess the money will be worth it." He nicked our palms across
the line fortune-tellers read for love.

Sookie and I cupped our hands and spit, watching the blood
ooze into the bubbly saliva. Then the three of us took turns
pushing our palms together in a promise of blood and spit.

Lobetto delivered the note quickly, swaggering into class while
Sookie and I watched at the window. When his father still lived
in Korea, Lobetto swaggered everywhere. One of the smartest
children in school—as well as the richest—he was able to present Respected Teacher with weekly gifts of coffee, cigarettes,
and nuts dipped in chocolate. Lobetto was chosen leader of the
class almost as much as I was.

But when his father left for the States and did not return, Lobetto stopped swaggering. The teacher stopped calling him to the front, then stopped seeing him at all. Eventually, Lobetto joined the other *ainokos* at the missionary school for children of GI whores.

Note gripped in his fist, Lobetto stood at the inside of the door, waiting for a break in the lesson, for the teacher to recognize him. The teacher glanced at him, then above him and kept talking. Lobetto flashed us a look; we pantomimed delivering the note, mouths open wide in silent and exaggerated instructions. After watching the teacher a few more minutes, Lobetto shuffled to the teacher's desk, head bowed, dropped the note, and slunk out.

We ran—away from the school and my father's shop, away from the GI girls draped in the windows and the hard-luck whores who danced in the "fish tanks," away from Chinatown herbalists and opium dealers—not stopping for breath until we reached the last butcher shop on Chinke-Chanke Road, at the edge of Chinatown. We puffed in front of the window where red ducks hung by their webbing and pig heads grinned on sharpened stakes. Around the corner from the butcher shop, the ocean opened before us, filling our eyes and noses: boats escorted by screaming gulls queued toward the pier where fishermen unloaded nets streaming with fish and eel and squid and clam. Wives and daughters squatted in the midst of the haul, hooking fingers under heaving gills and wriggling bodies, separating species into various baskets that they would later carry on their heads into the market tents.

Instead of continuing toward the docks, Lobetto veered to the train tracks, toward the coal factory that coughed its black smoke out to sea. Some days, when the wind stilled, a blanket of cinder hung over the pier, tinging the air with ash. "We'll follow the tracks north," Lobetto said as he stooped to pocket bits of coal.

"The Monkey House is in Seoul?" I gasped. It would take a week to walk that far.

Lobetto sneered. "They got Monkey Houses all over, *Dongg*-face. With all the GI girls in Korea, you think they got only one?" His pockets full, he began throwing chips of coal into his canvas bag, which was already packed with Lucky Strikes. "They probably sent Sookie's mom to the closest one, outside Pusan."

We walked parallel to the train tracks for a short while. The dust hung in the heat, and with the sun glinting off specks of rock, it was like walking through a glittered dream. I wished we had brought water. Sookie and I held hands until sweat pooled in our palms, salting the cuts Lobetto had made. Shaking the sting out, we dropped hands and continued to plod behind Lobetto. "He could kill us with his knife," I mumbled. "He could abandon us to die like dogs. He could have a gang of boys hiding in the hills, ready to beat us up. He could be plotting to sell us to Chinatown bandits or American slave owners."

Sookie kept her head straight, eyes on Lobetto's back, on the sway of the bag as it bumped against his hips. Without Sookie joining in, I dropped my game and became quiet. Finally, we crossed into a field of rice, a quilt of green and yellow. Mud squished between our toes and soothed our battered feet. Light shivered above the stalks like undisciplined rainbows. Sighing, the three of us knelt between the furrows to splash water into our faces, cup our hands, and drink.

"Watch for broken reeds," Lobetto warned as we stomped through the fields, up to our knees in the cool, brackish water. "They can slice into your foot like a spear."

"It's worth the risk," said Sookie. "After the tracks, this feels like heaven." But after a short while those fields became purgatory; the mud pulled at our legs, sucked them into the earth, and only reluctantly spat them out again as we trudged endlessly on.

We took only one break on the eternal trek to the Monkey House. Spying a small grape farm behind the rice fields, Lobetto motioned us out of the mud and onto our knees. We crawled in among the staked and stunted rows of twisting vines, glad for whatever shade was available during the hottest part of the day. Bellies to the ground, Lobetto and Sookie twisted cone-shaped clusters of grapes off the vine and shoved them— stems, curling tendrils, pits, and skin—into their mouths. Juice the color of blood dribbled down their chins and necks to stain the tops of their shirts. I nibbled at one, but gagged; grapes still tasted like vomit to me.

After eating his fill, Lobetto dug a shallow hole in the valley between two stakes, curled his body inside, and slept. Sookie and I lay head to head in the next row. The grape leaves only partially filtered the sun, dappling our skins. Under the leaves, I imagined Sookie and I—and even Lobetto—must look like siblings, their faces like mine always was, a pattern of light and dark.

"Sookie," I said, "did I ever tell you when my mother took me to this grape farm?"

"No." She stretched her arm out, groping for a small bunch of grapes above our heads. Most of the globes looked pink, sour, instead of purple. "This grape farm?" she challenged. "This very same one?"

I propped myself onto an elbow, squinted around. I didn't know if this was Grape Auntie's farm, but I nodded. "My mother carried me from town all the way on her back," I said.

"Your mother did that?" Sookie sounded sleepy, but surprised.

"Yes," I snapped. "She loved me so much, she carried me, then let me eat as many grapes as I wanted, just because I asked for them for my snack and we didn't have any at home." I paused to see if Sookie would question me again. When she didn't, I added, "That's how much she loved me." I scratched at a mosquito bite, scarping the skin until it oozed blood. "That was before you knew me."

"Ummh," Sookie grunted. "I can't remember a time I didn't know you."

I turned on my stomach to study her expression. "Are you saying I'm lying?" I demanded.

"Why would I say that?" she asked without looking at me. She sat up to concentrate on stripping the meat off of each grape she had picked. After sucking the seeds clean, she spit them into her hand and buried them in the ground.

In the late afternoon, we burst through the rice onto a dirt road carved by jeep tracks. "This is the last part of it," Lobetto told us. "The Monkey House is at the end of this road." Then he taught us American marching songs his father had taught him. Like soldiers heading home on leave, we shouted out:

> "This is my weapon, this is my gun.
> One is for shooting, one is for fun!"

and:

"I found a whore by the side of the road.
Knew right away she was dead as a toad.
Her skin was all gone from her tummy to her head.
But I fucked her, I fucked her even though she was dead!
I know it's a sin,
But I'd fuck her again!"

"Eh, Lobetto," we joked. "Do you even understand what you're singing?"

"Of course," Lobetto said. "I'm half-American."

"What's 'toad,' then?" Sookie challenged.

"Toggobi."

"What's 'fucked'?" I asked. I had heard Lobetto curse us with that word often enough to know that it was bad, but I wasn't sure how it translated.

"You don't know?" Lobetto hooted. "You don't know? Sookie, you tell her."

Sookie's mouth thinned, like she was holding something in, but she said, "It means, Hyun Jin, 'Your mama will die.' So don't ever say it."

Lobetto bent over, laughing, and held his sides like he was vomiting. I hated when he did that, acting like we were big jokes. "I bet," he gasped, "your mama wishes she was dead whenever she gets fucked." He laughed some more, then croaked, "Do you guys want to know what 'whore' means?"

Sookie and I pushed past him. We knew what whore meant; we knew whose mothers they were.

A jeep roared up behind us, silencing Lobetto's laughter, and we skittered to the side of the road. When it passed, we gave chase in the exhaust of fumes and dust. Without turning to look at us, the driver lifted his arm, releasing a handful of wrapped candies in the wake of the jeep. The candies landed like golden bullets in the dirt at our feet, and we laughed as we gathered them up. Unwrapping them, we sucked as we marched down the road, our mouths too full of sugar to sing again.

After a dip in the road, an abrupt hook, we came suddenly—almost unexpectedly, though that was our destination—face-to-face with the Monkey House. Gray and squat as a toad, the two-story Monkey House, ribboned by a chain-link fence, looked like any other government building. Except that this one, far outside the town, was half-hidden in the midst of nameless hills that rose around it like burial mounds.

In front of the padlocked gate, two guards pitched knives at the ground. Each time the knife quivered upright in the dirt, they would laugh. Then the thrower would step back and money changed hands. I could not tell if the soldiers were the same ones that had passed us on the road.

Lobetto pinched our elbows, then flicked his head toward the back of the building. In the shadow of the Monkey House, blocked from the guards, Sookie and I pulled and prodded each other over the fence. Lobetto, who had scaled it easily, puffed out his chest and grinned at us as our toes gripped loops of fence and our fingers slipped and slid off cold metal.

As we scrambled over the top, Lobetto scrounged on the ground for a handful of pebbles, which he threw at a window on the second floor. The rocks hit the window like a spattering of hail, then, rebounding, showered down on us.

"Ow, ow, ow," Sookie and I whispered as we danced around, trying to avoid the pelting. Lobetto stood under the window without moving, then shook his head free of pebbles when the quick onslaught was over.

"Shhwee, Lobetto!" A woman had lifted the window and poked her perm-burned head out. "You're early."

Lobetto swung his bag off his shoulder and pulled out a pack of cigarettes. "Eh, Mousie," he said, tossing one up. "My mother?"

"Not here." Mousie caught the pack and motioned for Lobetto to hurry. She was small and brown with the sharp, pointed chin of a rodent. "Heard she went up to Tongae hot springs with a rich GI."

Lobetto pitched two packs in quick succession.

"White guy this time," Mousie said, her hands darting quickly for the cigarettes. She flung them behind her, her eyes ready for the next one.

"Bet he don't know about me," Lobetto grunted as he threw the last of the Lucky Strikes.

"No," giggled Mousie, "I bet he don't." She faced the room and lifted her hand to close the window.

"Wait!" Sookie yelped.

"Shup!" said Lobetto, waving his arm to silence her.

"Ask about my mom," she whispered.

Mousie scowled down at us. "Does your girlfriend want to join us up here? We got plenty of space in the Rose Room."

"You know Duk Hee?" Lobetto asked.

Mousie turned to talk to the others in the room. When she looked back, she jerked her head to the side. "Try the Chrysanthemum Room. Two windows down, the one with the bars."

I didn't recognize the face that came to the window, not even when Sookie cried, *"Omoni!"* The face looked pale and gaunt, drawn with harsh lines of panic.

"What are you doing here?" Sookie's mother hissed.

"Mama," Sookie wailed. "I miss you. I'm scared. I'm hungry."

Sookie's mother pinned me with her black eyes. "Take her to your house," she ordered.

I opened my mouth to speak, though I wasn't sure what I would have said. In the end, I only stared up at her, gaping.

"No, Mama," Sookie said. "I'll be okay. Just give me some money so I can wait at home for you." Her arms reached toward the window, as if begging her mother to lift her into a hug.

"Go with Hyun Jin," she snapped.

Sookie dropped her arms and looked at the ground. "The mother doesn't like me."

Sookie's mother stared at her for so long, I thought she must have not heard her.

"She said my mother doesn't like her," I repeated, as loud as I dared.

When Sookie's mother's face reddened and her lips thinned, I stammered, "I'm sorry. It's not me. It's my mother, I—"

Without looking at me, she said, "Never mind about the mother. You tell Hyun Jin's father I said for him to take you in."

Stretching an arm through the bars, Sookie's mother held out a square of knotted silk. She dropped it, the red and blue tails of the knot fluttering like flags on the way down. Though Sookie stood under the window, ready to catch the purse, it dropped into the dirt beside her. Lobetto streaked forward, scooped up the prize and raced toward the fence.

"Hurry up," he said.

"Lobetto!" Sookie's mother scolded, though he couldn't hear her. "Sookie," she said, her face pressed against the bars as if she could squeeze herself out with the words, "don't let anyone steal that money from you. That's yours. That's yours. It's the only thing keeping you from this place."

After dividing the money into thirds—Lobetto clucking his tongue at the meager hoard and saying "pitiful" while he pocketed the won—Sookie reknotted the square of silk and wrapped it around her wrist with the weight of it cupped in her palm. Our shadows lengthening behind us, we decided to spend part of the money on train tickets back home. I was anxious to avoid questions from my parents; Lobetto was anxious not to miss out on his club circuit; and we took Sookie's silence as assent.

Sookie and I pushed toward the back of the train. *"Shillye hamnida,"* we repeated over and over again as we shouldered past other passengers and stepped on toes in our quest to find a handhold.

"Over here," said Lobetto. Tired of following behind us, ducking and weaving between bodies, he bulldozed a space near the windows. Sprawling in the foot space between two seats, Lobetto stretched his legs—stained by mud and sun and birth—into the aisle, ignoring the dirty looks of the passengers at whose feet he sat.

"Unjo." Lobetto pulled in his legs and motioned for us to sit next to him. "You might as well be comfortable." Sookie and I squatted by his toes. While Sookie looked out the window toward the hills shielding the Monkey House, Lobetto pulled a packet of colored papers from his bag.

"Homework?" I asked, surprised. I had thought all the *ain-okos* did was listen to stories about America and wait for their fathers to remember them.

"Work." Lobetto handed me a yellow sheet.

As I struggled to sound out the English: "See the Club Angel! Show. Pussy Pingpongball. Pussy smokecigarettes. Pussy writeletter," Lobetto explained. "I'm a bringer," he said. "The clubs pay me to bring in GIs. That's for Club Angel. Pink paper is for Club Rose, blue for Club Foxa. I make good money when the GIs come in with my programs." He tapped at his name scrawled in the upper corner of the paper.

"Pussy Openbeer bot-tle." I continued to wrestle with the words. "And 'dr-dr-I-ink-u'——"

Lobetto jerked the paper from my grasp. "You're pathetic," he snarled. "If you want to have a future, you have to learn better English. I'll read it to you." He puffed out his chest and cleared his throat, just as he used to do when preparing to read to us from his father's letters.

"See Fish Pushin sideher. Banana pushinto her. Egg pushin toher cunt——"

Before he finished reading the flyer, Sookie interrupted. "I'm hungry," she announced.

And suddenly we all were; that's all we could think about.

At the next stop, Lobetto stood up, leaned over the people in the seats and stuck his head out the window. *"Yogi-e, yogi!"* Lobetto waved at the grandmas selling food in the station. "Here, we'll buy something here," he called out. Women with backs bowed from food baskets crowded beneath our window, waving their specialties under the tips of Lobetto's fingers.

"What do you want?" Lobetto asked us. "*Kimbap,* sweet potato, eggs, persimmon, *hodu, cidah?*"

"Everything," I growled, suddenly hungry.

Sookie fumbled with the knot on her money pouch.

"Hurry, hurry." He motioned to the vendors with one hand and held his other hand out to us. We dropped money into his palm, and Lobetto passed it out the window. Reaching down, he grabbed up what was offered—rolls of *kimbap,* strings of yam, small woven baskets of eggs and orange persimmons, newspaper cups of walnuts, a six-pack of *cidah*—and hastily handed them off to us. Lobetto shoved his share into his canvas bag, while Sookie and I scooped the food into our shirts.

As the train began its slow roll out of the station, the three of us picnicked on the floor, stuffing rice balls into our mouths whole, washing down the bits of sticky grains clinging to our teeth with long gulps of bubbling *cidah*. We cracked open the eggs and nuts, devouring the meat and sweeping the shells underneath the seats. The *koguma* and persimmon we ate for dessert, smearing the fleshy fruits against our lips and tongues until the juices scented our faces and hair with their perfume.

When the passengers seated above Lobetto got off at the Pusan train station, Sookie and I scrambled into their seats. Relaxing into the cushions, we propped our feet against Lobetto's back. The sky outside deepened into the blue-gray of twilight, the time of magic and transformation. The windows turned into trick mirrors: I could see the countryside passing through my face. Sometimes a flash of light, like a lamp held by the dead returning for their annual *chesa,* winked from the fields and shattered my image.

As I tried to see my own face, I remembered how in my father's stories, reflection always reveals true nature. A fox demon disguised as a beautiful girl could be recognized by forcing it to look into a mirror, which would bare its real face.

Averting my eyes, I noticed the handkerchief from Sookie's mother hanging limply from Sookie's wrist. Digging through my pockets, I counted the money I had left: less than a hundred won. Less than a pound of rice. Ten times less than what her mother made in one night at the clubs. The picnic hardened in my stomach; I began to realize that, to Sookie, this day hadn't been just an adventure, a mere game, and I became afraid. For her, and for me.

I tried to catch her eye, waving at her face, but she ignored me. In the darkened window behind her, I saw my own flapping hand, a ghost straining to touch her through the glass. I ducked, trying instead to see Sookie's reflection. All I could see was the small cloud her breath made on the glass and above that my own face, pale and bodyless, hanging in the window like the moon in an uncertain sky.

6

"I don't know," I told Sookie as I blocked the doorway of my father's shop. I avoided her eyes, looking over my shoulder to make sure that my mother was not lurking behind me.

"Just ask," Sookie whined. Tired and dirty, her cheeks hollowed with hunger, Sookie crowded me on the top step. She tried to edge into the store. "My mother said your father said he would help me."

I stepped forward until Sookie dropped to the lower step. "When would my father have talked to your mother?"

Sookie scowled, jutting her lip. "He did."

"I don't know . . ." I said, twisting the shirttail of my school uniform.

"Hyun Jin!" Sookie pointed her finger at me.

I jumped, feeling as if I had been called out in class. "Yes," I said.

"I waited for you this morning," she accused. "And you never came for me. Again. How many times does this make?"

"I didn't want to be late for school," I lied.

Sookie narrowed her eyes. "You're not going to ask if I can stay even one night, are you?" she said.

I whirled around, stumbled into the sale table and scooped up some day-old rice cake. Holding the treat in my hand, I turned to Sookie. "Here," I stammered. "Something to eat."

Sookie stared disdainfully at the sticky rice cupped in my palm. "I told you I won't take scraps from you anymore," she said.

I let my arm drop. "Well, then . . ."

Her lip curled. "Yeah. Well, then." She turned and dragged herself down the steps.

I rushed after her. "Sookie!"

When she didn't slow, I hesitated, then hurried forward. "What're you going to do?" I panted at her back.

Sookie lengthened her stride. "Lobetto," she said, tossing the words over her shoulder. "He's been wanting to set me up."

"Oh," I said. "That's good." Pausing to watch her march away from me, I opened my fist and let the cakes drop into the dirt. One, softened from the heat and wet of my palm, clung to my fingers so that I had to wave and shake my hand like a crazy woman to get free.

———

I stopped walking Sookie to school, and Sookie stopped coming, but I never could stop myself from looking for her during the day. Over the next few months, whenever I took attendance, whenever I called out test questions, I was continually surprised by her empty desk, which remained vacant throughout the academic year. Nobody offered to fill the seat next to me.

When the other children rushed away after class, swarming into the streets to play together, I started staying late to assist the teacher in closing up the room, cementing my position as class leader. "A leader must always work harder than everyone else," Respected Teacher said approvingly one afternoon. "But today you can take a break. I don't need you."

Without Sookie, my days seemed too long, too lonely. I resisted his pushing me out the door. "I can wipe down the desks," I offered. "Or sweep the floor. What about—"

"No," said the teacher, not so kindly anymore. "Go home." He collected his papers, dusted off his hat, then stared at me until I followed him out.

Not seeing my father in the shop when I pushed open the door, I almost called out to him before I heard voices in the backroom. My father was saying, "No, no, no," almost begging. "I can't ask her to do it."

"You owe me." The words sounded like my mother's, but the voice sounded funny.

"I don't owe you anything anymore," my father said. "We're even."

"You made a promise to always help me," the woman insisted. "Just as I promised to always help you. We couldn't have survived the journey south without each other."

Inching quietly toward the backroom, I peeked behind the

beaded curtain, trying to catch a glimpse of the face that owned that voice.

I saw the back of my father's head. "We were children then," my father was saying. "Paekdu Mountain was a long time ago." His head shook. "I don't want my daughter involved."

I saw the woman's hands reach for my father. "Do you think I want Sookie—the only child I kept—involved?"

Gasping when I heard Sookie's name, realizing who the speaker must be, I rushed through the curtain to confront Duk Hee. "What are you doing here?" Surprise made me rude, but my father didn't reprimand me.

"Hyun Jin!" Duk Hee fell to her knees in front of me. "Sookie will listen to you. Tell her to return to school. Tell her to come home to me."

I gaped at her bowed head, unsure of how to talk to her. "She's, uh, not at home?"

Duk Hee grabbed my hands, her nails digging into my wrists. "She's—"

My father pulled Duk Hee up and away from me. "Go home," he said.

"But—" Duk Hee reached for me again, but my father propelled her through the curtain and out the door of the shop.

I ran after them. "Duk Hee, is Sookie okay? Does she miss me?"

"Hyun Jin!" my father barked. "Get in the house. Now!"

I stumbled at the harshness in my father's voice, looked from him to Duk Hee.

"Go to her," Duk Hee called out as my father pushed her away. "Please. She needs you, Hyun Jin. She won't tell you, but she needs you."

When Duk Hee hurried away, my father glared at me. "In the house," he repeated, and marched me up the steps.

What Lobetto told me, when I asked for his help in finding Sookie, was this: that it was Sookie who wanted to get into the clubs. "She begged me to help her get a job there," he said. "She said she knew how to work it."

I pursed my lips together. "Hmmm," I said, raising my eyebrows. We were sitting in his kitchen, sipping the barley tea his mother had boiled for us. Lobetto's mother, temporarily between men, hovered in the background, waiting to serve her son. Smoke from her cigarette wafted about her, ghostly arms swirling around her earthy bulk.

"You don't believe me?" Lobetto gasped in mock horror, then grinned when he saw my lips twitch. "I promise you, she did. I saw her waltz right into Club Foxa like she was hot shit." Jumping up from the chair, he thrust out his chest and minced on his toes. "'Oooh, you big GI Joe,'" Lobetto chirped in an English falsetto. He kissed the air. "'You like cocksuckie, butt-fuckie? Yum yum.'"

"Phah!" I said, blowing air at his face. "I don't believe you. You never heard her say that."

"Course I did," he laughed. "Who do you think taught her those words? She was pathetic when she came to me! I'm the one who taught her to walk, talk, use her body, use her mouth." Lobetto slouched back in the chair, and thumped his chest. "I should go into management, I think."

I snorted. "Where is she?"

Leaning forward, he slurped at his tea. "Eh, Mama," he said. Lobetto's mother jumped forward with a nod. "This tea is cold."

"Don't drink it," his mother fussed. "Cold tea is bad for the digestion." She bustled to the stove for the teapot and poured him a fresh cup. She looked at my empty cup, and walked out.

I clenched my teeth at her rudeness, then repeated, "Where is she?"

"Who?"

Lobetto irritated me. He often could not follow a story, even when he was the storyteller. Impatient, I rapped my knuckles against his arm. "Sookie," I said.

"That Sookie." Lobetto spat. "Now she thinks she's too good for me. I'm the one who got her started and she walks right past me without looking, like she's better than me."

"Lobetto," I joked, "everybody's better than you."

In the other room, I heard his mother slam what sounded like the blocks of wood they used as pillows against the wall.

Lobetto looked into his teacup. "I know you think that," he said. "Everyone thinks that. Remember when we were little and I was the one who could buy candy? I could buy anything I wanted from your daddy—the whole store if I wanted to. Remember when my daddy was in Korea?"

I waved my fingers in the air, wanting him to tell me what I needed to know about Sookie. "Yeah, yeah, you were the big shot then, GI baby."

"But you still thought you were better than me, didn't you? Because I'm half-black." He spoke the words coolly, as if they didn't matter, but when he took a sip of tea, he grimaced as if the tea soured his stomach.

"Not true." I shook my head. "Everyone was jealous 'cause you were half-American. We thought you would be the one to go to America."

"I will go." Lobetto reached into his pants pocket for his wallet and pulled out a letter written on thin blue paper. "Did I ever show you this?"

"Yes," I sighed, trying not to roll my eyes. Lobetto had

shown everyone that letter from his father several times since he had first received it just over five years ago.

A group of us had gathered around him that day on the dusty play yard, deserted for the summer. He passed out the Juicy Fruit bought with the money his father had enclosed. Sookie and Chung Woo and Young Sik shoved their pieces of gum whole into their mouths. They chomped noisily, tongues and teeth working the sugary rubber until spittle shot from their lips. I nibbled my gum stick, savoring the sugar in little sips as I chewed. We sat in a semicircle around Lobetto, all of us smacking and cracking until he raised his hand and ordered, "Shh," so he could read this letter from his father:

"'Dear Bobby,'" Lobetto read.

"Bab-bi? Bab-bi!" We screamed as we tried to snatch the letter from his hands. "Why does he call you little rice ball?"

Sookie leaned forward and rubbed the top of his bristly head. "Hmm, that is the shape of his head."

Lobetto shook her hand from his head, and—eyes focused on the thin paper, his fingers underlining the words—he struggled to translate what he read.

"'Bobby, I've been trying to find a place for you. My . . . fantasy, illusion, um . . . dream is that there will be a place for us in America. Dr. King—'"

"Who is Dr. King?" Chung Woo interrupted.

"Must be talking about the leader of America," Sookie said. "That's what *king* means in English."

I shook my head. "America doesn't have a king," I announced. "Their leader is called president. President Kennedy, for those of you who obviously did not memorize our map of the world assignment."

Young Sik sneered at me. "You think you know everything!"

"Maybe Lobetto meant to say *president* instead of *king*," Sookie offered.

"Shut up, you guys!" Lobetto snarled. "I am reading my father's letter, and it says King, whoever he is, says we are—shit, now here's a word I don't know, but I think it means . . . leftovers. Or maybe outcasts. Yeah, my father says we're outcasts in our own land."

"Shit," Chung Woo said, looking from Lobetto to Sookie. "He's talking about us. He's talking about America Town."

Lobetto frowned at the paper in his hand. "I don't know," he said. "My father says that the King was talking to all the Negroes in America, that there were so many *gomshis* in the street listening to him that it was like a living river. 'A river of humanity,' is what he calls it."

"Dirty river," Young Sik said under his breath. Chung Woo snickered.

"Which river, do you think?" I interjected. If the street there was as wide as the Ojum—what Sookie and I named the small trickle that ran down the hills behind her apartment like piss when it rained—then that wouldn't be very impressive for an American street. But, on the other hand, I could not imagine a street as wide as the Han river—it would be like living on an island.

"You are so stupid," Young Sik scolded me. "His dad is just talking pretend, like a story."

"My father is not telling a story!" Lobetto growled.

Young Sik narrowed his eyes and cracked his gum loudly. "Is, too."

"Is not." Lobetto held out his palm. "Give me back my gum then, if you think my father is a liar."

Young Sik closed his mouth, lips protecting his prize, and leaned back. "I never said he was a liar. I said telling a story—"

"Same thing, stupid," I said to him as Chung Woo whacked him on the head.

Young Sik pushed Chung Woo off before they could fall into a wrestling match, then he glared at me as he persisted in his explanation. "How could America have so many *gomshis?* I thought they sent them all here."

"In America," said Lobetto, flourishing his letter as if proving a point, "a lot of people are like me. Maybe most of them."

Young Sik looked down, unwrapping his pretzled legs so that his feet stuck out into the middle of the circle and almost touched me. I moved back.

"Could be," Chung Woo prompted and we all nodded, even Young Sik, in agreement. I kept my mouth shut even though I wondered if that was the case, then why did all the American magazines feature light-skinned girls? I supposed it was possible that in America the men were colored differently than the women. We hadn't covered that in our school lessons.

"Now let me read," Lobetto said, his words fast and impatient. "I'm coming to the best part."

Lobetto took a breath and tried to make his voice sound like his father's. "'I'm thinking of you. I haven't forgotten you. I been working hard to bring you to America, but the man is trying to keep us down.'"

"The man?" I whispered to Sookie.

Sookie shrugged. "I'm guessing it's the king."

Lobetto glared at us, but before his eyes returned to the letter, I could have sworn I saw tears in them. "'When you come,'" he read, clearing his throat, "'I will show you the America all American kids should see: the Grand Canyon, which cuts to the heart of this world; Yellowstone Park's Old Faithful; Hollywood with its walk of stars; and Disneyland, where you can ride Dumbo the flying elephant and visit Tomorrowland.'"

"Still think this is not a fairy tale?" hissed Young Sik.

Chung Woo laughed, but Lobetto just spoke louder: "'And, of course, I'd bring you back home to Maryland. You'd have to see Washington, D.C., and the Lincoln Memorial, the place where great King spoke to me.

"'Be good. I know you're still growing, but twelve years old is man enough. Take care of your mother, Your Father, Sergeant James Robert Williams.'"

I tried to look at Lobetto's mother as he reread his father's letter—more smoothly this time, after so many years of practice—and wondered if she would be hurt or angry at hearing the words of the American husband who deserted her. She stood half in shadow, just beyond the kitchen doorway. Her body, like her face, remained stiff and expressionless.

"My father said he was building a home for me," Lobetto said. "He's just waiting for 'the man' to come and get me."

"What are you talking about?" I gaped at Lobetto. "That wasn't in the letter."

"Yes, it is," Lobetto shot back, waving the paper in my face.

"Then how come you never read that part before?" I challenged.

Lobetto carefully refolded the letter, rubbed thin as onionskin and taped at the creases where they had split apart years ago. "I understand English better now. I've been working around the clubs, learning from the GIs," he said as he slipped the letter back into his eel-skin wallet. "When I get to America, I'm gonna be somebody."

I shook my head at him.

"You know the first thing I'm going to buy with the money I been saving?" He grinned. "A Chevy truck. I heard that's the best."

"How can you buy a 'lottery-ticket' truck? Isn't that something you win?" I asked, teasing out of habit.

Just as he always did at such questions, Lobetto scowled, saying I didn't understand the way things worked in America. I suppose I didn't; to me the country that Lobetto's father described seemed an impossible world, where the fantastical was commonplace. You could slip through a crack in the earth and find on the other side a land without a past, a land of the future where elephants flew and the streets were made of stars. It was a place where leftover *gomshis* were crowned king and girls looked like little boys. *Tweggis* posed in magazines and ugliness was beautiful. And in America was Lobetto's dream home: Mary's Land, the Land of Mary—which Lobetto assumed was the name of his father's American wife—the place where his father had disappeared into thin air.

After suffering through another interpretive reading of Lobetto's letter, followed by his analysis of American life—full of excess and worthless immigration officials, chief of which was "the man"—I finally convinced him to take me to Sookie. The word, he said, was that she was living with the darkie who had been her mother's last boyfriend.

"Chazu?" I blurted, shocked.

Lobetto smirked. "Starting to believe what I'm telling you about Sookie?"

I glared at him. "Let's just go."

Lobetto led me through the maze of streets that he worked, insisting on giving me a tour of the clubs he ran for. We ended up at Club Foxa, his favorite, he said, because Kitchen Auntie often gave him a small bowl of chicken wings and a bottle of soda after closing. Lobetto lifted an empty crate from a stack against the wall, turned it upside down and invited me to sit for a while.

"No, Lobetto," I grumbled. "I just want to find Sookie."

"She'll end up here sooner or later," he said. He had cracked the club's back door open and stuck his head in, clucking to get the attention of Kitchen Auntie.

"Shh, shup, Lobetto!" Kitchen Auntie scolded as she pushed Lobetto's head out of the doorway. "You know no Korean men are allowed in the clubs."

Lobetto laughed and tried to pat her bottom. "A lot of people don't think I'm Korean."

She knocked his hands away and blocked the entrance with her wide body. "You like to play with the women just like a Korean man." She looked him up and down. "Any man, for that matter—you're not a boy anymore," she said, shaking her head. "Tell your mama, now that she's back, to feed your skinny body so I don't have to."

Lobetto winked. "Can we get a Coca-Cola?"

"Hah, you're worse than a beggar." She slammed the door.

"Come on, Lobetto." I pulled on his arm.

Lobetto waved me away. "Just sit and wait," he said.

Before I could ask "For what?" Kitchen Auntie came back with a bottle. "What're you doing here this early?" she asked.

Lobetto flicked the top of his Coke against the door frame, knocking the cap off, then tilted his head toward me. "Her," he said.

"What's this? I'm jealous," she teased. "You bring me your girlfriend?" Kitchen Auntie, squinting at me, announced, "She's ugly."

"That's it," I said, standing up. "You're a pig," I spat at her, then added to Lobetto, "So are you!"

Kitchen Auntie cackled. "Just joking, just joking." Turning to reenter the kitchen, she threw over her shoulder, "Catch her,

Lobetto, that one is strong enough to make something out of you."

I thought I heard Lobetto groan, but when he caught up to me, he didn't say anything. He nudged my shoulder as he passed, his way of telling me I should follow him. I trudged behind him in silence, cursing him each time he tilted the bottle to his lips. I waited for him to offer me a sip, but he didn't.

When we reached a squat row of hillside apartments, Lobetto threw his bottle into the railing of one of the second-story balconies. It shattered and the sliding glass door screeched open. "Hey you shit head!" a woman yelled. When she poked her head over the railing, I saw that it was Sookie.

Lobetto yelled back, "I brung you a guest," and without saying goodbye, sauntered down the hill and into the streets of America Town.

"Come back for me later," I yelled after him, but he just put up his hand and waved; whether it was an agreement or a dismissal, I couldn't tell.

Sookie stared down at me from over the railing. "What do you want?"

"I just wanted to . . ." I stumbled over my words. "Say hi."

"Hi," Sookie said, her voice hard, careless.

"Your mother says 'hi,' too," I offered. "She's worried about you."

"Right," Sookie scoffed. "She's worried about the competition."

"She wants you to go back to school," I said, rubbing my neck where it was starting to ache from looking up.

"I bet she does," Sookie smirked. "Wants me out of the way."

I threw my hands into the air. "I give up," I said. "I'll leave you alone now." At least I had fulfilled my promise to Duk Hee about talking to Sookie about going back to school. I looked around, hoping to see Lobetto lurking in the shadows, waiting to take me home.

"Hyun Jin, wait!" Sookie leaned further over the railing. "I . . . I . . ."

"Are you okay?" I called up.

Sookie grinned. "Come see for yourself. I've been wanting to show you my new place."

When I trudged up the stairs, Sookie had the door open for me. "Come in," she said, "but we're done talking about my mother, okay? I'm fine right where I am."

"How can you live with a GI?" I frowned. "Don't they stink? Don't they clomp around leaving big messes? And you can't even talk with them."

"We communicate good enough. I tell him I need something, he tells me to get it. He tells me he wants something, I do it." She stopped me as I reached down to slip the rubber sandals off my feet. "We don't take off our shoes here," she bragged. "This apartment is American style." Sookie pulled me onto the carpeted floor. "Chazu taught me to keep the shoes on."

I crinkled my nose. "How dirty," I said, but I liked the way my feet bounced on the carpet. I liked everything she showed me: the living-dining room with its glass-and-metal table and chair set, its sofa and television; the bedroom with its American-sized mattress and its connected bathroom with toilet and shower and soap that smelled like lemons; and finally the kitchen, where she turned on all of the appliances as she named them— blendah, toastah-oben, hotu-platu, erectric can-openu. "In America," she boasted over the whirl of noise, "it's too much work even to turn your wrist."

I looked away, uncomfortable. For the first time in our lives, she had something I didn't, and I was surprised by the shift in our positions. I snuck a peek at her, trying to see if the months apart had changed her. She looked like the same old Sookie: skinny and ugly as me. But things had changed between us, throwing me off balance.

"Want a soda pop? Coca-Cola or ginger ale?" Sookie pulled open a refrigerator as tall as she was, to show off the shelves stocked with cheese and milk, beer and more American soda than my father could ever hope to afford. "Canada Dry. Real American ginger ale. Not cheap Korean *cidah.*"

I selected a brown bottle. "What does it feel like?" I asked.

"What?" She wrestled with the fancy can opener, clanging the Coke against the metal sides. I thought Lobetto's way was easier, and almost told her to pry the cap off against the door-jamb, when she handed me the bottle.

I took a sip. The overly sweet bubbles burned my throat and I could feel the sugar on my teeth. I licked my gums and belched. Feeling a sudden meanness, I repeated: "What does it feel like? Being a GI whore."

Blanching, she sucked in her breath and turned away from me, abruptly switching off all her cooking toys. "I love it," she said, her voice high and quick. "It's an easy way to get what I want."

I put the soda on the counter. "I heard it hurts when he puts his . . . soldier into you."

She grabbed a warm beer from the counter and, gulping it, moved toward the TV room. "You still believe my mother's stories?" she teased. Avoiding my eyes, she tried to laugh. "It only hurts the first time, and that happened so long ago, I can barely remember."

"What do you mean?" I asked. "It's only been a couple of months since you left school."

"A couple of months?" Sookie screeched. "It's been more like a year."

I looked down at my hands. "I'm sorry," I began. "I should have—"

"Besides," Sookie interrupted, "you think Chazu is my first man?" This time Sookie did laugh, tight and bitter. "I've been doing this since I was eight years old. One of Duk Hee's boyfriends thought it would be fun to have me join them."

"What do you mean? I don't understand," I stammered. "Duk Hee let—? Eight? Why didn't you tell—"

"What could my mother do? She kept me out of it as much as she could, for as long as she could." Sookie shrugged and, with a feral grin, pushed past me. "But I guess it didn't work; here I am with another one of her boyfriends."

Not knowing what else to do, what to say, unable even to look her in the eye, I guzzled down more of the soda. "Maybe I should go," I mumbled.

Ignoring me, Sookie waved me over. "You've got to try this," she said.

When I walked to her, she pulled me to a big chair in front of the television. "Here, sit," she commanded, nudging me toward the seat. "In America it's called a 'Racey Boy.'" Caressing the vinyl, she added: "I'm learning the American names for everything."

I climbed into the large chair, gingerly easing into the soft cushions. As I leaned back, Sookie pushed down on the headrest. I yelped, jumping up so I wouldn't fall.

"You did that on purpose," I yelled.

Sookie laughed. "I did that the first time, too." She pressed me back into the chair. "Relax." She rubbed my shoulders and I closed my eyes.

"The first night I worked at Foxa, I didn't know what to do," she said. "Bar Mama kept pinching me, telling me to ask one GI for a drink, another one for a dance." Sookie laughed and pretended to pinch my arms. "I had so many bruises from that night.

"The whole night she told me to smile, introduce myself, walk in front of their eyes, act pretty. I tried, but I was scared. Most of the time, I kept asking the GIs for Chazu." She laughed. "Lesson number one: Don't ever ask a man about another man."

"Is that why you wanted to work Club Foxa? Chazu?" I asked.

Sookie nodded. "The day he came to the apartment looking for Duk Hee, he told me to come to him if I needed help." She giggled. "He got more than he expected."

"He didn't remember saying that?" I guessed.

"Hyun Jin, he didn't even remember me. Or Duk Hee," she said. "But once I reminded him who I was, and told him I didn't have anyplace to stay, he brought me back here for the night. I decided not to leave."

I forced a laugh. "And he let you?"

"What could he say?" Sookie bit back a smile. "He's basically a nice guy. Really," she insisted when she saw my frown. "He's okay."

"And what do you have to do for him?" I studied her face, searching for the Sookie I used to know.

"Drink with me," Sookie said. She tipped the High Life into her mouth, then shook the empty beer bottle in my face. "It's boring by myself. I hate when Chazu leaves me by myself." She added the bottle to a row of seven she had started on the counter.

I held up my cola. "I am drinking."

"Ugh," Sookie grimaced. "Chazu said that stuff rots your teeth. Be healthy, drink beer."

I shrugged, then nodded. "Only if I can sit in a chair that doesn't move," I said, struggling to stand up.

Sookie lurched into the kitchen and brought back two beers. "How's your mother?" she asked, handing me a bottle. "Still as bitchy as ever?"

"Sookie," I warned.

"Still saying shit like, 'Blood will always tell'?" She mimicked my mother's shrill and disapproving voice. "As if her blood runs gold and mine—and yours—is just shit."

I was surprised that Sookie knew what my mother said about her, and though I didn't like it, I didn't want to hear Sookie's criticism. "I'm leaving now," I said.

"No, don't!" Sookie tried to grab my hand and dropped her bottle. Beer gushed onto the carpet. "Shit," Sookie muttered at the floor, then, looking at me, flung her arms wide. "Stay," she said. "You left me when I really needed you. Don't leave now."

"I didn't leave you," I said, shaking my head, denying her words though I knew they were true. "You're the one who left, remember?" When she continued to stare at me, I fluttered my hands at the spilled beer. "You better clean this up."

Ignoring the mess, Sookie threw herself into one of the chairs at the glass table. "Don't you know you've always been the one who left?"

Scowling at her, I demanded: "What are you talking about?"

"You left me," Sookie repeated. "Again. And again. And again."

I shook my head at her nonsense and watched the beer seep into the carpet. "I'll clean it up," I sighed. Marching into the bathroom, I grabbed a towel off the rack and returned to mop up the spill.

Sookie had gotten herself another beer. She took a sip, then frowned at me. "You were leaving me from the moment you were born."

"Sookie," I grunted, kneeling to dab at the puddle of beer, I have to tell you, you are not making sense." Most of the alcohol had soaked into the carpet. "You didn't know me when I was born," I pointed out to her. "You were only, what? Two?" I righted the bottle and, seeing that it was still half-full, took a swig.

She squinted at me, then nodded so hard she almost slipped off the chair. "I did know you. And at first I hated you," she said. "I hated you because I thought you were killing my mother. She screamed and screamed and I thought she was dying."

Shaken by her words, though I knew she was just on a drunken ramble, I threw the dampened towel at her feet. "Shut up. Shut up right now. You're scaring me."

"Then you popped out—pop!" Sookie rubbed a finger on the inside of her cupped mouth to make a smacking sound. "I thought, how could something so small cause so much trouble? I thought, I could crush you with one hand, that's how small you were."

I stood up and leaned over her. "Sookie," I snarled. "You're drunk."

Sookie tilted her head back and looked into my face. "One hand," she murmured, ignoring me. She placed her hand against my face, right against the birthmark. "I put my hand here, just like this, the day you were born. I was going to kill you for hurting my *omoni*."

I flinched at her touch, pulling away.

"But it fit my hand perfectly," Sookie continued, almost dreamily. "And I thought it was a sign that you belonged to me, that you were marked for me. Isn't that silly?" She smiled, then frowned. "It wasn't as dark then as it is now, though."

I felt dizzy, sick from the beer and the soda churning in my stomach. "You're fucked up," I croaked. "You don't know what you're saying. I don't know what you're saying."

She squinted at me. "For someone so smart, you sure are dumb. I'm saying Duk Hee's your *omoni*. We're sisters." She belched and reeled away from the table to add the empty bottle to her collection.

Stunned, I stared at her trying to place the bottle next to the others. It kept tipping over, threatening to topple the others in line. When I found my voice, it was weak: "What? What? What?" is all I could say.

She glanced at the bottle of beer I had left on the floor. "You done with that?" she asked.

"What!" I screamed, my voice gaining strength, exploding. Jumping up, I kicked the bottle, sending it clattering against the wall. The dregs from the bottom foamed up and dribbled out. "Sookie!" I marched up to her, grabbed her shoulders and shook. "Tell me the truth. Duk Hee's my mama? We're sisters?"

Stumbling against me, she wrapped her arms around my neck. "Duk Hee's your mother and my mother, too," she repeated, her words starting to slur.

I pushed her off me. "You better not be fucking with me," I yelled. "I know you're angry with me for not helping you last year, but if you're making up lies about me, about my mother, about my daddy—" I stopped, my heart suddenly in my throat. "Is my father really my father?"

Sookie sighed. "He's yours."

I let out the breath I'd been holding. It came out as a sob. Sookie wrapped her arms around herself and dropped her head. "I was jealous that you had him," she admitted. "I saw what he gave you, where you lived, and I was angry that Duk Hee gave you away instead of me."

I shook my head, trying to clear it, trying to think straight. "That means . . . Duk Hee and my father?" I whirled away from her and stomped to the door. "I don't believe you!" I shouted as I stormed out. "I don't believe you."

But I did.

It explained my father's affection for Sookie and my mother's hatred of me. And I believed because a part of me chose to believe; much as I looked down on Sookie, I loved her—even then.

"You do believe me," Sookie taunted as I ran down her stairwell. "And you'll come back—remember what your *mother* always says: blood will tell."

I searched for Duk Hee, wanting to hear from her mouth whether or not she was my first mother, my true mother. I wandered the streets until dawn, circling the bars she used to hang out at—Club Foxa and Angel, Club Rose and Tulips— eyeing the women emerging from the alleys nearby.

I stared at one couple, convinced that the woman was Duk Hee, until she broke away from her Joe and charged at me. "What?" she bellowed, thrusting her chest out. "What're you looking at?"

"How much-i? How much-i?" the GI called from behind her, whistling for me to join them. I tucked my chin toward my chest, looked down and hurried away. With nowhere else to go, I made my way back to Lobetto's house.

In the dim morning light, I pounded on the door and when no one answered, yelled, "Lobetto."

"Hey!" Lobetto hissed as he came up behind me. "Stupid, making so much noise."

"Sorry," I mumbled. I turned to go, but he grabbed my elbow.

"You okay?" he asked. "Not that I care, but if you start crying you might ruin my mother's time."

"Huh?" I asked.

He pointed his chin toward the apartment. "She picked up a Joe last night." Yanking my arm, he ordered: "Come."

We walked around toward the back of the house. Next to the pit where they hosed off their dishes, Lobetto had nailed blankets against the wall, creating a triangle of private space. Inside, tight and dark as a fox's den, was just enough room for a mattress.

Balancing a glass lamp on his lap, Lobetto groped under the mattress and pulled out an army lighter. "This is all that my father left behind," Lobetto said as he lit the lamp. He gestured to a small pile of junk on the mattress, then added: "Besides me, that is." He touched the mattress, the army lamp, the lighter, a compass with a limp arrow that hung south, a rusted knife, and two empty St. Paulie Girl bottles. "That's his favorite beer," he said, caressing the green glass. "Beautiful, huh?"

Then he looked at me. "What's wrong, Hyun Jin?" he asked, the first question he had ever asked me with compassion.

I opened my mouth, but I didn't know how to say that I wasn't who I thought I was because everyone in my life had been lying to me. I couldn't explain to him, or to myself, how I felt—betrayed and angry, but also pleased and guilty. It was ironic: when we were younger, I had harbored the secret fantasy that Sookie and I were really sisters. But now, to have that dream become a reality horrified me. I was disgusted to learn that we shared the same whorish blood, that the inside of my body was as tainted as the outside. The words became jumbled in my mind and stuck in my throat. "Soo-Soo-Sookie," I stammered.

"Huh," he grunted. "Don't worry about her. She's doing good."

I remembered his mother, who was at that moment with an American Joe, and worried that I had embarrassed Lobetto. I didn't want him to think that I judged him or his mother.

Lobetto lifted his hand and I flinched out of habit. But instead of thumping my head, he cupped his hand gently under my chin. He turned my head toward and way from the lamplight, so that I faced light and shadow in turns. "We are the same," he announced. "Half in one world, half in the other."

"I don't know what to believe," I said. "I can't tell what's true and what's not."

Lobetto pressed his thumb against my lips. "Shh," he whispered. "You'll know what's right."

I remember thinking only that my mother and Sookie were right. Blood will tell. Like the truth, it comes rushing to the surface, staining the body, a blueprint for life.

I had the birthmark to prove it.

7

I woke with my face pressed into the seam made by Lobetto's back and the bare mattress that smelled like sweat and grass. The blanket hung low over my head, trapping my breath hot against my face, but my feet felt cold, exposed to the open-air kitchen. I didn't know when I had fallen asleep; one moment I was ranting about Sookie, and the next I was wrapped around Lobetto's stinky body. Pushing away from him, I went to wash at the hose that hung from the kitchen wall. I sprayed my face with the water that screeched from the pipes, then aimed the water at my feet.

"What're you doing?" Lobetto grumbled. Holding one corner of the blanket up, he poked his head out of his tent.

I turned off the water. I looked for a towel to dry my hands, but when I didn't find any, combed my fingers through my hair. "I'm going to find Duk Hee," I said, wincing as I pulled through a knot. "I need to know if she's my . . ." I tried to make myself say "mother," but my throat tangled around the word. "I just need to know."

"Humph," Lobetto grunted, raising his eyes. He didn't seem surprised, but most times it was hard to tell what he felt. Scooting back, he let the flap of blanket drop between us.

I marched over to his tent and flung the blanket aside. "What do you mean by that?" I demanded.

Lobetto lay on his back, eyes closed. "I didn't say anything," he grumbled.

I kicked him with my toe. "I heard you. You said, 'Humph.' Like you always do when you think I'm being stupid."

Lobetto opened one eye. "You are stupid." He grinned, then held up his palms when I doubled my fists. "Joking, joking." Lobetto sat up and frowned. "But seriously, why do you want to see Duk Hee?"

I planted my fists on my hips. "Didn't you hear what I just said?" Taking a breath, I let the words rush out. "She's my mother. At least that's what Sookie said."

He stared at me. "So?"

I tapped my foot. "So?" I screeched. "So I need to find out the truth."

Lobetto yawned and rubbed his eye. "Why?" he asked, then added quickly before I could yell some more: "You got a good thing going where you are now. Why ruin it?"

I turned my back on him. I searched the dirt outside his lean-to for my slippers, found them, and, hopping up and down, jammed them on my feet. "Goodbye," I huffed. When I reached the corner of his house, I stopped and slowly turned back. Folding my arms against my chest and gritting my teeth, I asked, "Do you know where she is?"

Sookie's mother—my mother—now lived in the pit of America Town. Her apartment had already been rented to another bar girl by the time she returned from the Monkey House, so Duk Hee had no choice but to work and live in the street cubicles fringing the clubs.

The women who lived in these "fish tanks"—rows of boxes, really—danced naked in the glass doorways. As the GIs wandered in and out of the clubs, the women pressed themselves against the glass and, gyrating, touched themselves to get the men's attention. If one of the Joes was interested in a cheap quickie, she would open her door and take him to the cot. His friends could watch for free—good advertisement—or if he wanted privacy, she could pull a curtain in front of the door.

When Lobetto tapped on the glass to Duk Hee's booth that morning, I could see the curled shadow of her body, unmoving, behind the thin fabric.

"Duk Hee," he yelled. Still she didn't move. He pounded on the door and the flimsy structure shook. "Wake up!"

Duk Hee jumped out of bed, flapping her hands as she searched the sheets for a robe. Slipping it on, she stumbled to the front and pushed aside the curtain. As she squinted in the harsh morning light, I tried not to stare at her puffy-lidded eyes, at the deep gashes that bracketed pale and cracked lips. The lips smiled, parting to reveal a quick peek at a yellowing overbite, as Duk Hee hurried to unlock her new home.

"You've come to tell me about Sookie?" she asked as the

door swung open. Startled to see Lobetto looming behind me, she staggered a few steps back. She fumbled to keep the robe closed around her body, and grimaced. "I owe you something?"

"Yeah," he said. "You still owe me for that pack of cigarettes I gave you last week."

When it looked like she would close the door on us, I pushed Lobetto away and glared at him. "I'll pay you for it," I hissed at him. Then, turning to Duk Hee, I thrust out my chest and said, "I need to talk with you."

She studied my face, the lines on her forehead wrinkling in thought. "Sookie's not coming, is she?"

I shook my head. "No. This is about something different."

She raised her eyebrows at Lobetto.

"He'll wait out here," I said, answering her unspoken question.

"What?" scowled Lobetto. "You think I don't have anything better to do?"

"You don't," I snapped, then softened my tone. "Just wait, okay?"

"No."

I rolled my eyes. "Look," I said, "if you want to get paid for those cigarettes, you stay."

Lobetto muttered something under his breath, but he squatted outside the door, back propped against the wall. "Ten minutes only."

Duk Hee turned and, motioning me to follow, shuffled to the cot. She shook out the bedding, sending a large roach scuttling into the corner. "Please." Sitting, she patted the space next to her.

I perched at the edge of the mattress, tilting my head to look at her face. She licked her lips and plucked at the elbows of her robe. It looked like a long-sleeved men's shirt, shabby and frayed and missing its buttons. I stared at the loose threads at the cuffs while I wondered how to start.

"I'm sorry," Duk Hee said, folding the sleeves to hide the tattered ends. "I forgot my manners: would you like something hot to drink?"

When I nodded, she leaned forward, reaching for something behind my back. I jumped up, afraid the roach had returned.

"Relax," she breathed, and I caught the stench of rice wine and stale Juicy Fruit and decay as I settled back down. From a shelf on the wall, she dragged a thermos to her lap. Using the cap as a cup, she poured a drink. When she handed it to me, I sipped out of politeness. Lukewarm water.

"Duk Hee?" I asked. Then my mouth went dry. I drank again, then blurted: "Am I your daughter?"

"Hah?" Duk Hee said. "Where'd you hear a thing like that?"

"But I . . . aren't you . . . Sookie said."

"Sookie!" Duk Hee snorted. "That girl is always saying stupid things, getting the story wrong." She waved at the cup of water. "Pass me that." She drank what was left and gagged. "Yugh. How can water taste so rotten? Must be the taste of my tongue." She cackled, then, eyeing me over the brim, asked: "What did she tell you?"

My spit tasted bitter. "Sookie told me," I said, swallowing, "that she saw me being born—"

"That's true," she said.

The air left my body in a rush. "You are my mother," I whispered.

Duk Hee shook her head so hard, the barrette popped off and her frazzled hair whipped into her eyes. "No, no," she said. "That woman your father married is your mother."

"But," I began, then stopped. I chewed on my lip, peeling and eating a layer of thin, papery skin. I tasted blood.

Duk Hee slapped at my mouth. "Stop that," she scolded. "Your father does that all the time." She moved back against the wall and began to fiddle with the thermos. "I'm sorry; I shouldn't have done that." Tilting her head back, Duk Hee brought the thermos to her lips. Water dribbled down her chin. When the trickle slowed, she tossed the bottle to the ground.

I waited.

Duk Hee glanced at me, then looked down. "All right. I'll tell you what I can." She took a deep breath and let it out. "I've known your father a long time. We grew up in the same village, near Paekdu. I wouldn't say we were friends—he was a boy, and a few years older—but it was a small village and everybody knew everybody else."

"Sort of like America Town," I said.

"Yes. And no." Her lips twisted. "Anyway, during World War Two, the Japanese raided Korean towns and villages for boys to fight for them. And they took girls, too, to . . . to . . . take."

"Take where?"

Duk Hee ignored my question, continuing to speak, her voice wooden. "After the war, I returned to Paekdu. I had a mother, a father. A little sister. Two brothers. I thought I might be able to find them back home. But there was no one. No village. No home. Our house and fields were burned to the ground."

I reached out to touch Duk Hee's hand, wanting to comfort her, but she shifted away from me and gazed out the door. "I sat in the ashes of my family's home for two, three days, maybe longer. I didn't know what else to do, where else to go. I think I would have died there, if your father hadn't shown up. Together, we decided to make our way south; somehow it was easier for us to keep moving, to keep busy, to keep not remembering."

"Why didn't you marry each other?" I asked. To me her story seemed romantic, and a happy ending between the two survivors the most logical conclusion. "You should have been my mother from the beginning."

She stared at me as if I were a stranger, then shook her head suddenly. "Don't make me laugh," Duk Hee said in a way that sounded more like herself. "Neither one of us had anything. I had less than nothing. We each did what we had to, to survive."

I persisted with my fantasy, in my revision of the past. "If you had married my father, we could have been a family. You and me, Sookie and my father. Sookie always liked my house, she could have lived there, too."

Duk Hee gave me a funny look. "Hyun Jin," she said, "Sookie wouldn't be here if I had married your father. Sookie is Sookie because she doesn't have a father, at least not one that I can name."

I blushed at her frankness.

"And I can say for sure that she wouldn't have been living with you in your house, because that wouldn't have been your house; it's your mother's, remember?" She laughed at my confusion, then added more gently: "Besides, it wasn't like that between your father and me."

"Like what?" I asked, miffed at being laughed at.

"Like how a husband and wife should be."

I frowned. "But what about me? How?" I felt my face redden again. I couldn't even think the words I wanted to ask.

"Coming south, your father and I helped each other when and if we could. I guess it was habit that made him turn to me when he had trouble making a baby with his wife. I already had Sookie, so he knew we could help each other again."

"You 'helped each other,'" I echoed. "What does that mean?"

Duk Hee shrugged. Her robe gaped open, exposing her drooping breasts. "I carried his seed. He gave me some money."

"That's it?" I coughed, words choking my throat. "You sold me?" My eyes burned, but I would not let this woman see me cry. "Did you make a lot of money?" I asked, clenching my teeth to keep my mouth from trembling. "How much was this 'seed' worth?"

"Don't get me started!" she said, rolling her eyes. "I never did get paid the full amount! Your father paid in dribbles, a little here, a little there over the years, whatever he could wrestle away from your mother."

"She's not my mother!" I stood up. I wanted to move away, to pace, but there was no room to walk in the narrow space between the cot and the far wall. The floor was strewn with clothes, used paper plates, stained flyers.

"Hyun Jin," Duk Hee said, looking up at me. "She is your mother. What does it matter where you were carried?"

"What does it matter?" I stared at her. "Didn't you ever love me? Was it so easy for you to give me away?"

"Easy? No!" Duk Hee shuddered, misunderstanding me on purpose. "I had to fight to get her to take you in. Do you know that jackal of a woman said I tried to trick her?" She stooped to root through the pile of clothing and pulled out a short-sleeved red T. "Called you deformed!" Duk Hee snorted as she picked lint off the shirt. "Back and forth we pushed you until she shoved me backward and shut the door in my face. There I was, holding this newborn—" Duk Hee cradled the shirt like swaddling. "What was I gonna do? I left you at their door."

I felt dizzy, and swayed. "You just left me?" I whispered. "On the street?"

Duk Hee clucked her tongue. "Don't worry. I didn't really leave, I hid and watched. You cried and cried, my God, could you cry. Finally, just when I was going to give up and take you back, your father opened the door and pulled you in."

"My father wanted me," I said, my voice cracking.

"Never doubt it," she whispered. Then, tossing her head, she added: "He paid for you, after all." Her tone was mocking, though I couldn't tell if she was mocking me, or my father, or herself. Duk Hee wriggled out of her cover-up and into the T-shirt, then reached in to lift her breasts toward the neckline. "You know, these used to be happy before I had Sookie." She jiggled her breasts and sighed. "Time to visit the Monkey House for a *chi-chi* shot."

"What about you?" I demanded. "Did you ever want me? Did you ever love me?"

Sighing, Duk Hee said, "I knew I carried you for someone else. You were promised to someone better, to a better life. I thought of that every day, so that even though I carried you under my heart, I was able to push you away from it." Duk Hee knelt to rummage through her clothes once more and lifted out a pair of black shorts.

My own heart hurt as I watched her peel off her underwear and step into the shorts. Her butt hung out of the bottom. "Look," she said, pushing me toward the door, "I've got to find something to eat before work."

Gritting my teeth, I pushed her back. "I am your daughter!" I yelled.

Duk Hee pressed her hands over her ears. "There you go, crying again. So loud!"

I yanked at her arms. "I am your daughter!" I yelled again, louder. "That should mean something to you!" My voice broke, and though I tried to keep it strong, I could hear the pleading creeping into my words.

"Look at me!" Duk Hee snapped. "I am not your mother. I never wanted another child. I never wanted to bring another daughter into this world. I've even lost the one I tried to keep."

Panting, I fought the sobs that threatened to rip out of my throat.

Duk Hee rubbed her wrists, red where I had grabbed her, and touched my shoulder. "Go home," she nudged. "I'll walk you out."

Shifting away from her hand, I let myself be guided to the door, but I chafed at her easy dismissal of me. Wanting to show her that she meant as little to me as I did to her, I asked: "How can you stand living in this box?" High and squeaky, my voice didn't sound like it came from my body, but I was proud that the words sounded casual, slightly derisive. "All the people passing by, looking in?"

"I don't see them anymore," she said, seemingly not bothered by my impertinence. "Just like they don't see me." She tilted her head. "At least here I don't have to pay the bar owner a cut on every Joe I take."

Duk Hee opened the door and shoved me out. Spying Lobetto a few stalls down, she whistled him over. "Lobetto," she said. "Take her home. To her parents."

"Open the door!" I tried to keep the panic out of my voice as I pounded at the shop door that was locked for the first time in my memory.

"You're dead." I heard the voice of the woman who raised

me on the other side of the door. "You made your choice—a black dog who lies down with black pigs."

"I have nothing to say to you," I screamed back. "You're not my mother. You're nothing to me."

"That's right. We are nothing to each other. Did you hear that, husband? She said we are nothing to her—after all we did for her. She's no better than the fox girl in those worthless stories you forever told her. Eating up her own family."

"Let me speak to my father," I yelled. "I know the truth now."

"Truth?" she scoffed. "You don't know anything!"

"*Appah!*" I cried.

"He can't hear you," she said. From the other side of the door, I heard her fighting with my father: "No, I will not open the door. She's nothing but the whore she was born to be. Her blood makes her, marks her."

"Father," I called out. "Don't turn me away."

The door opened. My father lurched into the doorway, his wife clinging to his arms to pull him back into the shop. "Why did you do it?" His red eyes darted from Lobetto, who hung back on the street, to my rumpled clothes and disheveled hair. "How could you disgrace us like this? We tried to raise you right."

I reach for him. "I didn't—"

"We never wanted you," his wife screamed over his shoulder.

My father pushed her away. "We tried for years to have a child together," he started to explain, and I couldn't tell if he was speaking to me or to her.

"I wanted one of my own blood," his wife pouted. "A baby who could love me. Not her; she's not natural. She never did have human feelings, a human heart."

"Stop it!" My father shook his wife off his arm. "She is my blood. She is my daughter."

"That's what you think," she retorted. "But how do you know? You only have the word of a trashy GI girl. A whore that gave away her child for money."

"Shut up!" I screamed. The top of my head throbbed.

The woman I had called mother tried to leap past my father to claw at my face. "You see how she is?" she screeched at my father. "You see how she talks to me?"

I stuck out my chin. "You can't hurt me," I sneered. All my life I had tried to please that woman. All my life, I had hated myself, thinking I wasn't good enough to be her daughter. All my life, I thought she had a right to beat me, because I had failed her.

I wouldn't let her hurt me again.

"She's trash," my father's wife spat at me.

"She is my daughter," my father said. "My only child."

The woman shrieked as if in pain. "You don't know that! She doesn't look anything like you—and that mark! No one in your family has a birth defect like that. Something's wrong with her. You were tricked into taking her."

"Don't you have any feelings for her?" My father pleaded. "You raised her."

"Feelings?" The only mother I had ever known finally looked me in the eye. "Yeah, I had feelings," she said. "I had the feeling she was trouble. I had the feeling that she would hurt us and shame our family. I knew it the moment I saw her face. And I was right." She sounded proud.

My father dropped his head.

"I'm glad you're not my mother," I said. I wanted to sound mean, but my voice wavered and I tasted salt. When I brushed a hand across my cheek, I was shocked to feel my face wet with tears. "I'm glad I don't have your blood. You're an evil-mouthed, cud-chewing, infertile old cow."

"Stop it," my father said to the ground.

"You think you're better than me?" The woman laughed. "Nothing but filth runs in your veins. My family can trace its roots back to Prince Tan-gun."

"And your family will die off with you, won't it?" I taunted.

She howled, raising her upper lip not unlike a feral fox herself. "Get out of here!" she cried, her voice shrill. "Get out, be a GI whore like your sister. Like your mother."

"Wait!" My father grabbed my hand as I backed away. I couldn't feel him squeezing my fingers, they had gone so numb.

His wife scratched at our knuckles until he let go. When I turned to leave, he rushed into the backroom. I heard her goading my father: "I told you, didn't I tell you how many times over the years? She's evil. Evil. You cannot dress a fox as a daughter."

I stumbled down the steps, turning blindly toward the corner where Lobetto waited.

"Jin Jin!"

When I heard him call me by my baby name, I turned to see my father rushing to me. I opened my arms, thinking that he was going to take me back. Instead, he thrust an armload of dirty laundry at me.

"Appah?" I croaked, dropping the clothes and stepping forward. "Papa?"

He flinched when I embraced him. I smelled the father smell of him—soap and hair grease and sweat—for the brief moment before he pushed me away. Biting his bottom lip so hard it turned white, he pressed a wad of money into my hand.

"Appah," I whispered. "Please. I love you. Don't listen to her—"

My father closed his eyes, and in response I felt my own eyes burn. "I'm a good girl, *Appah*. Don't send me away, I'll be good—"

He backed away, shaking his head. "I did my best for you," he whispered. "Don't . . . don't come here again."

Doubling over, his quiet words kicking at my stomach, I dropped to my knees. "I didn't do anything," I said. "I didn't." I pressed my face into the clothes my father had brought out for me—T-shirts and school uniform and shoes—trying not to vomit. When I looked up, his wife was running toward me.

Swooping down, she grabbed at the clothes in my hands—clothes she would have no use for but didn't want me to have anyway. "That's mine," she screeched. "Not yours. That's mine. Nothing is yours. Nothing. You don't deserve it. You're dead now." She continued pulling at the things in my hands, even as I tried to leave. "Tell her," she ordered my father, who gazed above our heads, above the grappling near his feet. "Tell her what she is."

"You are what you are," my father said.

"See!" his wife gloated. "Blood will tell!"

My father searched my face, his scrutiny intense, fierce. He didn't skim over half of my face but looked at it all, the light and the dark. "She's right, Hyun Jin," he said. "Blood will tell."

I let go, suddenly too tired to fight. I dropped my arms, and air rushed through my fingers. Everything, everything that had once belonged to my old life, my old self—the daughter of these parents—fell into the street. "Take it," I said, rising to my feet though my body felt too heavy to move. "You are dead to me, too." I looked directly into her eyes, into his, contemptuous, before I forced myself to walk away.

Sometimes I think I could have changed my story at this point in my life, just by choosing how to interpret what my father said. When he echoed his wife, repeating, "Blood will tell," I thought at the time that he was acknowledging that I could be nothing more than a whore. But now, I can almost believe he was reminding me that I was his daughter, that I carried his heart, that I had choices. I could have chosen—can choose even now—to believe he loved me.

Other times, I think the maps of our lives are etched into vein and muscle and bone, and that mere words—however interpreted—don't have the power to change anything.

8

I went to Sookie. At first, I was hesitant, unsure of how to treat her. I imagined we'd fall into each other's arms. Weeping, she'd tell me how hard it had been not to claim me as her sister, how difficult to keep me—her own blood—far from her heart. I assumed things would be different between us. But Sookie acted as if nothing had changed—not us, not our relationship, not my life. It was as if she hadn't said what she said, as if I didn't know what I knew.

So I pretended as well, and soon I didn't have to pretend. We eased back into the tentative rhythm of friendship, enjoying the comforts of Chazu's apartment while he was away. After lighting candles in all the rooms, we'd turn off the lights in the bathroom and bathe in the private tub, the two of us face-to-face, knees pressed together. We made the water hot enough to scald our skin pink, soaked and rubbed dead skin off each other's back. Then with our hair wrapped in towels, our skin new and tingling, we'd eat ice cream and cookies on the bed and laugh about the days Sookie was so hungry she wondered what her shoes would taste like. But under the laughter, I would think: this is my sister. This is how it always should have been between us.

At night the two of us sat in the apartment, all dressed up with nowhere to go. Sookie said Chazu didn't let her out on her own in the evenings; she could only visit the clubs when he went with her. So we watched TV. We painted our nails. We dressed in the clothes that Chazu bought for Sookie and made ourselves up. We never once talked about Duk Hee, even though we wore the same brands and colors of makeup that Chazu had once bought for her.

When Chazu returned, he took us to the clubs. We avoided Club Foxa, where Bar Mama glared at Sookie and refused to serve us drinks. Though she fawned over Chazu, offering to pair him up with one of her girls, she ignored us and tried to pinch us behind his back. Sookie explained that Bar Mama was convinced Sookie had betrayed her, stealing one of her best customers. Sookie said this proudly, because it proved that Chazu never came in anymore.

Instead of the Foxa, Chazu arranged for us to meet his friends at Club Rose or Tulips. The first time I went on what they called a "doublu date," I sat in the booth, pressed against the inside wall. Chazu and his friend—a sharp-nosed and poky-headed man who looked like a grinning chicken to me—talked quickly in English.

Sookie, with her quick-swiveling head and mouth hanging open in a perpetual smile, looked like a small bird herself, trying to catch the worm of their conversation. I didn't smile or laugh at their jokes because I didn't understand them. Sookie kicked me under the table. I frowned, and that made her kick me even more.

"We go ladies' room," Sookie finally giggled. She crawled over Chazu slowly, fumbling over his lap until he helped her out by pushing on her bottom. His fingers cupped her cheeks, slipped into her crease. Embarrassed, I looked at the wall, and so I did not realize she was standing in front of the table until she said through a clenched smile: "Hyun Jin! Come."

I shrugged my consent and waited for my GI to get up so I could scoot out of the booth. He didn't move. I pushed his shoulder and he grinned at me.

"Please," I said to him.

"Good English," the happy chicken man said. "Polite."

I pushed Happy Chicken's arm again. "Ooh, now she's getting rough. I like that even better than 'please.'" He and Chazu laughed. So did Sookie, even though she narrowed her eyes at me. I smiled, too, even though I could not tell if the GI was complimenting or cursing me. I smiled and nodded, which made the men laugh louder. I could tell they thought I was stupid.

"Come on!" Sookie tapped her nails on the table. We had just painted them—Beach Peach—that afternoon. When I glanced at Happy Chicken, she pulled my arm so that I fell across his lap.

"Right on!" he crowed.

I climbed over him, but when his hands wandered over my breasts, I dug my heel into his shin.

"Shit!" he yelped and pushed me off of him.

Sookie dragged me into the bathroom and scolded me over the toilet. "Loosen up!" she said. "You are a *dragu*."

"What does that mean?" I asked, rubbing my arm where her nails had scratched me.

"That's what the GIs call a girl who won't have a good time." She pressed a pointy finger into my chest. *"Dragu."*

"Right, I'm not having fun with that Happy Chicken of a man."

"Happy Chicken?" Sookie laughed even though she wanted to stay mad at me.

I pinched up my hair and threw out my chest. I strutted around the stall with my arms flapping loosely at my sides. "Hello, kak-kak-akoo, call me Bil-lu," I said, trying to deepen my voice to sound like Chicken Man.

Sookie giggled, then suddenly pouted. "But it's not funny!" She looked in the mirror and smacked her lips. Her eyes flicked from her reflection to mine. "You have to learn to be like me."

I gazed at our images, studying the shape of our eyes, the slope of our noses, the colors of our skins. Closing one eye, I placed a hand over the side of my face without the birthmark. "Do you see what I see?" I asked her, willing her to acknowledge our similarities.

Sookie knocked my hand from my face. "Pay attention," she chided. "Make the men feel like big shots, but treat them like little babies—laugh, say, 'You are so funny!' Put your hand on their arm, say, 'You are so strong!' Dance with them, touch their face, say, 'You are so sexy!' When they buy you drinks, drink! When you start feeling good, lean into them and say, 'Let's honeymoon!'"

I crossed my arms over my chest. In Korean, *hunni* meant to "do anything." Sookie explained that in English it meant pretty much the same thing. "It's an easy way to make a few hundred won if you don't have a steady GI," she said. "Rub your chest against him; lick his mouth, his ears, his neck; put your hands down his pants," Sookie instructed. "Only when he can barely scoot off the seat do you take him to a backbooth for honeymoon. I promise, it'll be quick."

"No," I stammered. "I can't do that."

"You can," Sookie said. "You can do anything if you have to. And let me tell you something, Hyun Jin: it's easy. It's easy because the more you do it, the more you know it's not the real you. The real you flies away, and you can't feel anything anymore."

Sookie told me to invite Lobetto over to her apartment one night. "We can drink some beers," she said. "Hang out, watch TV before he has to work. It'll be a good time for us."

But he looked so uncomfortable, so out of place. He stood in the entrance hall fidgeting in his bare feet, flinching at the door whenever he heard a creak. Unwilling to sit on the couch or even step into the kitchen, he kept asking, "What if Chazu comes home?"

Ignoring him, Sookie threw herself on the couch and moaned, "I'm so bored."

"How can you be bored?" I asked. "You have everything here you could want. Even a TV. I could spend hours looking at TV."

"Try days," Sookie pouted. "Try weeks."

"Unngh," I growled, thinking she was spoiled.

"I hear someone coming up the steps!" Lobetto jumped toward the door. "What if it's Chazu?"

"I have no friends," Sookie whined.

"What about me?" I demanded. I marched to the front door and pulled Lobetto into the room. "Shit, Chazu's not even in the country. He's not coming home tonight!" From what I had heard, there was a good chance he was never going to come home; the word was, he was in Vietnam teaching farmers how to shoot guns.

"Exactly!" Sookie said.

I sat on the floor in front of the couch. Lobetto crouched beside me. "Exactly what?"

"Chazu never comes home anymore!" Sookie said. "I am always alone—"

"I'm here," I pointed out.

Sookie waved her hand in the air, impatient. "You know what I mean! I am a young woman! I have needs, I want to have fun!"

I twisted the knob of the television. The soap opera about the bathhouse flickered on. I liked that show. "So have fun," I told Sookie, flopping onto my stomach to watch the show. "Who's stopping you?"

Sookie dropped to her knees, blocking my view of the screen, and hugged my shoulders. "You're right, Hyun Jin!" she said, kissing the top of my head. "Thanks!"

When she jumped up and ran into the bathroom, I called out, "Wait, what?"

She didn't answer.

"I don't think this is a good thing," said Lobetto. "She's going to blow her ticket out of here."

"What do you mean?" I asked.

"I mean she's not playing it right." Lobetto, gingerly sitting on the edge of the Racey Boy, turned up the volume on the TV. The patriarch of the show was scolding his daughter for dating the son of his rival.

Sookie came out of the bathroom in a thigh-baring, sleeveless dress with a hole cut out of the middle and tangerine-colored platform wedges that matched her nail polish. "Let's go," she said, winking at me.

Lobetto and I followed Sookie toward the stretch of black clubs. "I'm going to try and set something up," Lobetto said. "Which club're you going to hit?"

"All of them," said Sookie. She walked away, dismissing him.

He scowled at her retreating back and I shrugged. "Foxa, I guess," I said, jerking my head at the club closest to us.

"Hyun Jin!" Sookie studied her nails and tapped her foot. "Hurry up." When I caught up with her she hooked her arm through mine and said, forgetting that she was the one who invited him to join us, "We've really got to lose him. He's a parasite."

"Hey, sexy!" Sookie opened the door and waltzed toward the bar. She blew kisses to a few of the men we passed, but I doubted they saw her through the thick smoke. She wedged her shoulders between two GIs hunched over the bar. "You buy me drink," she crooned to one of the men.

He scowled, and without even looking at her said, "Not interested."

Sookie pouted her lips sweetly and said, "Faggot." When the soldier turned to look at her she giggled. "Just joking, just joking. You a big man."

The man picked up his glass and moved down the bar. Sookie

waved me over to the empty stool and turned to the man on the other side of her. "Wanna buy two playgirls a drink?" she asked.

The baby GI, his head shorn into a soft fuzz barely visible in the dim bar light, had been watching Sookie since she sat down. He shrugged, smiled a crooked-tooth smile, and waved to Bar Mama.

Bar Mama nodded to the GI, but narrowed her eyes at me and Sookie. We were solo girls, unescorted in her territory.

When the GI waved to her again, Bar Mama bustled over with an apology for him—"So busy-busy! Sorry, yeah!"—and slapped two watery beers on the counter. She charged the man double.

Sookie threw back her head and thrust out her chest. "Where you from, handsome?" She scanned the room and before he could answer the first question, added: "What's your name, handsome?"

This time the Joe answered quickly. "Ernest."

"I feeling hot," Sookie sighed. Knowing Ernest watched her, she waved the air in front of her face and pushed her hair into a loose bun. She moved to the music, her breasts almost popping out of the dress.

The Joe named Ernest tapped his fingers to the beat. "Like this song?" he asked. "This was big back home last year. Reminds me of high school." He hummed, then began to sing the words: "'Stop, in the name of love, before you break my heart . . .'" He laughed. "Funny song for this place."

Laughing with him, or at him, Sookie shrugged. "Favorite song." Suddenly she hissed, dropping her hands, letting her hair fall back around her shoulders. "That shit!"

Ernest jumped back. "I'm sorry," he stammered. "I thought you liked the Supremes."

I turned to see what had Sookie so upset and spotted Chazu near the stage with a bar girl on his lap. He guzzled his beer, his free hand draped over the shoulder and dangling into the front of the bar girl's dress. He was laughing at something a friend of his said and didn't see Sookie.

Jumping in front of her, I pressed my hands against Sookie's shoulders, trying to hold her to the seat. "Wait," I said, "don't go over there; you're not even supposed to be here."

Sookie struggled away from me. "Why? I'm a free woman."

"This is America Town," I told her. "No one's free."

"Is something wrong?" Ernest asked. He looked worried.

I waved him off and smiled stiffly in his face. "Nothing, nothing, we're just going home." Instead of trying to push Sookie back down, I started pulling her toward the back door.

"Stop that," she snapped. "The nerve of him, to do this to me!"

"You shouldn't have come here without him, Sookie. He's going to be mad if he sees you here."

"He's not going to have a chance to get mad because I'm the one who's mad first." Whirling around me, Sookie stomped toward Chazu.

Reaching Chazu's booth, she dragged the bar girl off his lap by the hair. Up close, the girl looked familiar; we might have been in the same class together at school. It was hard to tell with all the makeup masking her features. "Get off of my man, pig," Sookie yelled.

Chazu's friends laughed and the men sitting behind them at the bar cheered. "Cat fight!" they chanted and called out bets.

The bar girl tumbled to the floor, red miniskirt slipping above her panties. Without bothering to right her clothes, the girl scrambled up and lunged at Sookie. Sookie rushed forward, baring her teeth and tangling her nails into the girl's hair. All the while she yelled at Chazu: "You liar, cheater, no good *gomshi,* Son of a Monkey, good-time boy!"

"Eh, Sookie," Chazu said, slurring a little. He smiled and held up his glass to her as the women fought. "Why're you so mad? We're all just friends here."

The GI sitting next to Chazu clapped him on the back. "Charles, you've got a way with women—they're fighting like dogs over a scrap of bone like you."

"I got ten on that wild one in the orange," one soldier from the bar called out.

Bar Mama scolded, "Stop that—betting only allowed through me!" She shouldered her way to the center of the crowd, splashing onlookers with water from a tub she held to her stomach like an overgrown, unwieldy baby.

Sloshing most of the water on the floor in front of her, Bar Mama tipped the tub over Sookie and the bar girl. "No fighting on the floor," she yelled. "Keep it on stage."

The women continued to fight. Bar Mama reached into the flurry of scratching nails and biting teeth and yanked on a scalp. Sookie came up wailing and swinging her fists at the other girl, who continued to kick at her. Bar Mama kicked back at the girl, telling her to stop, then told Sookie to get out of her bar. "You don't belong here anyway." Fist still knotted in Sookie's hair, Bar Mama shook Sookie like a wayward puppy. "You're not one of my girls."

Teeth clenched, Sookie said, "I'm not leaving without my man."

Bar Mama laughed. "You think you own one of these American GIs? Which one? Which one do you think is yours?"

Sookie pointed at Chazu. She looked him in the eye and said, in English, "He mine."

Chazu's friends punched him on the back and arms. "Chuckie, didn't you get permission from the little woman tonight?" they teased. "Can't go anywhere without that ol' ball and chain, huh?"

Chazu erupted out of his seat at their teasing. He yanked Sookie away from Bar Mama.

"Ow, ow, ow," she cried as strands of her hair, still tangled in Bar Mama's fist, ripped from her scalp.

"Go home," he ordered Sookie. To the bar girl, who stood in broken heels trying to tie the torn strap of her halter top back onto her shoulder, he said, "Get some beers for my friends."

The bar girl smirked at Sookie. Kicking off her ruined shoes, she turned to go, then stopped, fixed her hair and spit at Sookie. "Go home," she said in the same tone of voice Chazu had used.

As she sauntered away, Sookie tried to jump on her back. Chazu grabbed her and slung her over his shoulder. "You are one crazy bitch," he said. He winked at his friends. "What did I tell you, she's crazy for me!"

The men laughed. "Show her who wears the pants."

"No one's going to be wearing pants when he's done with her." The soldiers bantered back and forth, now taking bets on Chazu and Sookie.

Sookie kicked her feet. "Put me down," she growled.

Chazu spanked her. "Grow up, little girl." He carried her out the door and dumped her in the alley. When he turned to re-enter the club, she jumped on his back and started biting and scratching at his neck.

"I not throwaway trash," she screamed.

Chazu wrenched around, clawing Sookie off him and knocking her back to the ground. "What you are is a stray dog," he said, sneering. "I've fed you and now I can't get rid of you."

Sookie howled and tried to punch him.

He pushed her back. "Look at you," he said. "I'm looking for a real woman, not a spoiled little puppy."

"Well, you're not a real man," Sookie shot back. "Can't get it up, big head, small penis faggot."

Chazu lunged for her. Thinking he was going to beat her, I tackled him around the waist. "Run, Sookie, run," I yelled. Sookie, suddenly afraid at the effect of her own words, ran.

Chazu knocked me away, then chased her. Remembering how often we ran from Lobetto and his gang, I thought she could get away if she didn't have those tall heels. But Chazu, long legs and long arms pumping, reached out and wrenched her elbow. She jerked back as if on a leash.

"Bitch," Chazu panted. He struck her across the mouth, cutting it.

Sookie reached down to peel off one of her shoes and cuffed him on the head. When Chazu staggered back, Sookie tugged off the other one and ran toward her apartment house.

He stomped after her. I followed from the shadows, afraid he was going to kill her, throw her from the balcony when he was done with her the way his neighbor did to his girlfriend two months ago. Sookie and I weren't friends with the girl who died, but we knew who she was. Lobetto had said she thought she had it made; the week before he killed her the GI had proposed to her. The MPs ruled her death a suicide, even though she died with an umbrella wedged into her vagina.

If Chazu wanted to kill Sookie, I couldn't stop him, but at least I would witness it. I would know what happened to her, the ending to her story.

I crept up the stairwell and found their apartment door gaping open. Tiptoeing in, I heard muffled screams, crying, moans. Following the sounds, I tapped open the bedroom door.

Chazu was on top of Sookie. From underneath, Sookie gripped him to her, and cried, "Be a man, teach me good."

Looming over her, Chazu glanced up and saw me by the door. He was grimacing, but when I started to back out the door, he jerked his head. "Sookie," he panted. "I think your friend wants to join us."

I hurried to close the door on their laughter and went to sit on the couch. I switched on the TV but of course nothing was on that late at night except static. I turned up the volume and watched a flurry of black and white, trying to find patterns as I waited for the morning.

"He is a cheating fucker," Sookie screamed. Of course I'd heard that before, twice more since that night she found him with the Foxa bar girl. But I had never before seen Sookie act so desperate. "I can't take it anymore," she repeated as she paced the room, chain-smoking. Hitting the wall, she whirled around and stalked to the table where I was sitting. She stabbed the full cigarette out. It wasn't like her to waste. Even though she could get as much of anything she wanted from Chazu, a part of her always remembered having nothing. So she hoarded: food, cigarettes, soda cans, paper clips, gum wrappers, everything.

Her cigarette dead in the ashtray, Sookie crumpled before me. "I've got VD," she whispered.

"No!" I gasped. "What are you going to do?" I bit my lips, then, wincing, licked them instead. They were bruised and scabby from all my gnawing.

Sookie jumped up and headed for the kitchen. "I'm going to teach him a lesson," she sang out. "He's got to learn he can't treat me this way." She climbed on the counter, opened the cabinets above the refrigerator, and lifted out a jug of Jim

Beam. Cradling the bottle, she hopped off the counter and sauntered toward me.

She twisted off the cap and held the bottle to me. "Want some?" she asked.

I shrugged, heaved the jug to my lips and took a sip that burned my throat and the inside of my nose. "Aggh," I coughed, and sloshed whiskey down my chin and neck.

Sookie laughed and took the whiskey. Tilting her head back, she opened her throat and drank until she had to breathe. When she put the bottle down, her eyes were watering. "I'm going to drink this bottle," she gasped, "and then I'm going to kill myself."

"Right," I said. "That'll show him." I took another swallow when she passed the jug back to me.

"I'm serious," she said. "I can't live this life forever. I'll end up like Duk Hee."

I shuddered, picturing Sookie dancing naked in the fish tanks. I gagged; in my vision, half of Sookie's face was mine. "No!" I shouted, then added more quietly, "That won't happen. I won't let it."

Sookie peered at me over the bottle. "You won't let it happen? What do you have to do with anything?"

"I'm . . . I'm . . . we're sisters," I stuttered. "You're not alone."

"Hyun Jin," Sookie said, then belched. "Each one of us is always alone. You can't depend on anyone."

I watched her drink, taking the bottle only when she offered it to me, which became less and less as the night wore on. I took small mouthfuls when she watched me, letting the liquor sit on my tongue and holding it there while I forced my throat to swallow my own spit.

"My sister," said Sookie, offering a wobbling toast, "the only one who was ever good to me in this sad world." Grimacing, she raised the Jim Beam to her lips and poured the liquor down the front of her blouse. "Oops," she giggled, trying to mop it up with her bare hands. She licked her fingers.

Sometime after midnight, but before dawn, Chazu came home. "I should go?" I announced, my voice tilting up in a question.

"Shit back dowhhn," Sookie slurred. Eyes closed, she waved toward my chair.

"How long has she been drinking this time?" Chazu asked.

I shrugged.

He looked at the whiskey bottle lying on the table. There was still some left. Chazu righted the bottle and screwed the cap back on.

"'Cause you," Sookie mumbled.

"Aw, fuck," sighed Chazu, "not this again. Duk Hee never gave me this much trouble."

Sookie screamed, a long wordless howl.

"Shut up!" Chazu yelled. He looked at me. "Shut her up!"

"Don't mention my mother!" Sookie screamed. "I don't want to hear that woman's name!"

Chazu sneered. "Why not? Duk Hee. Duk Hee. Duk Hee."

Sookie tried to climb over the table to scratch at Chazu, but ended up sprawled in spilled beer and whiskey.

"Clean yourself up." He rubbed his eyes like he was tired.

"No!" Sookie wailed. "I dirty. Dirty girl!" She rolled on her back on the table, soaking in the liquor. She pointed a finger in Chazu's direction, her arm flailing wildly. "You made me dirty inside."

"Get a shot," Chazu said. "No big deal." He went into the kitchen and came back with a sponge to wipe the table. "It's what your mother did."

Sookie screamed again, over and over.

Chazu threw the sponge at her. "Shut up!"

"Fine, you want me to shut up, I shut up forever!" Sookie rolled off the table and, wobbling, reached into her shirt to yank out a plastic bag of what looked suspiciously like the dusty herbs I forced her to drink when we were younger.

Chazu's head snapped up. "What's that?"

Sookie shrugged. "Don't know in American—some shit, who knows? Who cares?" Sookie tilted her head, opened her mouth, and emptied the bag into her mouth. A cloud of fine dust billowed about her face. Her cheeks bulged and she gagged as she tried to swallow it.

Chazu ran around the table, reaching Sookie as she dropped to the floor. She began to shake and groan. She grabbed at her stomach, stuck her tongue out, and dry-retched.

Chazu knelt by her side and wrestled her into his lap. Her limp arms spilled over the sides of his body. "I'm sorry, baby, I'm sorry," he crooned. "You're my girl, you're my little wife. The others don't mean nothing to me." Chazu looked up at me and asked, "What do we do?"

I almost laughed, but I remembered how scared I was when Sookie first ate those herbs and began seeing colors on the road to school. I looked into her face, expecting to see a wink or a glare to silence me. Instead her eyes rolled back. My breath caught in my chest; I wasn't sure anymore that she was faking. "Carry her. Toilet," I said, gesturing to the bathroom.

He lifted her and rushed into the small room, placing her into the tub. He overwhelmed the space and I had to climb over his feet to get next to Sookie.

"Go," I told him, pushing him out the door. "I take care." I closed the door on his face, then turned on the shower, letting cold water drench through Sookie's clothes and hair, and stuck my finger down her throat.

She gagged and pushed my hand away. "What're you trying to do, kill me?" she slurred.

"Chazu thinks you're going to die," I said. My hands fluttered around her, unsure of where to land. I placed two fingers across her neck, and was reassured by the vibrant pulse of blood under her skin.

She moaned, then whispered, "Good. I'm teaching him a lesson."

"He's going to kill you if he finds out you're faking," I scolded, whispering.

"Who's faking? I feel like shit; I could die from that ground-antler crap." She stuck her own finger down her throat and threw up a stream of yellowish bile flecked with black clots.

Chazu pounded on the door. "You okay, Sookie? Sookie?"

Sookie panted, then wiped the drool hanging down her chin. "No," she said, answering in Korean. "I will never be all right again." She closed her eyes and let herself fall back into the water. "Get out of here."

"You want me to leave you alone for a few minutes?" I asked.

"No," she said. "I want you to leave for good."

I frowned at her face, willing her to open her eyes, to face me. "I don't understand. Why—"

"Hyun Jin," she whispered, "I am becoming my mother. I have to go to the Monkey House."

9

"I can't believe your father would send you out into the street with nothing," Lobetto said. He put his arm around me and clucked in sympathy. "I remember when we were little, how he would give you everything. You were so spoiled."

"You were the spoiled one." Irritated, I shrugged his arm from my shoulder. "Always flashing your money in my daddy's store, buying stuff for your friends." I turned on him, wanting to make him hurt like I hurt. "Well, where are your friends now?"

Lobetto cocked his head, eyeing me from under his bangs. "Guess I'm like you, Hyun Jin," he said. "I've got nobody."

My stomach felt sour. I looked up, a last glance at Sookie's apartment.

"That's why you called for me, isn't it? You've got nowhere else to go?" He started walking, dragging his feet in the dirt. The sun hadn't yet struggled above the horizon; the dust he kicked up, the air, the streets, our skin, everything was tinged gray in the pallid light.

I jogged to catch up. "What do you mean, nowhere to go?" I demanded, acting cocky to cover my fear. "You have an apartment. We're going there now."

He raised his eyebrows. "Think you're going to live there, too?"

I felt my face grow hot.

"Go home to daddy," urged Lobetto. "He'll take you back."

I narrowed my eyes, stuck out my chin. "Well, I won't take him back."

"Easy words," said Lobetto, "but you couldn't make it out here. You don't have what it takes."

"What?" I snapped, letting words fly from my mouth without thought. "I wouldn't be able to pass out flyers as good as you? Or run cigarettes up to the Monkey House fast enough?" When Lobetto sped up, refusing to look at me, I sucked in a breath and rushed forward. "Wait, I didn't mean . . ."

He whirled, pushed his nose into mine. "You don't know what I've had to do," he hissed, spittle flecking my face. "You don't know what you'd have to do."

"Doesn't matter," I said, moving back a few steps. "I can do anything you can do. I was the best student in school."

Lobetto shook his head. "Give up, Hyun Jin. This isn't school. You don't know what you're talking about."

"I know about honeymoon. What's the big deal?" I said, repeating what Sookie told me. "You close your eyes and the real you flies away."

"You think it's that easy?" Lobetto challenged.

"I know it is," I shot back. "Sookie taught me."

"Sookie?" Lobetto scowled. "What'd you do? Watch her with Chazu? Join them?"

I blanched, remembering Sookie pinned under Chazu's dark bulk, his hips pumping into hers, their mocking laughter as he called out to me.

"Fine." Lobetto spat as if tasting something bitter. "I'll set something up at my place. Tonight."

"Tonight?" I yelped. I almost confessed that I was merely parroting things I had heard. I almost backed down. But I thought how Lobetto would gloat, how he would taunt my big talk. I squared my shoulders and followed him home.

I was embarrassed to face Lobetto's mother, but I didn't want to show it. She had prepared a simple soup and rice for her son's dinner and complained when I sat at the table next to Lobetto. "I didn't expect a 'guest,'" she grumbled.

Lobetto shoved some rice into his mouth, then washed it down with the spicy soup. Sucking air, he muttered, "Hot, hot, hot," as he reached for a glass of water.

Lobetto's mother ladled a second bowl of soup from the pot and sighed. "I guess I go hungry tonight." She dropped the bowl on the table in front of me and glared.

I scooped up a spoonful and blew.

Her eyes narrowed as she watched me lap up the soup. I glared back, reasoning I was working for this meal.

"You don't have any manners," she snapped at me.

Placing my spoon next to the bowl, I bowed my head in exaggerated politeness. "Thank you for the soup," I said. "It is delicious." I picked up the bowl and tipped it to my mouth, slurping. The pungent heat cleared my nostrils.

Lobetto's mother looked from me to her son. She glowered at Lobetto as if expecting him to scold me. Instead Lobetto ate faster. Finishing the meal, I wiped my mouth with the back of my hand and smiled.

Lobetto smacked his lips as he finished his soup. "Any more?" he asked.

"No! Your friend"—Lobetto's mother grumbled, sneering at the word "friend"—"took the last bit right out of our mouths."

"Huh," Lobetto grunted, then pushed up from the table. He stared at me and pointed his chin at the kitchen door.

Feeling myself redden, I frowned at Lobetto, then risked a glance at his mother. She was scowling at her son as well, her mouth gaping over the empty bowls. When he left the room without looking back, her head swiveled to me and her mouth flattened in a thin line. I looked down to avoid her gaze and hurried to follow Lobetto out the door and into the tent.

Stumbling into the darkness, I hissed: "You made it look like we were, we were . . ."

"Fucking?" Lobetto laughed. "Do you want to do it?" He licked my neck, making me jump.

"Sick," I grumbled, wiping my neck. "Get the lamp." I heard the strike of a match, then light flared, piercing the shadows.

Lobetto turned the wick, softening the firelight. "Why are you worried about what my mother thinks?" he asked.

"I'm not," I blustered. "I just, it's just . . . I want her to know that this is just business. That I'm working. That's all."

"I'm sure she'll figure it out," he sighed, backing out of the tent. "Get ready."

"Lobetto!" I grabbed his shoulder. "Where are you going?"

"Ow, ow!" he complained. "Get your claws off me."

Loosening my fingers, I tried to sound nonchalant. "What a baby."

"I'm going to work, try to get something set up for you." Lobetto rubbed his shoulder. "That is, if you still think you can do a job." He mocked me, but his eyes—shuttered and serious—questioned.

For some reason, I felt like crying. I shrugged and forced a laugh. "Let's make some money," I said. "Set up something big." When Lobetto left, I curled in on myself, closed my eyes. I felt the heaviness of the birthmark across my cheek and willed the dark stain to spread. I imagined the blackness creeping over the rest of my face, erasing all that I was.

I fell asleep waiting for Lobetto to come back.

"You're supposed to be ready!" Lobetto panted, rushing into the tent and pulling me by the arm.

Dazed, I rubbed at my eyes, touched my hair. "I am."

"What?" He scowled, eyeing my wrinkled shirt. "You should have borrowed something from my mother."

I sniffed, wanting to imply that nothing his mother had would fit me. Though her dresses were tight enough on her to make her resemble an overstuffed sausage, they would have hung on me. I might as well have draped Lobetto's tent across my shoulders.

"Never mind," Lobetto grabbed at my shirt and tugged at the buttons.

I smacked his hands. "What are you doing!"

"Take your clothes off," he snapped. "Hurry!"

We wrestled over the shirt. "Stop it, Lobetto! I thought I was going to work!"

Lobetto yanked and the last few buttons popped off. "You are, dummy!" he said. "But you can't wear this."

"Oh." I let him take the shirt. "Don't look at me," I said, fingering the button of my pedal pushers. "You have something for me to wear?"

Turning his head away, he muttered under his breath.

"What?" I asked. "What did you say?"

Groaning, he raised his voice. "I said: yeah, I have something for you. It's in my mother's room."

Stripped down to my panties, I crossed my hands over my breasts. "Bring me the outfit," I hissed.

Lobetto swore and threw his hands in the air. "Get over there! You're late." Grabbing my arm, he dragged me out of the tent and toward the apartment door.

The open air bit at my nipples as I hustled after Lobetto and into the cover of the apartment. I scanned the room. "Your mother isn't home, is she?" I asked. My voice sounded small and shaky.

"I sent her to the clubs tonight," he said.

When we approached the closed door, I heard a man's voice, then laughter. "Lobetto," I balked, digging my nails into his wrist. "No. I changed my mind."

Lobetto turned on me, his eyes glittering. "No?" he snarled, twisting his arm so that he was the one gripping my wrist. "You told me you wanted this! I busted my ass landing this job, and it's a big one. I got the money up front and I'm not giving it back."

I backed away, trying to break free of his hold and cover myself at the same time. "Lobetto, I thought I could do this, but I can't. You were right."

"Hyun Jin," he said, his voice quiet and almost sad. "It's too late. Please do this job; it's really important. Look—" His words rushed out, more forcefully, "it's nothing you haven't done before. Just do what you did with Sookie's Joes and you'll be fine."

"I didn't—" I started to say, but by then Lobetto had yanked the door open and was pulling me in after him. Keeping my head down, a veil of hair shielding my face, I closed my eyes and bit my lip to keep from screaming.

"Hi, GI! Hello Joe!" Lobetto blustered into the room, smiling and waving his thumb. His other hand held my wrist so tight that I would sport a bracelet of bruises for over a week. "Got a good-time girlfriend for you."

"Not bad," said a man who came to stand in front of me. "But a little small." Knocking away the shield of my arm, he cupped my breasts and jiggled them in his palms. "Mmm, mmm," he smacked his lips. "Hel-lo Jell-O."

I heard chuckling and, closing my eyes, whimpered.

"What's wrong with her?" a second voice said.

Shocked at hearing more than one Joe, I snapped my head up and saw that there were three of them, and that they were white. I shot a glance at Lobetto, realizing why he seemed so insistent, so desperate I do this job; to pull in these fish meant that he was poaching outside of his territory. He was trespassing, crossing over to the white sections of America Town.

The man who was fondling me, the meanest-looking of the three with small, quick-moving eyes and hard, calloused fingers, released my breasts and grabbed my face, tilting it to the light. "Hooo, boy!" he spat at Lobetto. "She dog. Bow-wow, understandie?" He squeezed my cheeks. "You cheatin' us?"

My teeth cut the inside of my mouth. I twisted my neck, trying to bite his hand. He shoved my head back so hard I bit my tongue instead.

"No, no cheating." Lobetto, a smile pasted on his face, tried to reassure the men. "She's really, really good. The best." Lobetto pinched my arm, in warning. "Keep a good attitude," he hissed at me in Korean. "Smile!"

Tasting bile, I swallowed what I wanted to say to him: go to hell.

"What you say, boy?" the man asked. "You giving me a hard time?"

"She looks young," said the man who had asked what was wrong with me. Glancing at him quickly, I saw him hunch his bony shoulders. He looked young himself, his rounded eyes and protruding ears making him seem unsure and vulnerable. His gaze skittered away, refusing to meet mine. "I don't know about this," he mumbled.

"Them Orientals all look young," said the man I already hated.

I looked at the boy man, and at the third man—a pudgy, older man with curling red hair—who sat on the bed. I let my eyes fill with tears. I shook my head at the red-haired man. His gaze dropped from my face to my breasts, and the pale skin between his freckles reddened.

The skinny boy man moved toward the door. "I don't think she's into this," he said, reaching for the doorknob.

Lobetto dropped my arm and moved to block the door. He waved his hands at them. "It's her act," he said. "She always does this. Makes it more exciting for you."

The young GI frowned, unsure, and looked to his friends.

Lobetto spoke fast. "I give you guys a good deal," he said. "One thousand won for all of you. Three for the price of one."

The man who touched my breasts started laughing. "Why not?" he said. "We don't need to look at her face." He sneered at the boy. "Don't be a sissy, Remmy. You heard the guy: this is her act. She probably done this a hundred times afore now."

"Right, right," Lobetto agreed quickly. "You have a good time, tell your friends. No one better than her, she love to fuck you anyway you like."

The red GI shrugged. "I think it's their culture or something; they cry so they won't feel guilty when they enjoy it."

"Okay, then," Lobetto said, turning to leave. "It's a deal."

"Wait!" I yelled. "Don't leave me here." I tried to run out with Lobetto, but Lobetto pushed me back in.

"Don't mess this up." He gritted his teeth in a fake smile. "This could be the start of something rich. It's a new market; these white *miguks* wanting to try something from the other side. Besides," he added, "it's not like you haven't done it before. After the first, it doesn't matter how many you have."

"Lobetto," I cried. "It is my first time! I haven't done honeymoon before."

He stared at me.

"What's going on?" The GI looked from me to Lobetto. "Do we have a deal or not?"

"Why didn't you tell me before it got to this point?" Lobetto hissed. "I could have gotten more money for you." Glancing at the GI, he said in English, "Yeah, yeah. It's a deal."

The GI slammed the door on Lobetto's face. "Go on then, boy. We'll let you know when we're done."

The mean GI swung me over his shoulder and whacked my ass. I kicked.

"Are you sure she wants this?" one of the men said. I think it was the baby-faced one.

"No!" I yelled.

"She's just fucking with us." The GI threw me onto the bed. "It's part of the game. You too much of a faggot to play?"

Jerking off his pants, the man stood in front of my face. He pressed himself against my lips. "Suckie, suckie," he coaxed.

Jaw clenched, I swatted him away.

"Fine," he said. "I'll start this way." He got on top of me. I shifted under him, trying to turn away from the stench of his body: smoke and stale beer and an animal sourness. He rolled my panties down my hips, opened my legs and entered me, swift and sudden. I arched, crying out in shock and pain, and tried to buck him off. "That's it, sugar." He grinned at his friends. "She's tight as a virgin," he said. "Join in."

"Stop," I cried, in English and Korean. I tried to focus on the baby-face Joe—the Remmy Joe, the faggot Joe, the Joe who wanted to leave—but the man wedged his arm under my chin to shut me up.

The red GI angled my head so he could shove his penis into my mouth. I gagged, but he moved himself in and out, thrusting against my throat. He called out to the boy man, teasing him, urging him to have some fun. After a short while, the boy man took my hand and placed it on his body. "Like this," he whispered, folding my hand in his and pumping.

After a while, the men rotated, shifting from one orifice to another, taking turns at the stations of my body. They pumped, grunting and grinding themselves into me while I whimpered and tried to get away. It didn't matter what I did; they pinned me down, moving my arms and legs as if I were a doll.

"Sandwich!" one of the GIs called out.

I thought for a moment they were going to take a break. I knew what "sandwich" was from Duk Hee. Once she had brought home a Spam and egg sandwich from the PX. I remember thinking that the fried pink meat and bright yellow yolk folded between the crusty white bread was the most deliciously beautiful food I had ever tasted. Better, even, than *jajie* dogs.

But instead of leaving me, the men lifted me up so that one

of them could slide under me. After the other two positioned me on top of him, one climbed on my back.

I cried out, realizing he was trying to put himself into my anus. Struggling to get away, I twisted and bucked my hips. The man under me moaned and the man on top jammed into me. I screamed. And then went numb. I could barely hear them above the whimpering, the small animal cries. When I grasped that the inhuman keening was coming not from a cat cornered in the alleyway, but from me, I gave up the struggle of trying to decipher what the GIs were saying. And I gave up trying to hold on to my body, the body that disgusted me with its crying and mess and pain.

I finally understood what Sookie told me about letting the real self fly away.

From far away, the real me watched them open the shell of my body, ramming and ripping into every opening they could. I watched them spread the legs open, splitting the inner lips wide enough to fit two of the men at the same time. I watched them bite at the breasts and *poji* till they drew blood, and saw them shoot themselves into and over the belly, take breaks, then come at it again.

I watched, and, other than a vague sense of pity, didn't feel a thing.

After a while, I realized they were done. I lay on the bed like a stone. I heard them talking and joking as they got dressed, heard them open the door and talk with Lobetto outside the door. When it was quiet, I opened my eyes and, disoriented by the change in perspective, saw Lobetto looking down at me.

"You did good," he said, awkward in his attempts to pat my shoulder. "Especially for your first time." Then he wrinkled his nose. "You better clean yourself up."

I blinked at the ceiling, refusing to acknowledge him, refusing to acknowledge myself. I didn't want this body, this lump of meat on the bed to be me.

"Get up," he said, tugging my arm. "You've been in here a long time."

My arm flapped, loose and limp, in his grip.

"You know, if you wiggle around and moan like you like it, it'll go a lot faster." He poked a finger into my belly, steadily pressing the breath from my body. I fought the inhale, refusing the air, until my body kicked and lunged, gulping without permission.

"Fuck you, Lobetto," I gasped. My voice echoed, flat and far away in my own head.

"Now that's the Hyun Jin that I know and love." He clapped his hands. "Up, up," he said briskly. "I'll wait for you outside, come out when you're ready, but don't take too long; my mother wants her room back. She's tired."

Only the thought of Lobetto's mother seeing me like this, weak and broken, forced me to sit up. I eased my legs off the bed, wincing when I saw the streaks of blood on my thighs. "She's not out there, is she?" I croaked before I realized Lobetto had already slipped away. Grimacing with each baby step, I shuffled toward the kitchen.

Lobetto's back was to me. As I approached, I saw him tuck the money the Joes gave him into a plastic bag, then shove it elbow deep into the rice jar. Suddenly he jerked his arm out of the jar, scattering a few grains across my path, and spun around, startled by my presence. He scanned my face.

I concentrated on my feet, watching them inch past the minute pellets of rice. I looked up only when I had crossed the kitchen to stand directly in front of him. I kept my expression blank, pretending not to see his hiding place. "I won't do this anymore. "I–I can't." The words cracked my throat, came out as sobs. "I'll die, Lobetto. I want to die now."

Lobetto opened his arms, guided me away from the rice jar. "The first time is always the hardest," he murmured. "I know it hurts, but soon you won't feel it at all." He led me to the hose, positioning me over the drain, and grabbed the nozzle.

Bow-legged, blood and semen smeared across my belly and dripping down my legs, my hair tangled and sticky with bodily fluids, I waited for Lobetto to hose me down. I couldn't stand the feel of my own skin.

"Those pricks should have paid full price," he complained when I didn't answer. He turned on the water and squirted me. "Next time," he said, "wear makeup. Cover up your face so they won't have anything to grumble about."

I picked up the wire brush they used to clean vegetables and scrubbed between my legs. "No more," I growled as I ground the metal into my flesh. "No. No. No." My skin, already raw, broke open and bled.

10

At first we ignored each other, Lobetto's mother and I, as we orbited around her son. Stalking the apartment—wary, watchful—we were careful never to confront the other directly. I waited until she had prepared and eaten her dinner of rice and soup before I left the shelter of Lobetto's tent. She waited until I washed myself before cleaning the dishes. I waited until she turned on her television soap opera before eating her leftovers. She waited until I snuck out the door before mopping the floors.

And we both waited for Lobetto, who came home sometimes with the sun, and sometimes not for days. With Sookie in the Monkey House, I didn't go into the clubs, so when Lobetto ran jobs outside of America Town, I didn't talk to anyone for almost a week at a time. And Lobetto's mother didn't leave the house as long as I was there, so who knew if she talked to anyone either. When Lobetto came home, we both jumped at him, eager to exercise our rusting voices. I made mental lists of things to talk about, things that might have happened days before. Lobetto's mother stored her grievances about me in a similar way.

"Lobetto," she'd say as she served him rice, "that girl ate the last of the steamed fish you like so much."

"Lobetto," I'd say, "I saw Mousie on Market Day. She was looking for you to run something to Pusan."

Lobetto would shrug, shovel the rice into his mouth, and say something like: "Fine," or: "It's handled." Which both Lobetto's mother and I, smirking over his head, would take as a response to our own comments.

"When do you think you'll be ready for another job?" Lobetto asked one morning, waking me when he returned.

"When do you think your mother will be ready for another job?" I retorted, pulling the blanket to my chin.

Lobetto flopped down beside me. "Try to be patient with her," he said. "She's getting too old to work the clubs."

"Sookie says grandmothers work the clubs," I said, without adding that I didn't think it was age that kept his mother from being successful at the clubs, but her weight. For someone who constantly complained that she was hungry, she was enormously fat. GIs didn't like fat women.

"Sookie!" he barked. "The same girl who pushed her own mother out of work?"

I sat up, picked at a thread in the blanket. "Did you know," I asked, "that Duk Hee is my mother, too?"

Lobetto rolled onto his belly, wiggling until I began to rub his back. "I hear stuff," he mumbled into the pillow. "But I don't pay attention if it doesn't involve me." He groaned as I elbowed a knotted muscle. "What's it matter anyway?"

"What's it matter?" I gritted my teeth and pinched his skin, trying to make it hurt. "That's what she said, too."

"That feels good," he sighed.

"Duk Hee abandoned me," I sniffed. "I was a baby and she left me."

"No," Lobetto grunted. "She gave you to your father."

"Sold me." I pounded on his back with my fists. "I was a baby, her baby, and she should have loved me!"

"Ow!" Lobetto sat up and grabbed my hands. "She made sure you had a better start than most," he said. "Now the free ride's over and you've got to work. Speaking of—"

"You don't understand." I wrenched away from his grip, bitter.

"I understand," he answered. "It was hard when my father first left, but not anymore. Now I'm doing good."

I stared at him, then let my eyes roam the dingy makeshift place he called home. "You think you're doing good?" I scoffed.

"Yeah, I do." Lobetto leaned back on his arms and thrust out his chest. "I got my running jobs, I got my mother working, and you, too. Soon I'll have enough money to buy my way into America."

"Me?" I croaked. "I'm not working. I'm not doing that again." I felt dizzy, out of breath. Speaking used up too much of the air in the tent. I grabbed onto Lobetto.

"I know, I know," he crooned. "That was a hard job—too much, too fast. Next time—I'm not pushing you yet—it'll be

FOX GIRL 159

better." Lobetto pried my fingers away from his arm. The nails left a cluster of indentations—half-moon eyes peering out of a darkened forest.

Time seemed flexible, rippling and doubling so that each day passed with excruciating tedium but the weeks disappeared without notice. Lobetto's mother and I were like fish in a tank, endlessly circling, both joined and divided by the medium of water that was Lobetto.

One morning she asked me to chop the vegetables for the breakfast soup; I thought she was trying to build a friendship. Grateful for the overture, I cooked the way I was taught; I cleaned the parsley, peeled and cubed the turnips, minced the garlic, and set everything to boil.

"Ugh," she grumbled at the first spoonful. "The turnip is still crunchy raw in the middle—cut too big to cook through."

I stuffed a turnip into my own mouth to keep from snapping at her. As I crunched, she slurped from the bowl, muttering, "Tasteless." But when it was empty, she held the bowl to me and waved her jiggling arm toward the stove for a refill.

I should have knocked that bowl from her imperious hand. I should have ignored her. My mistake was that I took that bowl, carried it to the stove, ladled in a second helping, and placed it back on the table in front of her like a dutiful daughter-in-law. She didn't say thank you, didn't even look up to acknowledge me, but when she bent her head to smell the steam, I saw her secret smile.

From then on, she lorded it over me. Lounging on the mat in front of the television Lobetto had scavenged or stolen from somewhere, she continually ordered me to refresh her glass of water, to cook and bring her her meal on her tray, to rub her tired calves. If she could have, I believe she would have ordered me to piss for her.

After I complied with each order, she would say, "You are not good enough for my son." Her eyes never left the television screen as she needled me. "When he goes to America, do you think he will take you?"

Inside, I thought: "Witch! Fox demon! Hag! Do you think he will take *you*?" But I never said anything. I never believed any of us would go anywhere. We were drowning, dying in America Town and it was all I could do to hold on.

I tried to hide in Lobetto's tent, but his mother would bang the dishes together and hose off vegetables so that the water sprayed against the blanket, leaving it damp and musty-smelling. And all the while, she'd complain about having to support a pretend daughter-in-law too lazy to work.

Flushed from my retreat, I spent more time out of the house, first sitting on the step, then, when boredom set in, venturing farther. With Lobetto's house the center, I spiraled away until I was walking the perimeter of America Town—following the wall past the school for the throwaway children, past the tombs where Duk Hee pushed her buttocks against the transparent door, toward the row of apartments where Sookie used to live. The back of Sookie's old place brushed against the wall which enclosed America Town—I could just wedge my body in the space between. Turned sideways so that my discolored cheek scraped the side of Sookie's old house and my back rubbed against America Town's wall, I forced myself along that narrow pathway.

I stumbled through, but didn't break contact with the wall until the wall itself broke away. Through the gap was my father's candy shop and the life I could have had as a shopkeeper's daughter. I craned my head, trying to catch a glimpse of my father, then ducked. I didn't want him to see me, to see what I had become. I looked instead toward Chinatown and beyond, at the docks and the water littered with boats. Then I stepped through.

When I felt people staring at me, I assumed it was because of my ugliness. I ducked my head and covered my face with hair which, loose and tangled, felt sticky with sweat. Then I noticed my clothes, borrowed from Sookie: blue tank top that tied at the waist; skirt that ruffled above the knee; orange sandals open at the toe. I was dressed like a *kichiton* girl. An America Town whore. But instead of cowering beneath their glares and smirks, I threw back my head and looked each passerby in the eye. I could almost hear the mothers whisper behind their hands: Dirty. No class. Throwaway Korean.

I wandered toward the pier and watched the slow queue of boats vie for position at the docks. Seagulls screamed at the boats and dived for the trash thrown overboard. Once tethered, the vessels coughed up their loads of fish and crab, shrimp and squid. Squatting in front of one of the boats, I watched two women drag nets full of what looked like squiggling silver fingers onto the shore. I studied the way these women—possibly mother and daughter—worked together, easy in each other's company, efficient in their routine of culling anchovies, of laying them in the sun to die and dry.

The days without Lobetto, I filled with the sea, walking to the ocean to watch the harvest of fish. Disguised in a long-sleeved shirt and a pair of Lobetto's pants, I found and followed that same family as often as I could, so often that the daughter pointed me out to her mother. The daughter, close to my age, put up her hand to wave as if she knew me, but, suddenly unsure, she tucked her hair behind her ear instead. Her mother scolded her without lifting her head to look at me; I couldn't hear the words but her tone was sharp.

One afternoon I saw the daughter without her mother. This time the girl waved. I looked behind me, then back at her. She waved again, motioning me toward her. "You, do I know you?" she demanded.

I shrugged.

"You must be in love with me then." The girl laughed.

I scowled, then laughed with her. "You remind me of someone," I said.

The girl stared at my face, and when I tried to hide myself from her, she announced: "My mother said you were a GI girl. But I told her you were too ugly. I was right."

I spat at her feet.

She jumped back and huffed. "Don't get mad."

"I'm not mad," I growled, hating her shining bob of hair, her neat clothes, her rubber shoes that somehow stayed bright white even walking through the muck of fish.

"Good." The perfect girl smiled. "Then do me a favor— watch the fish for me. I need to go somewhere."

"I don't do favors," I snarled, and turned away.

She caught my arm. "Of course I'll pay you," she said.

So I stayed and patrolled the small army of anchovies lined up like troops. Stepping between the rows of baking fish, I waved a rolled newspaper at the determined flies swimming through air thick with heat and the stench of the sea.

Occasionally I rested in the shade of the girl's makeshift tent, where she had a bucket of octopus soaking for the night's dinner. I crouched over the bucket, poking desperate tentacles back into the cold, murky soup. Every once in a while, I pulled out an octopus by the head, giving it a taste of freedom. Its legs twining about my arm, sucking at my skin, I would look into its purple, lidded eye, the same eye—with its tail of guts—I would later pluck out. The eye and entrails, a bucket of guts and leftovers, this was the payment the girl offered me for a day of work.

Like a cat with her half-devoured prey, I dragged that bucket up the hill into America Town, back to Lobetto's house. I should have dumped it over that girl's head, but I was so tired that all I could think was that I had earned it without lying on my back. Exhausted, I stumbled into Lobetto's house and spilled the fish guts onto the steps.

Lobetto's mother screamed and swooped to whack me on the head. I dropped into the slime at my feet and dizzily looked at the octopus eye staring back at me. The streamer of its purple stomach looked almost like tentacles. My vision blurred and the tentacles squirmed toward my knee.

"What's the matter with you?" Lobetto's mother shrieked. She pulled at my elbow, perhaps suddenly worried she had gone too far. "I didn't hit you that hard," she stammered. "It was just a tap, really."

"I'm just so tired," I said. Then I threw up.

Lobetto's mother dropped my arm. "You stupid, stupid girl," she wailed.

"I'll clean it up." I wiped my chin and only succeeded in smearing either octopus blood or vomit across my face.

"You won't trap my son," she said. She shook her head and her whole body quivered.

I couldn't follow her train of thought. I thought of fishing, bait, nets, and baskets that tricked octopus into getting caught. "I said I would clean up this mess," I snapped. "Just be still." All I wanted was for her to shut up so I could rest my brain.

"Damn right you're going to clean up your mess," Lobetto's mother said. She kicked the slimy entrails out the door. "And I'm not talking about this crap."

I fumbled to my feet. "Then what are you talking about? You're always griping about something," I complained, yawning. I nearly gagged as the smell of fish and vomit burned my throat.

"I'm talking about why you're so tired, why you're so fat, why you're so much stupider than usual." Her voice scratched at my ears.

I folded my arms over my head to muffle her noise. "I'm tired because I've been working, something you keep nagging me about."

"You were tired when you woke up this morning," she said. "I thought you were just lazy—which you are—but now I know. You can't hide it anymore." She looked at my stomach, where the button to my jeans skirt had popped open. "I've been there myself; you think I don't recognize the signs?"

"Shit," I said, splaying my hands against my stomach and trying to remember when I had last bled.

"Didn't anyone teach you about protection when you started in this business?" Lobetto's mother scolded. "That's one of the first things every girl in America Town should learn."

"I . . . I . . . what?" Choking, I struggled to my feet.

"When can you fix this?" Lobetto's mother demanded.

"Fix it?" I still couldn't think straight.

"Are you as stupid as you look?" She marched up to me. For

the first time, I realized I was taller than her; she had to look up to meet my eyes. "You need to do it soon."

"Do it?" I echoed, then shook my head when I realized what she meant. Most of the girls in the clubs had had abortions, some as many as six or seven times. They got pregnant with each GI boyfriend, but when the GI left town without marrying them, they got an abortion and started all over again. But I didn't want this child for bait; I wanted it for myself. Suddenly, savagely, I wanted it. "I'm going to keep this baby," I told Lobetto's mother.

"Why? You think you can hook a GI into marriage?" she taunted. "That's what I did." She reached up and grabbed me by the shoulders. "But you know what? It didn't matter. In the end, he still left me with a brat to take care of."

I gasped. I had never heard her speak this way about Lobetto before, would never have guessed she felt this way since she doted on him, spoiling him rotten.

She dropped her hands. "Don't think I don't love Lobetto," she said. "He's all I have left. But I'm telling you for your own good: get rid of it."

I stepped away from Lobetto's mother and narrowed my eyes at her. "Since when have you cared about my own good? You're just worried I'll mess up any plans Lobetto has."

Lobetto's mother scowled. "I'm warning you," she said. "Throw it away before it drags you down. Before it drags us all down."

I smiled. "This baby is not a piece of trash," I said. "This baby is mine."

"Then God help you," Lobetto's mother said, eyeing my hands still protecting my belly, "And God help it if it's a girl."

————

"A drink to your son." Lobetto filled our glasses with warm beer. He and his mother slurped their drinks, but I only pretended to swallow. The smell curled and kicked in my stomach.

"How are you going to take care of him?" his mother asked me. Her tone was polite, but her heavy-lidded eyes were mocking. "Where are you going to live?"

I smiled despite my dislike of her, a vision for a new life forming in my mind. "I'd like to get a place in the country. Move out of America Town."

"What a great idea," said his mother.

I looked up, wary of her support.

"But, tell me: outside of America Town, where else in Korea could your child, your little GI baby, fit in?" She bared her pointy teeth in what was supposed to be a smile.

Lobetto pushed away from the table. "Stop, Mother."

"Stop what?" His mother batted her eyelashes. "I'm just making conversation."

"Then stop making conversation," Lobetto ordered. "Leave her alone. She hasn't been feeling well."

His mother sniffed. "I don't see why you should care. You're off to meet your father in America any day now."

Lobetto sighed. "Don't worry, Mother. I won't forget about you."

"Of course you will, dear." His mother took another sip of beer. "That's the way it is with children." She raised her brow at me. "You'll see."

Lobetto stopped asking me to work. I should have been suspicious. Instead of urging me to make money until I began to show, he insisted I rest and asked his mother to take care of me.

To further ensure the health of my baby, Lobetto brought

home American pills. "'One a Day,' it says," Lobetto instructed, shaking the bottle. "Take one every morning."

"Lobetto, thank you." My eyes teared at the unexpected kindness.

He shrugged. "No big deal. Leftovers from the PX." He wiped a tear from my cheek. "Now the baby will grow big as a GI."

I opened the bottle and sniffed. The smell reminded me of Chinatown herbs. I groaned when my stomach rolled, but tried to joke: "I don't want to have to push a GI out from between my legs."

Lobetto scowled. "Don't talk like that anymore," he scolded. You're going to be a mother."

"I just meant I don't want the baby to grow too big," I said.

"But the baby should be big," Lobetto answered. "He's an American, isn't he?"

I frowned. "No. He—or she—is Korean."

Lobetto raised his brows, then handed the bottle to his mother. "These are called vitamins," he explained. "Make sure she takes one every morning."

And though his mother smiled at him, nodding her compliance, when she brought me the vitamins along with my morning soup and fruit, I'd hear her grumble: "When I was pregnant, I didn't have special medicine, and my baby turned out fine."

I assumed the tea his mother prepared for me was also Lobetto's idea, but that was something I later discovered she had thought of on her own. Every morning, after my fruit and vitamin, she carried a cup of tea into Lobetto's tent. Crouching beside me, she'd wait and watch me struggle to force down the bitter tea. When the scent and taste would make me gag, I would push it away. "I can't finish," I'd gasp.

Lobetto's mother would shove the cup back into my hands. This will make you feel better."

"It's the tea that makes me sick," I pouted, feeling like a child.

"It's for your own good," she'd say, goading me until I choked it down.

One morning, five weeks after I realized I was pregnant, I drank the tea and couldn't hold back the nausea. I threw up, my stomach cramping, emptying itself until I spit up only yellow bile. Still my stomach cramped. I curled in on myself, taking the shape of the fetus within me. "Help me," I cried as I reached for Lobetto's mother. I grasped her knees and, looking into her face, saw that she looked neither scared nor surprised.

I gritted my teeth at another wave of pain and crossed my legs to try to hold back the thick tide of brine and blood gushing down my thighs. "You did this!" I howled at Lobetto's mother. "You made this happen!"

Lobetto's mother didn't answer, didn't even look at me as she pulled the blanket from the wall. She wiped the blood from my body, then covered me as I cried. When I woke the next morning, she was still sitting beside me, quiet and stern.

"You did this," I croaked. "You killed my baby."

She remained silent, but she reached over to massage my belly.

I shoved her away, kicking even though I felt cramps and blood. "Lobetto will hate you for this as much as I do," I lashed out, ranting. "He will finally know what a monster you are."

"It wasn't the tea," she murmured. She dropped the bottle of vitamins onto my belly and stood to go.

Grabbing the pills, I shrieked, "Are you saying this is what killed my baby?" I felt dizzy, flooded with hatred for Lobetto, for his mother, for myself for not guarding against their gifts.

"No," Lobetto's mother snapped. "That's not what I'm saying." As she held the flap open she paused, trying to gentle her tongue. "Sometimes these things happen for no reason. It really is for the best."

"It was you!" I screamed. "It was you!" over and over until the words became meaningless and I no longer knew if I believed them myself. When I couldn't squeeze any more sound from my throat, I wrapped my arms around my belly, protecting the child that was no longer there.

11

Immersed in the dark and dank of Lobetto's tent, I felt close to my child. In my half-sleep, I could almost imagine her in there with me—twins in the womb rather than mother and child. Off and on I slept, for days and weeks, unsure of the boundaries of time, space, self. In that dimness, I felt I could call her back into my body.

When Lobetto tried to crawl into the tent, I ignored him and lay still, afraid that any movement, any acknowledgment of the outside world would threaten my concentration, breaking my link with the baby. But when Lobetto touched my feet, I kicked him away, hating his intrusion and his betrayal. And each time he spoke, he killed my child all over again.

"Get up," he'd growl. "Get out. Get back to work." And I could feel the baby's quick skitter away from me.

"Shut up," I'd howl, lashing out with tongue and feet. "You're scaring her away."

Jumping back from my kicks, he said, "Losing that baby must have scrambled your brain. My mother said you might feel strange for a while."

I lunged at him. "I will kill your mother," I snarled. "You tell her I'm going to kill her. And then I'm going to kill you."

"Fuck," Lobetto said, backing away. "You are messed up." Later I discovered that Lobetto found some job for his mother on Cheju Island. He was worried enough about my threats that he settled for only a portion of his usual cut in order to get her out of the apartment.

With each of his visits, I could feel the baby shrivel into herself, becoming a black dot that would disappear if I blinked. It took a lot of concentration to coax her to emerge again.

I was coaxing my child back to life, nudging the nub of her body to sprout legs and arms, fingers and toes when Lobetto threw back the covers of the tent and said, "She's in there!"

The light shattered my child's body and I squeezed my eyes closed against the shock of light and pain. "Get the fuck away," I said, and was surprised to taste the salt of my own tears. I turned my face into the mattress.

"Move, Lobetto," I heard Sookie scold, her voice loud and grating. "Phew, it stinks in here."

"I'm going," Lobetto grumbled.

"Take her with you," I yelled into the mattress, refusing to flip over to face Sookie.

"Whah, whah, whah," Sookie blabbed. "I can't understand a word you're saying. At least sit up so I can see you."

"No," I mumbled, my mouth tasting the cotton beneath me.

Sookie knocked on my head. "Where is Hyun Jin? Hyun Jin, are you in there? Hi, hi! I'm back from Monkey House hell!"

I wanted to sleep. I could feel the baby hovering at the edge of that dark unconscious. I held my breath, hoping Sookie would give up and go away.

She didn't. Instead she jumped on my back, smashing the air out of my body.

"Great, you're back," I said, coughing.

"I brought you a present," she sang. Something thumped onto the mattress next to my ear.

Shifting my head, I cracked open my eye to look at her gift. A glass ashtray. "I don't smoke," I said. When I was pregnant, the smell made me vomit.

"Since when?" Sookie rummaged through her purse and pulled out a bent cigarette.

"Don't light up in here," I said. I meant to sound mean, but instead sounded tired. "There's nowhere for the smoke to go."

"Suck it up, baby." Lifting a match to the stick, she inhaled, then blew. Smoke feathered around my head.

Fanning my hand in front of my face, I coughed to hide my need to gulp it in.

"If you don't want to get up, fine," Sookie said, "but at least turn around and take a good look at me." She prodded my back. "Come on, you'll barely recognize me. I've changed."

Body aching, I flipped over. She seemed like the same old

Sookie to me: long, burned-tea face framed with hair that had frizzed when she dyed it red. She was skinnier, maybe, her eyes more sunken, her cheekbones sharper.

Then I looked lower and jolted upright despite myself. "Shit, what the hell happened to them?" I croaked. I pressed my hands against my temples, dizzy from the rush of blood and smoke. I closed my eyes and then opened them again to stare at her chest.

Sookie giggled, straightening her back so that her swollen breasts jutted toward me. "Like 'em?" she asked. It's the newest thing at the Monkey House."

"You look like a cow," I mumbled.

"Thanks," she said. She pinched her nipples. They stuck out like buttons. "I can't feel them anymore, but I figure Chazu will like them. He was always complaining at how small I was before."

She cupped them, holding them out as if in offering. "Go ahead," she said. "Touch them."

I pressed a finger across the top of her breast, where her shirt dipped into her newly formed cleavage. "It's hard," I said, poking at what felt like a rubber ball just under her skin.

"Yeah," she grinned. "I know some GIs who should get it done to their penises."

"Did it hurt?" I touched my own breasts, still swollen and tender with the memory of child.

Sookie shrugged. "Doctor just took a needle and shot something in there to pump it up."

I lay back down. "I'm tired," I told her. "Go away."

"You should get it done yourself," she said. "It'll help you get the GIs when you start at the clubs. The competition is tough."

"I'm not working." I tried to ignore Sookie so I could listen for the baby's cries.

"Hungh," Sookie grunted. "That's not what Lobetto said."

"Lobetto can go to hell," I murmured.

"Lovers' quarrel?" Sookie teased. "Only makes the sex hotter."

I glared at Sookie. "Is that what he told you, that we're lovers? I hate him!" I shouted. The volume made my head ache, so I whispered. "I think he killed my baby."

"Baby, what do you mean 'baby'?" Sookie waved her hand as if chasing away a fly. "It was nothing, yet."

"It was a child." I clenched my teeth. "And Lobetto killed it."

"Oh, please," Sookie said. "It was a smart thing not to have it."

When I opened my mouth to argue, she held up her hands and talked fast. "What, you were going to raise it in this hell-hole? Hyun Jin, listen: our only hope is to marry U.S., and no GI is going to want you with that weight dragging you down." She took a breath, then grinned. "At least not that kind of weight." She bent forward and swung her chest at my face. "You need this kind of weight. I'm telling you, use this for bait and some GI is going to gobble you up."

"You think those'll make Chazu marry you?" I sneered. "You think those'll make him love you?"

"Chazu or some other Joe," Sookie said, shrugging. "I'm not going to be like my mother, waiting until Chazu gets bored and dumps me. I'm going to help myself before I get too old."

Sookie returned the next day, and the next, and each day she came, my baby retreated farther and farther into the darkness. I still felt her at the edges of my skin, in the flicker of my blinking eyes, but I couldn't conjure up her image anymore.

Instead, it was always Sookie that I saw, Sookie bearing gifts she smuggled from Chazu's apartment. She lured me out of the tent with them. "Come into the kitchen to see your present,"

Sookie cajoled, and I hobbled into the light to see what she had brought for me. They were inconsequential things at first: a few American coins, cuff links, shot glasses, Hanes underwear, which I wore, unwilling to give them to Lobetto though he constantly asked for them.

"Sookie," I said, fingering my presents. "Won't Chazu know these things are missing?"

But Sookie would shrug it off, saying they were little things. And they were, to him. "Chazu has so much why would he care or even notice if he's missing a pen or a pair of underwear? He can always buy a new one."

When Sookie got more daring, bringing me reading glasses, a pair of men's shoes, and a blender, I got nervous. "I don't need any of these things, Sookie," I said. The glasses did look good on me, making me look as smart as I was, but they gave me a headache. The men's shoes became a burden I had to keep hidden from Lobetto who coveted the rich leather. And the blender, its tail of cord hanging limp and useless without an outlet, sat neglected in the middle of the kitchen floor. We became so accustomed to its presence, it became invisible even as we stepped over it to prepare meals or shuffled into the tent to sleep.

Sookie laughed. "Who cares if you need it? It's American!" Sometimes Lobetto would convince us to sell some of the things on the black market, but instead of giving him the money like he wanted, Sookie would buy clothes or candy, cigarettes or liquor.

"Why take the risk?" I asked her as she piled the goods around me. "Chazu would give you all this stuff if you asked."

"I don't like to ask," she said, cracking her gum and popping a can of High Life. "It tastes sweeter this way, don't you think?"

She plucked the gum out of her mouth and tilted the beer for a long swallow.

"I don't know, Sookie." But she was right, it did.

The last gift she brought over from Chazu's house was the camera. She came to Lobetto's at dusk, dressed in a halter top and denim cutoffs, and swinging that Pentax by its thin black strap. I could tell she had been drinking, but she didn't seem drunk.

"Don't you ever change clothes?" she asked, wrinkling her nose.

I wore an undershirt and the pair of boxers she had stolen from Chazu's apartment a week earlier. I was lying in the middle of the floor, listening to Lobetto sing—"Come on baby, light my fire, time to set the night on fi-i-re"—as he hosed off, showering before hitting the streets.

Sookie pinched my shirt between her toes and tugged. "Why don't you make yourself up?"

"For what?" I pushed her monkey toes away and crossed my arms across my chest.

Sookie lifted the camera to her face and pointed it down at me. "For this," she said. She giggled and snapped the button.

"Stupid," Lobetto drawled from the kitchen doorway. His hair still dripped water, but he already had a Tootsie Pop wedged in his mouth. Since Sookie bought a bag from the black market, he ate them nonstop. He swizzled the thin white stick and added: "You got to use the flash. When you're inside, you got to use the flash."

"Go on," Sookie said to me. She didn't even turn around to acknowledge Lobetto. "Change clothes. I want us to take some pictures. It'll be fun."

Lobetto sauntered over. "That's a nice-looking camera—expensive. Does Sir Black know you're playing with his toy?"

Sookie jerked away from him when he tried to touch it. "Look but don't touch." She laughed. "I bet you hear that a lot around the clubs, don't you? It's what all the girls tell you, huh?"

"Shut up," Lobetto said. "You're just as ugly as you always were."

I stood and combed the hair away from my face. "Do you know how to work that thing?" I asked her, although I didn't really care.

"Ah, how hard can it be?" Sookie frowned. "I watched Chazu use it hundreds of times. You know, he treats it like a baby." She held it to her face, smacking her lips against it. "Oooh, aren't you sweet?" she crooned to it. When she saw my face, she stilled. "Oops," she said. "Sorry. I was trying to get your mind off that whole thing."

I staggered back. "I'm . . ." My voice trailed off. I thought I heard the wail of an infant. "I'm tired. Going to rest."

Lobetto shoved Sookie, grabbing the camera from her. "Stupid!" I heard him hiss under his breath. Louder, he announced: "Stay, Hyun Jin. I'll take the pictures."

"Give it back, you black dung boy," Sookie protested, but it was weak, halfhearted, and Lobetto didn't let go.

"Really, let me take them," Lobetto said. "I can make you look good. You and Hyun Jin both. You girls'll be two foxy mamas, I promise."

Sookie bit her lip, then let go of the camera. "You better do a good job, Lobetto," she said.

"I guess I should change," I said, planning my escape.

I turned toward the tent, but Lobetto held my arm. "Wait," he said. "Just take off the shirt."

"What?" I put my hands on my hips.

"Okay," said Sookie. She pulled at my shirt.

"Stop it!" With the shirt tangled around my arms and head, my voice came out muffled.

"It's not like we don't know what you look like," Sookie said. "It's nothing. We're all family here."

I yanked off the shirt and glared first at Sookie, then at Lobetto, who was hidden behind the lens. "You're right," I said, throwing my hands out in surrender. "It's nothing. I'm nothing."

"I'll make you guys look good," Lobetto said. "Sookie, get behind her and hold her breasts."

Sookie stepped back and wrapped her arms around me.

"Don't cover them," Lobetto ordered. "Lift them."

I looked down, shamed by Sookie's touch and the relentless eye of the camera. "I don't want—"

"That's good," Lobetto said as the camera flashed. "That hides your birthmark."

As the light continued to burst from the camera, Sookie took off her top and moved next to me. I noticed that her chest was looking a little lopsided and then she pressed against me. Lobetto was talking—"I'll develop these, see if I can sell them. You guys really look foxy"—and Sookie was touching me, and the camera was blinking, the shutter moving and clicking, and I had to close my eyes against its shattering brightness.

When Sookie and Lobetto dragged me out of the house that night, I forced myself to ignore the tug I felt, the sense that I was leaving my child alone in the dark of the tent. The streets seemed surreal, a dream compared to the image I had held close of that perfect baby. But I let go and almost fell down, feeling light-headed-drunk on air that smelled like piss and smoke and beer and trash.

Out of habit, we headed toward Club Foxa. We waited out-side until we could hook up with a group of GIs, looping our arms around the waists of two of the men and sauntering in with them. Sookie and I downed two vodka tonics each—mostly water since the bartender saw who the drinks were for—and Sookie pulled a quick honeymoon. Pocketing the money, we ran out before Bar Mama could track us down and demand her cut. Outside, we ducked into a corner alley and Sookie bent over and got sick.

I'd seen Sookie drink half a bottle of vodka without puking, let alone two glasses of watered-down shit. But I figured she could have started drinking before she came to Lobetto's. She could have started days ago.

We tried Club Angel next, but its Bar Mama saw us as soon as we tried to walk in the door and wouldn't let us in. "You guys aren't even wearing your tags," she scolded. "I can't let you work even if I wanted to." She pushed us out into the street. "And I don't want you to. You'd just be stealing money from me."

"Fuck you," I said, and Sookie pulled out a roll of bills from her purse and waved it at Bar Mama.

"We were going to buy our own drinks," Sookie said.

The Angel's Bar Mama spat at us. "You're so stupid you think I don't know that you'd never pay for drinks? You think I don't know you just want to steal business from my own girls? Get the fuck out before I call the officials."

Sookie stuck her finger out at the closed door of the bar. My feet hurt and I could tell Sookie was still woozy—she kept wip-ing at her mouth and holding her stomach—so I said, "I'm done. I want to sleep."

Chazu was waiting for her at his apartment. As soon as we stag-gered through the door, he leaped from the couch and pinned

Sookie against the wall. She dropped her purse and the money she made honeymooning spilled out.

Chazu swooped down and scooped it up. "It's true?" he asked. "You been screwing around on me?"

Sookie tried to walk around him. When he didn't move, she pushed him. "I never cheat on you," she yelled back.

"You're such a liar." Chazu flung his arm toward me. I flinched though he was far away. "I give you enough so you don't have to work, and you pay me back by fucking around, then lying about it?"

"Hooo, you give me so much?" Sookie screamed. "A few won here, there and you think you big shit! Here, I pay you back." She threw her purse at his head.

Chazu didn't duck and the purse hit him on the forehead. It bounced and landed near my feet. I picked it up and stood, offering it lamely first to Sookie, then to Chazu. Both ignored me.

"When I met you," Chazu was saying, "you seemed so nice. So quiet. I thought I could help you be something better than your mother." He shook his head, sneering. "But you are more a whore than she ever was."

Sookie shrieked and flew at his face, clawing at his eyes. "Don't. Talk. About. My. Mother," she snarled.

Chazu twisted his head and pushed his arm against her throat.

I held the purse against my chest and backed away. I had seen them do this too many times. I decided to wait in the doorway, out of their way but close enough in case Sookie needed my help, until they finished fighting. When they moved into the bedroom, excited by their anger, then I would leave.

"Nothing I do is ever going to change you," Chazu said. "You're a whore to your bones; it's in your blood."

"You think you better than me," Sookie wheezed, "but your

blood tastes just like mine." She angled her head against Chazu's bicep and bit into his skin.

He yelped, jumping back, but Sookie held on, jaws locked on muscle. Sookie's orange hair was tangled in Chazu's fist; he pulled some out at the roots. Tears leaked from her clenched eyes, blood oozed from between her teeth, and Chazu shook her and slapped her in the head.

Finally, Sookie's mouth gaped open and she dropped to the floor. She wrapped her arms around her head as Chazu struck her with his boot. "I would have given you everything you stole from me," he grunted. "Why didn't you just ask? Why did you have to make me look like a fool?"

Sookie rolled onto her back and opened her arms, leaving her belly unprotected. "That the best you can do? Pussy kicks," she panted. "Try harder."

Chazu's foot hovered above her abdomen, and then he put it down, slow and gentle, next to her ribs. "I can't do this anymore," he whispered. "I'm not like this. I'm not this kind of person." He dropped to his knees beside her and bowed his head. Get up," he said, looking at Sookie sprawled in front of him, "and get out. Take anything you want, but don't ever come back." He rose then, stepping over her to the bedroom, where he closed the door behind him.

I inched into the living room. "Sookie?" I whispered to her prone figure. "Aren't you going to go in after him?"

"No," Sookie said. "This time, it's over. I knew it before I came here tonight." She held out her hand and I helped her up.

I handed her her purse. "Um, here," I said. "I guess we should leave."

Sookie waved the purse back. "Hold it." She staggered into the kitchen and pulled the dish towels off the rack. Then she opened up drawers and cabinets and refrigerator and packed whatever she could into the towels: silverware, shot glasses and plastic tumblers, canned Spam and tuna, rice bowls and lemons, grapes and several cans of soda. She knotted the towels, handed me one of the packs, and then marched out of Chazu's apartment.

I figured Sookie would return, if not the next morning then within the next few days, but until then the only place she could go was Lobetto's. Since he would be working tonight, I thought we would be alone until at least the next afternoon.

I wasn't expecting to see his mother, back from Cheju with her hair cut short and permed into a tight afro—which meant she had made enough cash to spend on extras. "More trash?" she said, blocking us from entering. "I won't support any more freeloaders."

I stopped breathing. I hated her so much I couldn't move, couldn't speak. My ears started ringing and my vision blurred until all I could focus on was a tiny black dot swimming above her head. As I stared, that black dot sprouted a head, then little squiggles of arms and legs. The black dot floated toward me and Sookie, hovered above us, and in that brief moment before I had to blink, I saw my child.

"—go on, go," Lobetto's mother was saying as she waved Sookie away. "You belong with your mother—heard she had a place in the fish tanks," she said. And then she laughed.

I roared and stalked toward Lobetto's mother. "She stays here."

Lobetto's mother placed her hands on her hips, squaring herself within the door frame. "You're nobody here," she spat. "What makes you think you have any say here? You're just some stray that Lobetto let in, one of his pets."

I pushed my face into hers and breathed: "I paid with my child, my body, and my blood."

Lobetto's mother looked at me and her smug smile wavered, then faded when I bared my teeth. I wanted to bite her, to feel her blood against my teeth. I imagined how satisfied Sookie must have felt when she bit into Chazu's flesh.

Lobetto's mother sniffed. She looked away from me, past my shoulder to Sookie, and said, "Fine. Lobetto can deal with you." She marched away, and we heard the whine of the television warming up.

I pulled Sookie into the house, past the front room where Lobetto's mother faced the TV, determined to ignore us as we moved through the kitchen and into Lobetto's tent. Under the shelter of blankets, I struck a match to light the lamp, then looked at Sookie.

She looked like shit—hair wild, her face and arms red and swollen where Chazu had slapped and kicked her, neck ringed with purpling bruises.

"Want a cigarette?" I asked, already rummaging under the mattress for Lobetto's stash. Instead of cigarettes, I pulled out a handful of headless Tootsie Pop sticks, the candy sucked and chewed off so thoroughly that the ends were frayed.

Sookie covered her nose and turned away. "I'm tired," she groaned, and lay down. Hunched in on herself, her hands around her head and knees pulled in to her chest, she looked small, a tiny seed.

"How do you feel?" I asked.

Sookie, eyes closed, didn't answer. I watched her breathing turn slow and even. And then I noticed the pictures Lobetto must have developed spread out next to the mattress. I picked them up, looking at Sookie and me in frame after frame.

It was then that I finally saw: her pale skin, her sickness, her tired eyes, her thickening waist.

All the time I had been calling my baby, Sookie was blocking the way. While I was the one making the wish, Sookie was the one to catch it. She was pregnant, my child in her belly.

12

When Sookie began to swell past the binding of her skirt and could not work the clubs, she slouched around Lobetto's house. "How did I get stuck with so many useless mouths to feed?" Lobetto would grumble when he stumbled home each morning to find his mother, Sookie, and me stationed in an uneasy truce around the television. "This is begining to look like the inside of the Monkey House."

"What do you know? You never been inside," either his mother or Sookie would snap back.

If Sookie was the first one to point this out, Lobetto's mother would scold her before Lobetto could fire off a retort. "Don't talk back to my son," she'd say, wagging a finger in Sookie's face. "Show him respect as the man of this house."

But if his mother had been the one to reply to Lobetto's greeting, he would answer, "I know enough to know it's a zoo full of menstruating women."

"I should be there," Sookie would moan, rolling back on the floor mat, her mound of stomach pointed toward the ceiling. "I don't know how I let Hyun Jin talk me into having it."

"I could have fixed you up here," his mother would say. "If you came to me earlier."

"Stop it." I knew they tried to goad me, but I responded each time, afraid if I didn't speak up they might take my silence for agreement. "This baby is you and me, Sookie. It's our chance to be a family."

"Phah," Lobetto's mother spat. "What a bunch of shit."

"I'm getting rid of this thing right now," groaned Sookie. She made a halfhearted attempt to roll to her feet.

I nudged her back down. "Besides, I told you I'd pay you for your time. I want this child."

Sookie threw an arm over her head. "And what Hyun Jin wants, Hyun Jin gets." Her words, muffled, sounded tired. Without bite.

"What's to eat?" Lobetto asked.

"Rice soup. What else?" I opened the drawer of the TV stand and pulled out the bottle of Johnson's Baby Oil I had bought from an ex–bar girl who had married a Joe. The girl liked to flaunt her status as a military wife, and she offered to get goods from the PX at a fraction of the price charged on the black market. Dribbling oil into my hand as Sookie raised her shirt, I began to massage her belly.

"How you going to take care of a baby when you can't even take care of my son?" Lobetto's mother said. "You should get up, get him his food."

Sookie and I looked at each other and shrugged, unsure of who she was scolding. I swirled the oil into Sookie's navel, which had grown shallower as her belly grew larger. "What does it feel like, inside?" I asked.

Sookie grimaced. "Uncomfortable."

"Did you hear me?" Lobetto's mother demanded, raising her voice. She struggled up from her knees and made a show of hobbling into the kitchen. "Lobetto," she called, "sit, sit. I will be the one to serve you."

I rested my hands on the drum of Sookie's belly, feeling the soft moth-wing movements against my palm.

"Poor Lobetto," I heard Lobetto's mother whine. "We have so little to eat, all the food going into those beggars you brought home. Kick them out, wasting money."

"Black dog bitch," I muttered.

Sookie sighed. "But she's right," she whispered. "What are we doing here? How long will they let us stay when we're not pulling in any money? Especially when there'll be another mouth soon."

"Don't worry, Sookie," I said, pressing my lips into a grim line. "I know what I have to do."

I agreed to start at Club Foxa the next night, and Sookie and Lobetto's mother joined forces to fuss over me. "Remember, pick the shy uglies. They're easy." Sookie played with my hair, pinning it away from my face with bright silver clips. "And get to them first before all the cows grab them up."

Lobetto's mother knocked Sookie's hands from my head and

pulled the pins out. "She should wear it down, cover up her face more," she said.

"Or maybe you should wait till the end of the night when everyone is drunk," Sookie frowned, rethinking her strategy. "Then you can pick up leftovers. No one is choosy at the end."

I turned away from both of them. "I know what I'm doing," I snapped. "Back off."

"Don't have to bite," Sookie sniffed. "I was just trying to help."

"You need to make some money tonight," Lobetto's mother grumbled.

To keep from shaking, I tugged at the straps on my shoulders, smoothed the fabric over my thighs, then called to Lobetto, who lounged outside the door, gnawing on a Tootsie Pop stick as he waited to take me to the Foxa. "Let's go," I said. I wanted to leave before I ran back to the tent.

Lobetto tucked the stick carefully behind his ear and tugged at the waistband of his pants, which hung low across his hips. From around his neck, he took off a chain and handed it to me. The plastic card on the chain was Sookie's working ID, on the back of which was a record of her shot dates, her menstrual cycle, her visit to the Monkey House. That card, doctored by Lobetto to fit me, was my passport into the clubs. Over Sookie's picture, Lobetto had pasted one of the shots of me he had taken a few months before. I looked naked and feral, an animal hunted for meat.

Lobetto checked me over, then unbuttoned the top two buttons of my dress. I knocked him away and clutched at the opening of my dress. When he tilted his head in question, I dropped my hands.

Lobetto called himself a modern-day matchmaker; for every

girl he brought in, the club paid him a couple hundred won, a commission off her earnings. He'd make that off me, and still get whatever I managed to wrestle away from Bar Mama. But it was worth it if it meant shelter for me and Sookie, a safe place for the baby to be born.

"Do like I told you," he said when he opened the back door of Club Foxa. He shoved a bag of eggplant into my arms.

My arms felt numb; I fumbled the bag. I bent over, hands on my knees, forcing myself to breathe.

"I remember her." Kitchen Auntie stomped over and leaned down to look into my face. "She didn't look like much when you first brought her by and she looks like even less now."

"She'll do okay," Lobetto said, patting me on the back.

I straightened, picked up the vegetables. "I'm better than okay." I tossed my head, trying to assume a mask of bravado. "It doesn't matter what you think. I know I can make these GIs think I'm the most beautiful girl here."

Kitchen Auntie laughed. "Yeah, Lobetto. I remember her. That girlfriend of yours got a mouth on her. Wait, before you go, eat something." She handed him a bowl of chicken wings. "Just leave the bones and the bowl at the door when you're done. The cats'll clean it up."

My stomach growled.

Kitchen Auntie pulled me into the kitchen, closing the door on Lobetto. "If you want to eat," she said, "you got to pay for it just like the other girls. It comes off your earnings."

"Not hungry," I lied.

"Ate too many eggplants?" she hooted.

Sookie had warned me that bouncing up and down to the music would not be enough for the stage at Club Foxa. I needed a hook, she had explained. Props. She stole a few vegetables from Lobetto's mother and showed me what to do with them. As she waved the eggplant and cucumber, thrusting them around her distended belly, we had laughed until tears ran down my cheeks, until she had shrieked that she was about to birth the baby.

But on the stage, bumping and grinding, naked except for the tassels swinging from my nipples, it wasn't funny. The eggplant felt awkward and slippery in my sweaty hands, and when I started stroking the long purple shaft, I heard the drunken slur: "Old news! Boo with the vegetables." Someone barked like a dog and someone else yelled, "Do something new."

I stood there, gaping into the light, knowing that there was nothing new but that if I didn't come up with something, I would lose my chance. I would lose the baby. American hits radio blared—"Honey, Honey," boomed through my head, Bobby Goldsboro shouting at me to "do anything, do anything"—so I couldn't think above the music, and just when I saw the angry face of Bar Mama coming to yank me off the stage and throw me out of the club for being so stupid, I spun toward the big-mouth man and yelled, "Do anything! What you like?"

"A cock suck," he tossed out, and his friends laughed.

I marched over, grabbed him by the collar and pulled him onto the stage with me. "You got it," I said. I could taste my fear, bitter at the back of my tongue, smell the acrid smell of it. But like a puppet, I tapped my feet, jerked my hands into the air, shook my hips in front of the man. The man acted up by groping my breasts and crotch and for a long horrible moment, it was the three GIs from Lobetto's apartment grabbing me. Shaking my head to block them out, to turn off my mind, I placed my hands on the hips of the man in front of me. The GIs hooted as I unbuckled his pants and the man's grin wavered. When I yanked them down, his face flushed red.

He tried to push me away before I could reveal his penis, which was still soft, but I held on, putting him into my mouth the way Sookie had taught me. I pretended he was a zucchini, an eggplant, forcing my mouth to slide up and down. I needed to do this show. I needed the money for the child.

From then on, I became the "Hunni Girl," the bar girl called on for requests, doing what the other girls didn't want to do—at least not on stage. I was the GIs' life-size doll, always smiling, always bendable, always able. I had sex on stage with whoever and however many marched up. I poured beer and shot cherries from my vagina into men's mouths. I got pissed and shit on. I had oral sex with a dog that someone pulled in from the streets. The mangy thing kept trying to run off with its tail between its legs. I was afraid it was going to ruin the show until I came up with the idea of rubbing chicken grease between my legs. Then I was afraid it was going to bite me. But I built a name, a reputation as the girl—that freak—who would do anything. They paid to push the limits of what Hunni would do.

Lobetto wrote up some new flyers talking me up, and the more business I brought in Foxa, the bigger chunk of money I brought home. Lobetto took most of it, but I hid some money that I planned to spend on my child, which Sookie was growing. Remembering what I craved the short time I was pregnant, I hunted the fish markets for the right taste to coax Sookie to eat.

I dressed as what I was, not bothering to try to hide that I was an America Town girl. Though the fishwives would look at me as if I were trash—they in their grimy, gut-stained rags—I flashed my money. Enough of it to make them hide their scorn and smile at me. Enough to make them greet me like a celebrity, and to compete for my attention. "Here, lady, here," they would call to me. "Fish just pulled in today. Someone like you should have only the best."

I suppose they must have felt like choking on their words, steeped in false praise, but I wouldn't buy from them unless they said them. The more they catered, the more they groveled, the more I minced around their stalls, teasing them with what I could buy. I paraded through the maze of stalls, selecting only the choicest and most succulent offerings: fetal octopus, sea cucumber, abalone, and oysters, knowing Sookie would consume them as soon as I walked in the door. Hands dripping with brine from the bucket, she would devour the slippery morsels as if starved for the salty fish, savory as primal memory.

But I always made sure to visit the anchovy girl and her mother, buying a small packet of their dried fish for soup. The mother never spoke to me, never came forward to greet or acknowledge me in any way. The girl, however, bubbled as if we were old friends. She was, I think, dazzled by the clothes I wore, by the jewelry that flashed from my neck and fingers.

The closest the mother came to speaking to me was when I offered to give the girl one of my bead necklaces. I had seen her eyeing the shiny strand and, remembering how much I had loved the fancy things Duk Hee wore when I was younger, I pulled it off my neck and placed it around hers. The mother jumped up and yanked the necklace away. The string broke and the glass beads clattered to the ground in a dizzying shower of color. "Trash," the old lady spat, directing her words to the ground, "from trash." The girl cried and bent to salvage the beads, but the mother kicked them away, crushing as many as she could under the heel of her slipper.

After working the club, I hosed off in Lobetto's kitchen, attempting to scrape myself clean as I tried not to remember the first time I honeymooned. Lobetto had thrown away the wire vegetable brush after that night, replacing it with a plastic one with softer bristles. I used that to try to scrub the dirt off, but no matter how hard I pressed, I could never break the skin.

I kept the water pressure low so that the water wouldn't bang through the pipes and wake Sookie. Sookie and I had set up a bed outside the tent, taking half the floor of the kitchen. I was careful to stand directly over the drain as I washed my body, careful to keep the water away from the nest of blankets where Sookie slept.

I crawled into the blankets with Sookie, loving the way she turned toward me even in her sleep. It always took me a while to fall asleep those mornings, with Sookie shifting constantly to get comfortable. She used me like a pillow, throwing her arms and legs over me. Sometimes she woke briefly to complain: "I cannot stand this body. I cannot stand being so fat and helpless. I promised myself that I would never have to depend on anyone to feed me, and look. Look at me now. Gigantic and ugly as a sow, can't even flip over without help."

I helped her turn onto her side, and she fell back asleep. When she slept, the baby swam inside of her, tumbling in the ocean of her womb. If I pressed my belly against Sookie's, skin to skin, I could almost pretend it was swimming in me.

One night I had a dream: I am walking by the docks, looking into the sea, the light silver on the water. Ripples quicken on the surface, slap into the pier in an excited chatter; a spiraling shell of magenta pierces the waves. I focus. The conch shell reveals itself to be the nose of a dolphin, small and very pink, a baby. Unable to resist, I bend down to touch her downy head. The baby smiles, cooing, then flips back, taking my hand in her teeth. She pulls me under, deeper and deeper, and in the distance, I can see where we are going: to an underwater city, a flash of gold and silver stars.

When I described that dream to Sookie in the morning, she said: "If that thing bit my hand, I would have beat it in the head until it let go."

When it came time, Sookie did beat it in the head until it let her go. She began screaming as soon as her water broke, and didn't stop until thirteen hours later when Lobetto's mother reached between her legs to pry her vaginal lips open. During each contraction, Sookie arched her back, cursed, and slammed her hips back down onto the floor. "Rub my back," she'd yell at me, "harder!"

I pressed until I could see bruises flowering on her spine, and still she yelled at me to squeeze, to punch, to hurt her. During the labor, Sookie and her baby battled each other. As she struggled against the waves of pain, Sookie chanted, "Get it out, get it out, I hate this, get it out."

Lobetto's mother forced Sookie to squat over the drain. "Push like you're taking a crap," Lobetto's mother said as Sookie crouched on all fours, whining like a dog.

Finally, I saw the baby's head, crowned with thick black hair, at the bulge of Sookie's vagina. When Sookie bore down, the top of the baby's head squeezed through then receded repeatedly, as if pulled by the tides. After surfing the contractions for a long while—long enough that her skin reddened and wrinkled in the brine—the baby's flattened nose popped out, and then the rest of the head. Mother and baby rested, then fought again; after a brief skirmish, the baby's body shot out, slick as a fish, and Lobetto's mother almost dropped her.

"Better that this one died," said Lobetto's mother as she toweled blood and mucus away from its eyes and mouth.

"Why?" I demanded. "What's wrong with it?" I grabbed the small body, checking for two arms, two legs, ten fingers, ten toes. Then under the cord, I saw the vagina. "A girl," I breathed and loved her even more. I loved her fiercely, this being I had called back to life. But I was shocked at how ugly she was. The girl's head was long and lumpy, cone-shaped, with blackened eyes that made it look as if she had been hit repeatedly.

"What's wrong with her?" Sookie groaned. "She's a monster, isn't she? I felt it inside of me."

I placed the baby, still connected to the womb by the birth cord, on Sookie's chest. Sookie craned her neck to look at her child and grunted at me: "Ugh. She looks like you."

After Lobetto's mother sliced the cord with a kitchen knife and tied the ends, I snatched the baby back. "She'll grow out of it," I retorted, though I doubted it. I didn't care if she was ugly the rest of her life; I knew how to love the unlovable. Cradling her in my arms, I could not help wondering if the baby I had carried would have looked like this one. She resembled both Sookie and Lobetto, a blend of Korean and American, in the way that all mixed-race babies—the *tweggis*—resemble each other, siblings in a way.

Sookie put off naming the child, careless with it. When I brought the baby to her to nurse, she'd wrestle with her, crying that the sucking cut her breasts like knives. The baby would fuss, straining for the nipple while at the same time butting against it. In frustration, the baby would wail and Sookie would shove it away. "It's a stupid little animal," she'd spit out. "Something's wrong with it. Or with me," she'd complain. "It hurts too much."

I took the screaming infant, soaked a rag in sugar water, and let her gum that till she fell into an exhausted sleep. I slept with the child, and if it woke during the night, I let it suck on my own dry breast. I would have cut myself open if the baby had drunk my blood. Still, she probably would have died if Lobetto's mother hadn't relented and stepped in.

In the middle of the third day of the battle between mother and child, she intervened, taking the crying baby on her back. "Better I should let it starve to death. Better it's put out of its misery early in life. Better it dies now before it knows anything," she muttered as she paced the room. When the child quieted down, she returned to Sookie. She taught Sookie how to cradle the baby, how to lead her to the breast, how to push her mouth onto the nipple. "Don't worry about the milk," Lobetto's mother explained. "That will come when your body knows your baby is eating."

Lobetto's mother ordered me to bring home seaweed. Every day, she made Sookie a bowl of seaweed soup and rice. Though she guzzled it without restraint, Sookie complained about the food, how she could not stand to eat the same thing every day, several times a day, the only variation being whether or not it was clams or anchovy in the soup. Despite her grumbling, she always devoured whatever she was served.

Her own stomach soothed, Sookie began feeding the baby with milk that came in so fast and plentiful that at each nursing the unused breast shot out streams of milk, drenching the blankets. In the mornings, we lifted the sodden sheets, dragged them into the sun to dry like fishing nets. Still, it was as if in the first three days after the birth, something between mother and child was irretrievably lost. Sookie began to get restless, resentful of the baby and its groping, greedy mouth that constantly strained to latch on to her.

After three months, Sookie got up one afternoon, fed the baby, and placed the unsuckled breasts over a jar. As the baby ate, her extra milk sprayed into the jar. Then, the baby and jar both full, she announced she was hitting the clubs. "I'm bored," she said. "I'm ready to play."

"Why, Sookie?" I felt so tired. If I could have nursed the baby, I would have been grateful to stay home, to quit working the stage, the booths, the back alley honeymoons. "The baby needs you."

"Well, I need to get out of here," Sookie said, holding the baby toward me. "I heard you're pulling in good money at Foxa."

I shrugged, gathering the child into my chest. "I don't see much of it," I said in a singsong voice, trying to make the baby smile.

"I'd make sure I kept all of my money," Sookie bragged. Crawling to a pile of clothes, she began to rummage through it for something to wear.

"Stay home, Sookie," I coaxed, trying to keep the irritation from my voice. "Rest." The baby whimpered, her arms flailing. I propped her against my shoulder. "Wait until the baby is a little bigger."

"Why?" Sookie said. She had found a strip of cloth which she began to wind around her breasts. "You afraid of the competition? You afraid I'll take all the GIs?" She grinned at me, adding: "You never did like to share."

I turned away, tapping on the baby's back. I knew she was

teasing me, but I was still irritated by her comments. "You don't know how lucky you are. You don't know what I'm giving you. You don't know what you want."

"I know what *you* want." Sookie looked pointedly at the baby. "What is she worth to you?"

"Is that all she is to you? Money?" To hide the fierceness of reaction, I buried my face in the underside of the baby's neck, inhaling the sweaty milk smell. "What are you going to name her?" I murmured.

"Nothing," Sookie said as she tucked the cloth around her chest. She looked down at the lumpy wrapping and shook her head. "What a waste," she sighed. "I'll have to get them pumped up again."

Myu Myun. Nothing name. Holding her small body close to my mouth, I whispered, "Myu Myu." My little no name.

Sookie wiggled into a tube top that left her belly hanging over her orange patent-leather hot pants. When she realized that the tube top's stretchy material outlined the chest binding, she screamed in frustration. "Name it whatever you want. It doesn't matter to me." She rolled the band of material down her body and kicked it off her legs. "I'm getting out of this zoo," she muttered. She slipped on a loose blouse, shimmying so that the sleeves draped off her shoulders.

"If it's money you want," I said, still thinking we were working out a deal, "I can pay you now."

"Yeah, yeah, whatever." Sookie dropped to her knees, rummaging under a pair of jeans and several tank tops for her makeup kit. "Just give me what you think she's worth."

"I'll give you what I've made so far," I started. "So you don't have to leave tonight."

Sookie held up her hand. "You don't get it. I can't stay

cooped up with that crying, puking brat any longer. I won't."
Eyes narrowed on me, she plucked a tube of lipstick from her
bag, smeared the frosted bronze across her mouth. She smacked
her lips, then asked: "Remember when Lobetto called this
place the Monkey House?"

When I nodded, rolling my eyes, she said, "He was wrong."
Pulling a stained tissue from the bag, she pressed a kiss on it,
then tossed me the rubbish. "It's worse."

13

One morning after working the club, I returned to Lobetto's house to find Myu Myu alone in the tent. Tangled in the blankets, she wimpered and kicked listlessly. "Myu Myu," I crooned, but she refused to look at me.

I picked her up, and as I cradled her, I was hit with the stench of feces. Greenish diarrhea oozed from her diaper onto my blouse. "Sookie!" I yelled. "Lobetto!"

Responding at last to my voice, my touch, Myu Myu wailed, high pitched and angry.

"Poor baby, poor baby." I tried to soothe her, but anger choked the kindness from my words. Peeling the soiled cloth from Myu's bottom, I dumped it on Lobetto's mattress, then grabbed his blanket to wrap her squirming body.

"Sons of bitches!" I yelled as I stomped through the kitchen, jiggling Myu on my shoulder. I bumped her so hard, the breath left her body, leaving the air suddenly still. After a moment, she screamed again.

I looked in the ice chest for a cup of milk, then through the cabinets for some of the powder mix I had bought on the black market. Not finding anything, I grabbed a fistful of cold rice from a bowl left over from last night's meal. I shoved the rice into my mouth, grinding the pellets into a soupy mush which I spit out for Myu Myu.

I placed a pinch into the red wound of her mouth, where it sat in the middle of a scream. Taking a breath, she quieted for a taste and then pushed the gruel out with her tongue. It dribbled down her chin, but at least she stopped crying. I fed her, rice and spit on my fingertip, until the bowl was empty.

Leaving my finger in her mouth for her to gum and suck, I unbuttoned and wiggled out of my top. I dropped the blanket, wadded up the blouse to find a clean patch to wipe at Myu's bottom. Some of the shit had dried to a crust. Afraid to scrub hard because I could see a bouquet of raw sores blooming under the mess, I held Myu Myu under the hose.

She started screaming again, the water cold enough to tinge her body with splotches of blue, but I washed her quickly and wrapped her in the blanket. Propping her against my shoulder, I walked her through the house, in part to soothe her again, in part to convince myself that no one else was there. I rehearsed in my head how I would yell at Sookie when she returned, how I would beat her for leaving a baby alone. I would twist her ears with my words until she felt the pain Myu must have felt.

When Myu Myu's body settled heavily against my shoulder, weighted in sleep, I laid her down on the mat in front of the television. Curling up around her, I watched her sleep, her head nestled near my heart. When she stirred, I shifted my nipple in front of her mouth. She latched on, soothed by the feel of meat against her tongue.

I must have fallen asleep, because I woke to the television. Sookie was clipping her toenails, laughing at a game show host challenging a contestant to perform a pop song. Lobetto's mother was cracking sunflower seeds and spitting the shells into a pile by my head. I could hear Lobetto chuckling behind me. When I sat up, I felt a few stray splinters of sunflower shells drop from my hair. I almost forgot why I felt angry, but when I reached for the baby and she wasn't there, I remembered.

I swiveled around, searching for Myu and glaring at everyone.

"So, the princesss awakens," Lobetto's mother sniggered, a small zebra-striped seed caught between her front teeth.

I ignored her and looked at Lobetto. He had Myu Myu propped on his knees. "Where were you?" I growled.

"Working, where else?" Lobetto asked. He blew against Myu's belly and she laughed.

I took a breath, trying not to yell. "I came back, and the baby was alone."

"Oh yeah?" Lobetto shrugged and blew against Myu's toes. She gurgled, waving her foot in the air. He put her toes in his mouth and she squealed, eyes shining.

"I don't think she's pretty." Lobetto's mother stopped cracking sunflowers and pointed at the TV screen. "That one there," she said. "The one with the fat face."

"Could you guys shut up?" Sookie whined. "I can't hear what the girl is saying." She shook a bottle of pink polish.

"What about you?" I yelled at Sookie. "You're supposed to take care of her when I work."

"Who?" Sookie asked, her attention caught between the TV and her toes.

"We had a deal." I gritted my teeth. When she didn't say anything, I added: "The baby."

"I think someone should clean her up," Lobetto said, holding Myu up. "She stinks."

I grabbed her, more roughly than I meant to and she wailed. "No one except me loves you," I scolded Myu Myu as she reached for Lobetto. "That one will kill you if I don't watch out for you."

"What?" Lobetto frowned. "Why would you say a thing like that?"

I slapped Myu Myu's hands down. "I said: Don't love him. Don't get used to him," I told her. "He doesn't want you."

"Good advice," Lobetto's mother said without looking away from the television. "His father was good with him, too. Said he wanted lots of babies. But in the end, it didn't matter; he left us."

"Quiet," Sookie complained, turning up the volume. "I missed why everyone is laughing."

I marched in front of the TV.

Lobetto's mother threw a handful of seeds at me.

"Hey!" Sookie shouted.

"We had a deal," I said to her.

"Me?" Sookie jerked her arm and polish splashed across the floor mat. "Shit!" she said as she tried to blot the color with the palm of her free hand.

"A deal. About the baby," I insisted.

"I don't think so," Sookie said, wiping her hand on her shirt and staining what I recognized as her old school uniform. "You told me what you wanted but that's not what I wanted."

"You wanted money," I argued, "and I told you—"

Sookie twisted the nail polish closed and tossed it down with a bitter laugh. "Yeah, you told me," she taunted, standing up. "You're always telling me something. But you know what? I don't have to do everything you say. You're not class leader anymore."

I stared at Sookie and I shifted Myu Myu to the other hip. Myu Myu twisted, beginning to whimper as she strained toward Lobetto. "You're joking," I said to Sookie. "I'm giving you a chance to take it easy."

"She wants me," Lobetto said. He took Myu Myu back from me and, pushing at the pile of damp sunflower shells with his foot, moved to sit closer to the television. "The baby is not even a year, and she is already like all other women."

"Stay away from her!" I yelled at him without taking my eyes off Sookie.

"Oh great," Lobetto's mother grumbled. "Now I can't hear or see."

"You're giving me a chance to 'take it easy'?" Sookie said. "Let me tell you something for a change, Hyun Jin: You cannot pay me enough to stay home with that whining trash-baby. I'm bored, and I'm tired of waiting for your scraps. I'm missing my chance out there. You can't make me stay in this dump, you can't keep me down any longer."

"Keep you down?" I laughed in her face. "I hold you up. Without me you'd drown."

"That's what you think, isn't it?" Sookie stomped her foot,

smudging the polish against the insides of her toes. "That's what you've always thought—that you're so much better than me, so much smarter. Well, Hyun Jin, take another look." She crossed her arms over her chest and scowled at me. "Maybe you don't want me working with you because the GIs think I'm pretty—to them, I'm not an ugly dog. But you, you're ugly to everyone."

"I may be ugly, but you're stupid," I snarled over Myu's head. "Didn't you learn anything from Duk Hee? What you look like doesn't matter in America Town; you can make those Joes see what you want them to see."

"She only said that to make you feel better." Sookie tossed her hair, flounced through the kitchen, and ducked under the flaps of the tent.

My hands itched to yank that burned mop from her scalp, but I forced them down. Instead I yelled back, "You still look like a black dog to me." I sank to the floor, tired from the night before and from Sookie's words.

"You know, she may be ugly," Lobetto's mother said—and for a moment I thought she was talking about Sookie instead of the game show contestant—"but that fat moon-face girl sure can sing."

That night I took the baby to work. Kitchen Auntie grumbled: "I'm not running an orphanage. I'm only supposed to cook."

I slipped her a handfull of bills. "Please, for your trouble."

"Bar Mama's not gonna like this," she said, but she tucked the money into her shoe.

"Myu won't be any trouble," I told her, lugging an egg crate toward the countertop. I unstrapped the blanket from my waist and swung the baby into the box. She stared at me with un-blinking eyes, stunned from the sudden drop.

Kitchen Auntie clucked. "Of course she will be trouble. All

babies are trouble." She picked Myu Myu up, wrestled her onto her own back, and warpped the blanket around them both. "But my own mama worked with me tied to her, and her mama did the same with her. I did it with my own children, and I can do it for this one."

"Thank you," I murmured.

Kitchen Auntie groaned, hunching her back as if it ached with baby weight. "But only for a little while," she warned. "I'm not young anymore."

"Of course not. I understand," I sighed. "I'll cut you ten percent of my honeymoon tips tonight."

"Twenty percent, each night you bring her in," Kitchen Auntie negotiated. "For when I retire."

"Okay," I nodded slowly, calculating the numbers in my head, dividing the money between Bar Mama, Kitchen Auntie, Lobetto, Myu, and myself.

That first night, I had to stop myself from running into the kitchen every few minutes. Even though I worked extra hard—laughing with the GIs, dancing, keeping my hands and mouth busy so that they continued ordering rounds of drinks—I kept imagining Myu Myu crying. I pictured her abandoned in that decrepit egg crate, soiled and fretful as she had been when I found her alone in Lobetto's apartment. I saw her burning herself on the stove, or getting bitten by a rat. But when the bar closed and I rushed to collect her, I found her sleeping, nested in the crate, fist curled around a boiled chicken bone. Kitchen Mama, who had stayed past her shift, lay slumped against the crate snoring, one arm flung across Myu Myu, guarding her even in their dreams.

I had to work harder than the other girls to make myself popular with the Americans. I didn't have the looks the other *yong sekshis* did, but I could read what each GI wanted. The problem with most of the girls in the club was that they thought all the GIs were the same, so they stuck to the same act. But me, I could be either a shy and submissive maiden—looking at them from the corners of my eyes and smiling from behind my hand—or a hair-flipping, loud-laughing, wild-dancing sex queen. I could be their idea of me—at least for the amount of time it took to buy six rounds of drinks and a honeymoon in the backbooth.

I'd been having a good night, entertaining a group of three GIs with two other girls from the bar. The men were trying to teach us a drinking game with quarters that we would bounce onto the table and into the cups. I had been "taught" this game countless times and missed on purpose so I would be forced to drink my glass. That way, they kept adding to the tab and to my commission for the night. Even though the drinks were heavily watered, I was feeling good. Unfortunately, my bladder was feeling bad.

On the way back from the outhouse behind the kitchen, I was surprised to see Bar Mama sitting in a backbooth, away from the stage and bar. She usually liked to stay upfront, keeping an eye on her girls, making sure that the GIs were happy with us.

Bar Mama was sitting across from a woman, and I raised my eyebrows at the platters of food between them—not the small bowls of boiled soybean or salty chicken wings for which she overcharged the *miguk* men, but *kalbi* and *bibimpap,* oxtail soup and kimchee pancakes. We sometimes got women GIs in the club, and no one I knew was so against honeymooning with them that they would turn down an offer, but this woman wasn't a GI. She was Korean—maybe forty, rich-looking. Dressed in a

Western suit that looked like a man's except for the long skirt, she looked out of place in Club Foxa, but she didn't look uncomfortable.

"Hyun Jin—" Bar Mama grabbed my hand as I walked past.

"Her?" the lady frowned, looking me up and down. "She ugly. You trying unload the bad ones, keep good ones for yourself?" I was surprised that the rich woman sounded like she came from the countryside, her accent rough and poor.

"How long have we done business?" Bar Mama huffed. "I promise you, this girl is one of my best workers. You've been watching, so you know."

I tried not to squirm. I would have been irritated, being kept away from the shy ugly I had marked—even as I stood there, I could see another girl had slid into my place—but I could see this woman was important.

The woman said nothing, just looked me over. I felt like I was seven again, being inspected by my mother—by my father's wife—and found wanting. Finally she nodded. "She clever," she said. "I never seen anybody work with the audience before—you think quick. In America, we call that 'think on your feet.'"

She slid over, motioning me to sit next to her. "Looks're important," said the woman. "But that can be faked. You know the tricks."

I nodded, then, to be polite, perched at the edge of the booth. The rich lady grabbed my chin, spit into a napkin, and began to rub at my face.

"Stop!" I grimaced, trying to wrench away.

"Disgusting," she clucked, looking at my birthmark without its cover of makeup.

I knocked her hands down. "I'm leaving," I said.

The woman snatched my hair before I could slide out.

"Good hair though. Good teeth, too, I think." She spoke to Bar Mama and tapped her fingers on the table as if considering. "Good teeth important. One girl I brought over a couple years ago had all rotten teeth. I had to take her to the dentist, put in all new teeth—gold in the back, you know. She still working to pay me back." She sighed and pulled my hair so I was forced to look at her. "Open your mouth," she ordered.

I kept it shut.

"Hyun Jin," Bar Mama growled.

The woman tugged my hair until I grunted. "I thought you said she was smart," the woman accused Bar Mama.

Bar Mama laughed. "I said she was a hard worker. I don't know how smart that is. Go on, Hyun Jin. Say something smart."

I narrowed my eyes at the woman, then with my lips covering my teeth I said, "Who are you?"

Bar Mama slapped my arm, but the rich woman laughed as she threw the ends of my hair in my face. "I'm Mrs. Yoon," she said. "I'm looking for girls to work for me in Hawai'i."

I gasped, my mouth falling open.

"Okay," the lady nodded. "Teeth look good."

I shut my mouth, swallowed. "Is she for real?" I asked Bar Mama. "Hawai'i? Real Hawai'i?"

Bar Mama grinned. "Real Hawai'i. Not Cheju Island."

The woman lifted her glass and smiled with her lips against the rim. She took a sip, then grimaced. "You know, in my bar—in Hawai'i, which is in America now, you know—I serve much better whiskey. Seagram."

Bar Mama ground her teeth like she wanted to say something but couldn't. She looked down at the table to hide her eyes.

"What would I have to do?" I asked, dubious, trying to guess her angle.

"Oh you know," the woman said, waving her hand in the air. "Same things as here. My bar is just like this, its twin sister. I call it Club Foxa Hawai'i." She belched. "But it's better than this, because it is, you know, in America. Hawai'i. Paradise."

Bar Mama grunted. "Yes, we know."

Yoon reached into a briefcase on the seat beside her and pulled out a stack of folders. "See this? Each folder is a man. They good men, but lonely. They cannot find nice girlfriend for themselves. American girls so fussy, hardhead. So I tell them, 'Pay me. I find you one good Korean girl.'"

"I can be that," I told her.

"Maybe," said the lady. "Maybe not. Maybe they no like you."

"They'll like me," I said. "If I want them to like me."

"I tell you what. I buy you from Bar Mama, take you to Hawai'i. You work my place, get to know the men. If they like you, you stay in America, work for me till you pay back what you cost me. Including transportation, visa fees, rent, clothes, food."

"I heard it was very difficult to emigrate to America," I hedged, even though I knew and she knew I would go. "How come you make it sound so easy?"

The woman picked up a sliver of beef and popped it into her mouth. "You ask a lot of questions," she said, her cheeks bulging. When I continued to stare at her, she swallowed her food. "All right, you want to know: I get you a tourist visa. You come in, but you don't leave. Easy."

"Easy," I repeated, narrowing my eyes, thinking it through. "Except I've got to hide, stay quiet," I said. "I've got to live like your slave, under your thumb."

"Shut up, Hyun Jin," Bar Mama snarled. "This could be good for all of us."

"No slaves in America," the woman said, waving her chopsticks in the air as if in dismissal. "If you not happy at this chance . . ."

"How long will it take to pay you back?" I asked. Only after the words were out of my mouth did I realize I spoke too quickly. I sounded desperate.

Yoon smiled, a green onion wedged in her front teeth. "Some girls, they get some man to love them so much, he pays for them right away. Other girls work two, three, five years maybe."

I inhaled, blew out sharply. "That's it?"

The woman drained the rest of her whiskey, then rattled the ice. "That's it."

I laughed, giddy at the prospect of getting out of America Town. I would be able to start over, make something of myself. And then I stopped laughing, guilty that even for a moment I had forgotten about Myu Myu. I reasoned it would be best for her, too, if I left, to make a new life for the both of us. Once I established myself I would call for her, fit her back into my life. Five years was not so long. In that time, I would find that small place in the country for the two of us, only it would be in a new country.

On the walk home, my mind continued to trip over what to do with Myu Myu until I was dizzy with guilt. I didn't want to leave Myu Myu behind, but I knew that my taking Yoon's offer would be the best chance for us both to escape America Town. I just needed to convince someone to care for the child in my absence. I would pay the guardian well, and once my debt to Yoon was repaid in full, I would send for Myu.

Sookie was Myu's birth mother, the natural choice; I was

counting on her having some basic maternal feeling for the child. I didn't let myself think about Duk Hee, about how easily she was able to give me up. I wouldn't let myself wonder if Duk Hee's daughters inherited the talent for walking away. I dragged my feet, bending like Kitchen Auntie under the baby's weight. Myu Myu felt like a rock, heavy on my back.

.

14

When Myu Myu cried, I tried to harden myself to her in order to prepare for leaving. I pictured myself moving away from her and, looking at her through the distance of that long tunnel, I began to see that she looked more and more like Sookie each day. Her skin darkened into the same chocolate brown; her hair sprouted into the same frazzled black-cherry nimbus surrounding the moon of her face.

"Sookie," I said. "Don't you care that Myu Myu is crying?"

"Why should I?" Sookie wouldn't even look up from her magazine.

But I felt the baby's cries cutting into my own heart. "She's your blood. Don't you feel anything?"

"Why should I feel anything?" Sookie said. "I didn't want her in the first place." She held up a hand to stop me from arguing. "Look, if I pick a scab off a cut, I'm not going to cry over that scab, mourning because I miss it."

"It's that easy for you, isn't it?" I said, suddenly angry. "To cut away from this baby, just like you cut away from your own mother."

"What? What did I do?" Sookie grumbled, then shuddered. "Duk Hee, living in the fish tanks. I'm embarrassed she's my mother."

"I'm not talking about Duk Hee." I turned away from her to tend Myu Myu, who was choking on her own screams.

"Yes, you were—" Sookie called after me.

I grabbed Myu from her nest of blankets and plopped her onto my shoulder. "No, I wasn't," I said to Sookie, jiggling the baby. Her crying eased into hiccups.

Sookie eyed the child, then grinned. "Are you mad because you've changed your mind about the kid?"

"No!" I snapped, but looked down, fussing with Myu Myu's coverings so Sookie couldn't read the doubt in my face.

"You are changing your mind." Sookie nodded, smug. "I knew having her was a mistake. You should have let me get rid of it when it was still nothing. It's not too late to get rid of it," Sookie said. "Remember Apple?"

"Yes," I said. Apple had been four years ahead of us in school, so we hadn't been close. But she was someone I would never forget. The girl's real name, Sang Won, sounded like the word *apple,* but we called her Sagwa mostly because she looked like one. She never lost the red-cheeked roundness she had had as a child; in fact, if anything, she had grown redder and rounder with each year.

"You know what happened to her, right?" Sookie asked.

"Everyone knows." I fidgeted and licked my lips. "She married her Joe and went to America." Apple was one of America Town's success stories. Pretending to be a student at Ewha University, she had been set up by a matchmaker who found girl-friends for GIs.

"Yeah, yeah." Sookie waved her hand, impatient. "But remember what happened to her baby?"

I frowned and turned away. "I'm done talking about this," I said.

"Well, I'm not." Sookie smiled a big cat smile. "She killed him."

"No! I don't—" When Myu Myu whimpered, I crooned to her: "Shh-shhh-shhh."

"Apple, that big fake, playing such an innocent. She couldn't tell her Joe she had a throwaway baby, so when it came time to leave, remember what she did?" Sookie didn't wait for me to answer. "Drowned that kid in the bathwater at the *moyokton.*"

"Stop!" I spun away from Sookie, as if to shield Myu Myu. "I still don't believe she did it on purpose. She loved that boy." I remembered how Apple doted on her son when he was born, how she showed him off—that fat and shiny-faced boy. She didn't even pretend to be ashamed that he didn't have a father. She loved him so much that, like a mother dog, she would lick him clean with her own tongue.

I felt light-headed, disoriented as if I was in the steam room too long. I used to love going to the bathhouse. My father's wife and I would go almost every weekend so that she could relax in the steam room and I could swim, alternating between the cold and hot pools. I would paddle between the clusters of women, dodging breasts and hips and floating hair, ducking under the clouds of steam that hovered above the surface of the water.

On the day Apple killed her baby, there was so much steam in the bathhouse you couldn't even see your hand in front of your face. Because of the steam, it was a while before the crowd of women realized that something was wrong with Apple. She was holding her boy, rocking and crying, rocking and crying, while his head swayed under the hot water.

"One less," my father's wife had commented when she looked over, dismissing the turmoil. She tried to pull me away, but I couldn't stop staring at the small body, cradled so tenderly in his mother's arms.

"She loved him very much," I whispered again.

"She loved herself more, I guess," Sookie said. She looked at me, then at Myu Myu before turning back to her gossip column. "Doesn't it always come down to that, in the end?"

Yoon sent the visa papers to Club Foxa, and whatever I made performing was funneled through the club as down payment for my new life. My body continued to work the routine of stripping and honeymooning at the club, but my mind whirled through the details of leaving: pictures for the passport application; birth documentation; student records; interview responses; and mostly, the problem of Myu Myu.

Afraid of revealing my plans before they were set, I avoided talking to Sookie and Lobetto as much as possible during this time. When I did speak with Sookie, I would contrive to mention our childhood, how much we loved each other, how sisters should never abandon each other in time of need. "And after all, we are also mothers together," I told her once.

Sookie grimaced. "What are you talking about?" Her eyes darted past me, scouting the bar for Joes who showed up for the early evening happy hour. In truth, it was always happy hour at Foxa; the prices for drinks or women never went up or down.

I forced myself to smile, to be patient. "In a way," I explained, "Myu Myu is a daughter to both of us."

"Whatever you say," Sookie answered, shrugging. She had spotted a shy ugly and, having scooted off her bar stool, was already moving toward him.

Perhaps, looking back, I should have paid more attention to Sookie. I should have noticed how preoccupied she was, how she almost doubled her work in the backbooths and the alleyways. I should have noticed, too, how she was suddenly on better terms with Bar Mama, apparently more willing to line her pockets. I assumed they had worked out an under-the-table agreement that benefitted both of them: Sookie working Foxa without hassle; Bar Mama getting double commission off the same set of registration papers—two of us for the price of one. In truth, Sookie *had* worked out a deal, and if I hadn't been so distracted with plotting my own strategy, I might have realized that she had her own secrets to hide.

The night before my interview in Seoul, I dressed in a plain shirt and long gray skirt reminiscent of my school uniform. I braided my hair and scrubbed my face free of the makeup I had worn the night before. The birthmark gleamed, a dark sea in the landscape of my face. Yoon had laughed when she realized that the birthmark would be my best proof of morality—they would not think I was pretty enough to be a prostitute. "Don't hide it," Yoon had told me. "Make sure you expose that side of your face as much as possible."

In contrast to my outfit, I dressed Myu Myu in her fanciest clothes. Even though it was warm, I layered her silk *hanbok* and her embroidered Western-style dress over her nightgown. I tucked an envelope of money into her clothes, against her chest. Rising to leave, I thought of one more thing. I knelt back down and reached under Lobetto's mattress and pulled out a stack of photos. I flipped through them and found one of Sookie and me, our faces tilted toward each other. A little blurred, my birthmark seems a trick of the light, an illusion of shadow. I placed a finger over the photograph, covering half of both Sookie and myself. Searching for similarities, I compared our faces feature by feature, piece by piece.

Then I held the photograph next to Myu Myu, wanting to be able to see what part of the baby was Sookie, what was me, what was neither, what was both of us. I saw Myu Myu only as herself. I folded the picture until it was small enough to slip into the money envelope. That way, she would have something to remember me, her second mother, by.

I planned to leave Myu Myu with Kitchen Auntie, catch the train to Seoul, and stay there until I left for America. I reasoned that Kitchen Auntie, though she acted gruff, loved the baby and would make sure she was cared for. She could watch Myu Myu at night, since she was already doing so anyway, and when I told her Sookie was the baby's first mother, she would force Sookie to take responsibility during the day. The money in the envelope would be payment enough until I was able to send more from Hawai'i.

Entering the kitchen door of Foxa, I hurried to Myu Myu's box. I held her close, letting myself nuzzle her, soak in her scent. "Bye-bye, my sweetheart," I murmured into Myu Myu's neck. I rubbed my teeth against her skin, tickling and tasting. "My little rice cake."

Kitchen Auntie, who was soaking cabbage leaves in brine, looked up from the sink at Myu Myu's laughter. Frowning, she scanned my outfit, my hair, my face. "You come to work dressed like a missionary?" she scolded, flapping one of her hands, reddened from the salt water, at me. "How much money you going to make like that?"

I nestled Myu Myu into the box. "I have my reasons," I said, stroking Myu's hair, her cheeks, her fingers that grabbed mine.

"Something for your show tonight?" Kitchen Auntie guffawed. Then, with a swift intake of breath, she knew. "Don't you dare leave that child here," she said.

I loosened my finger from Myu Myu's grip and turned to face Kitchen Auntie. I made my face, my voice, my heart hard. "I need to go to Seoul for a few days."

Kitchen Auntie slapped at the sink full of water and cabbage. Water sloshed onto the floor and across her blouse. "Shit," she swore. Patting at her clothes with her equally wet hands, Kitchen Auntie rushed to Myu Myu's box. "Take her with you." She grabbed Myu and tried to push her into my arms. "You're her mama."

Squirming, Myu protested the wet and rough handling. Her arms flailed and she yowled, opening and closing her hands, as she looked at me.

I backed away, refusing to acknowledge the baby's cries. "No," I told Kitchen Auntie. "I can't."

Kitchen Auntie continued to push, thrusting Myu Myu at me. "I'm not stupid. Yoon's been here before, taking girls with her." She scowled. "Good for you, but don't leave the baby with me. I'm too old for this."

I crossed my arms. "I'll make it worth your while—"

"No." Kitchen Auntie shook Myu in front of my face, making her scream louder.

"I'll send you money from—" I yelled.

"No," Kitchen Auntie yelled back. "You're the mother."

I pushed Myu Myu away, hard enough to make Kitchen Auntie stagger back a few steps. "I'm not," I screamed. "Sookie is! She'll take the baby when I'm gone."

Kitchen Auntie scowled like she didn't believe me, then whirled out of the kitchen. "Sookie," I heard her calling, "Sookie!"

I opened the back door to leave, but Kitchen Auntie hurried back, the baby tucked under one arm, dragging Sookie, who was too shocked to balk, with the other. "Stop!" she bellowed at me. Turning to Sookie, she demanded: "You the baby's mother?"

Sookie frowned at me—eyes flicking a quick question at my clothes—then glanced dismissively at the baby. "No," she smirked. Prying her arm from Kitchen Auntie's claws, she turned to leave.

"I knew it!" Kitchen Auntie crowed.

"Sookie!" I yelped, scrambling to catch her. "Wait."

She stilled, looking at my hand clutching her shoulder, her brow raised in question.

"I have a chance to get out of America Town," I said, words tumbling out in a rush. "Now it's your turn to take care of the baby—your own flesh and blood. You need to be a mother. You need to—"

"I need to be a mother?" she snarled, trying to shake me off. "Me? I never needed it and never wanted it! You're the one— you were always the one—so don't you try to dump this kid on me now!"

"One of you needs to be the mother," Kitchen Auntie grumbled. She had finally begun rocking Myu, trying to quiet her. "One of you take her so I can finish making kimchee."

I hurried on, ignoring her: "I'd pay you. You wouldn't have to work here or anywhere—"

"Stop it!" Sookie screeched. "I'm not staying behind! I won't be pushed aside by you or anyone else! I saw what was going on so I talked to Yoon, too. You think you're the only one she wanted? I paid to make sure I was one of the girls she picked." She whirled on Kitchen Auntie, wrenching Myu Myu from her arms. "I knew this child should have died inside me."

Startled, Myu started squalling again as Sookie stormed to the sink. Sookie shook her like a rag doll. "Shut up! Shut up!" she raged. Her head whipping back and forth, Myu stuttered into silence.

I howled, long and wordless, and leapt forward to rescue Myu Myu.

After a sharp look at me, eyes wild and fierce, Sookie plunged Myu Myu into the sink, shoving her head under the leaves of cabbage that floated at the top of the water. "It'll be better for everybody." Sookie panted. "You'll thank me later."

Scratching at Sookie's arms, I called Myu's name, over and over, while her belly skimmed the surface, buoyant in the salted water, and her arms and legs lashing out, struggling through the pickling vegetables to grasp air. She squinted, blinked, opened her eyes wide, black marbles in the murky water.

I slapped Sookie, pulled her arms and her hair, screamed at her to stop. "Help me!" I shrieked at Kitchen Auntie, but she stood, rooted in shock, her hands covering her mouth.

"How dare you try and force this on me!" Sookie gritted her teeth and pushed harder, stiffening her arms. I could see the muscles of her arms strain, the veins in her hand popping blue, as she wrestled with the baby's surprising, slippery strength.

Wrestling past Sookie's arms, I reached for Myu Myu. Her body slid against my fingers as Sookie elbowed me in the ribs. "You're fucking crazy!" I snarled.

"I'm fighting for my life," gasped Sookie.

I clawed at her hands. Myu's mouth parted, a silent mew that propelled a cluster of bubbles into the black seaweed of her hair and the white limbs of the cabbage. "Sookie," I sobbed, "I'll take her back. I'll leave her with Lobetto."

"Lobetto!" Sookie spat. "She's better off dead than growing up as another black mutt in America Town."

Letting go of my hold on Myu Myu, I punched Sookie in the head. She stumbled forward, bellowing, and pressed Myu Myu deeper into the water. I bit her in the arm. When she reared back in anger and pain, I scooped the baby out of the water.

Myu Myu sputtered, retching water, her harsh gasps racking the sudden silence of the kitchen. I rocked her, cooing, and backed slowly toward the door, keeping an eye on Sookie.

Sookie stood, head bowed, hugging herself. I had bitten through skin; the water dripping off her elbows was tinged with blood. She was breathing almost as hard as Myu; I realized with a start she was crying. "That baby is yours," she croaked. "She's dead to me."

"Get out."

Glancing away from Sookie, I saw Kitchen Auntie, ashen under the bright pink of her blush, swaying in front of the stove.

For the first time, I saw her as the old woman she was, feeble and broken. "Get out," she repeated, her voice shaking.

I couldn't tell if she was talking to me or to Sookie or to both of us, but I clutched Myu Myu to my chest and rushed out the door. I knew if we stayed—at Foxa, in America Town, in Korea—Myu Myu would die.

15

I had prepared, going over the questions and answers regarding family, schooling, and employment Yoon had me memorize for the interview. I thought I knew what to expect. But the American who greeted me at the door spoke Korean, not English. "Please, sit," he said, pointing to the chair in front of his desk.

Disconcerted by his unexpected language, I took a moment to decipher his words. I stared at his mouth as it repeated, "sit," and then moved woodenly toward the chair across from him.

Settling Myu Myu into my lap, I perched on the edge of the seat.

"Thank you," I murmured. Breathing deeply, I glanced down to reorganize my thoughts, and out of habit, licked my palm to smooth Myu's curls.

The interviewer's eyes followed my hand, scanning Myu's face. Tilting his head, puzzled, he asked the first question I had no memorized answer for: "Yours?"

I almost jumped from the chair. Instead, I forced a smile. "No, no." I chuckled and shifted to attempt to hide the way Myu Myu clung to me like a baby monkey. "I'm only a student . . . her *nanny*," I added, testing the American word.

"You know some English," he said. "I suppose you practiced with her family." Staring at Myu Myu, he clucked. "Do you like it?"

I held her to my chest and turned my face down to hide my anger. "It? I love *her.*"

The American laughed, showing all his teeth. "I meant the job."

"Job?" I squeaked, thinking that he knew about the clubs, the backbooth honeymoons, the stage shows, about everything Yoon said must be hidden from him.

"As a nanny?" He was back to cooing and smiling at the baby. "Will you return to the job when you come back?"

"Yes," I said. "I would like to." Yoon had told me to emphasize anything that would indicate I planned on returning to Korea. "As long as it doesn't interfere with my coursework."

"I see from your transcripts you are an excellent student." The man looked at me sharply, his smile gone. "You don't want to go to an American school? In Hawai'i perhaps?"

I shook my head. Yoon had warned me to expect this question; in addition to weeding out prostitutes, the consul worried about students who posed as tourists, then disappeared into the American education system. "No," I said. "My father wants me to go to Ewha University."

"Excellent school," he said. He studied my face intently. I let him look, returning his gaze the way Yoon had told me to do, so he could believe he saw the truth. "I'm sure your parents are proud of you. Not every young lady can get into that school."

When he looked down, satisfied with my answer, I blinked my eyes quickly, surprised at the sudden sting of tears. My father had often urged me to study hard, telling me that I was smart enough to attend Korea's most prestigious women's university. It had been one of my father's dreams for me. "Yes," I murmured. "It's a dream come true."

The man beamed at me, easy and relaxed once more. "Her father," he asked, gesturing to Myu Myu, "he is American, right? The baby is mixed. What you call . . . *tweggi?*"

I nodded and forced myself to smile at the offensive term.

"I knew it!" he crowed. "If you've been here long enough, you can tell!" He tapped at his desk. "What did you say her father's name was?"

"I . . . I . . ." I gulped, then blurted the first American name I knew: "Lobetto Williams."

"Riyams?" His fingers drummed at the desk, then he repeated, "Robert Williams." He shook his head and smiled sadly.

My stomach dropped to the floor. I clenched Myu Myu so hard she cried out.

"No. Williams is a common name, but I don't know him." He stood suddenly and extended his hand.

I stared at his outstretched hand and slowly stood. I could tell he wanted me up and out, that the interview was now over, but I couldn't tell if I would be granted my visa.

When I didn't take his hand, he turned it and patted Myu Myu on the head. "Enjoy your visit in the U.S.," he said.

I almost slumped back into the chair in relief. Instead, I straightened my spine, hefted Myu onto my hip, and moved toward the door. Then, the weight of the baby triggering a thought, I turned back. "Excuse me, sir," I stammered.

He was shifting through the papers on his desk, and looked up as I spoke. "Yes?"

"My friend has a baby who wants to go"—I jerked my chin toward Myu Myu—"but not this baby." I stopped when he frowned, confused. I took a breath, ordered my words, and started again. "Sir, I have a friend who is also thinking of traveling to the U.S. I told her, since I was coming here today anyway, that I would ask what she needs to do to bring her baby."

"Sorry, no kids allowed," he said, and laughed.

Not realizing he was trying to make a joke, I stared. I could barely keep from crying, thinking my plans had just collapsed.

The man cleared his throat. "No, really, it's just an amendment to her passport," he explained. "Only a matter of paperwork and money. Tell your friend to pick up forms from window number two, outside, and send it in with her application and payment."

As simple as that, I was welcomed into America. But when I walked down the embassy steps, I was still in Korea, with nowhere to go except back to Lobetto's.

"You think it's that easy?" Lobetto, his chin up in challenge, snapped his fingers. "You think you can leave just like that?"

"Yes." I didn't try to stop grinning as I wandered through the apartment, looking for things that were mine or Myu Myu's.

"It's not just the money," he said. He paced around me, then stopped to dig into the back pocket of his pants. "Don't you remember my father's letter? Don't you remember how difficult he said it was to get into the country? The Immigration Man doesn't just give visas away."

I sighed. "I remember the letter."

He flipped open his wallet and pulled out the square of paper. Without bothering to unfold it, he quoted his father's words: "'I'm working hard to bring you to America, but it's not easy; the man wants to keep you out.' It's not easy, that's what my daddy said. It's all the laws and paperwork. You can't walk into that country anytime you feel like it."

"Lobetto," I said. "Yoon arranged the paperwork and I've got the visa."

"No!" He grabbed for me. "I don't believe you." When Myu Myu whined, startled by his intensity, he asked: "What about the kid?"

"I'll figure it out." I shrugged. I didn't let him see that I was worried; Yoon would front me the money needed to get there, documenting each penny spent, but she wouldn't pay for Myu Myu. I didn't even want Yoon to know about the baby until we arrived in Hawai'i.

Lobetto crowed. "See? There're things you haven't planned for. I've been planning for years. Everything I've made, I've saved for when I go to America."

"How can I forget?" I spat, remembering the first fistful of money I made for him, hidden at the bottom of the rice jar. I wondered if that money was still there, buried under the pearls of rice. I figured I worked hard for that money, that Lobetto might have been the one to find the men and bring them to me, but I was the one they paid for.

"There's always something to hold you back, isn't there?"

Lobetto nodded his head as if I were his prize pupil. He put his arm around me and I tried not to stiffen. "Let me help. I've got a plan, something good for both of us."

I put Myu Myu onto the floor and shook him away from me. I watched Myu Myu rock on her hands and knees in an attempt to propel herself forward.

"What's the matter?" Lobetto said. "Why you got to be like that for? My idea is a win-win." He took a breath, and released his words in a rush. "Leave the kid with me."

"What?"

"I hear you tried to unload her on Sookie," he said. "This way, you can go. And when you get to America, you can send me money until you bring us over."

"I thought your daddy was going to send for you," I taunted.

Jaws clenched, Lobetto ground out: "He will." Then he forced a smile, relaxing his mouth. "But I'm thinking for myself, too."

I shook my head. "I've decided to bring Myu with me. Get her out of America Town."

Ignoring me, he swooped, scooping Myu Myu into his arms. "I'll take care of her," he said, and continued embellishing his plans. "I'll get a birth certificate, put you down as mother and me as the father." He rolled his tongue, blowing spit bubbles off the tip, and she gurgled, smacking his face with her hands. "See how she loves me? I'll treat her good."

"Lobetto," I growled. "You don't get it. I can't arrange for you to come."

"I'll be nineteen soon," Lobetto said, his voice quiet, intense. "Too old for my father's help."

"Well, I can't help you either," I snapped.

"Can't or won't?" Lobetto narrowed his eyes. "You're just

like your daddy, aren't you? You think I'm not even good enough to be this kid's baby-sitter?" he spat. "You better think again, considering there's as good a chance as any that I really am her father."

I gasped. "What?"

"Sookie didn't tell you?" he asked, smirking. "I been doing her a long time."

"She would have told me," I said, "if it were true."

Lobetto placed his face alongside Myu's. "What do you think?" he said, grinning. "Look alike?" Myu Myu wriggled around to face him and bit his nose. Lobetto grimaced at the drool, then laughed when Myu Myu tried to mimic him.

"Give her back," I said, holding my arms out to her. "You know you don't really want her."

"Now why do you say that?" He swung her into the air, away from me. "Right now, I want nothing more than to keep her. She's my new ticket out of this place."

"Please, Lobetto," I begged, as Myu Myu, arms and legs paddling air, squealed with delight. "Please."

"What do you think of my idea?" he demanded, holding Myu just above my reach.

I looked up at her face. She smiled, and slobber oozed down her chin. When she gurgled, holding out her hand to me, I told Lobetto what he wanted to hear. "Okay, Lobetto. You win."

He smiled, patted the baby on her bottom, and plopped her on the ground. "Right," he said. When the baby tugged at his knees, wanting him to pick her up again, he nudged her with his toe until she fell onto her belly. "I'll bring her to you, I promise. With Sookie there, it'll be just like home."

And that was just what I was afraid of: Lobetto dragging his world along with him.

Later, after Lobetto walked me to Club Foxa's kitchen door and sauntered toward his corner on the street, I handed Myu Myu over to Kitchen Auntie.

Kitchen Auntie lifted the baby to peer into her face. "I'm surprised to see you alive," she sang to Myu, her voice light and high-pitched. "Yes, I am. Thought that Sookie would have turned you into soup by now."

Myu Myu giggled and kicked her legs. When a thin line of drool threatened to splash into her face, Kitchen Auntie hugged Myu to her bosom.

"I'll be back," I said. "Five minutes."

Kitchen Auntie glared at me. "Don't try what you did last week. I will let Sookie go through with it." She turned her back on me, shuffling to Myu Myu's crate. Kissing Myu on the head, she said, "I'd be sad to see it happen, but it's none of my business."

"I'm coming back," I repeated, then added: "Don't tell anyone I was here."

Kitchen Auntie shrugged. "Who's gonna ask?"

I doubled back to Lobetto's apartment, and after grabbing the small bag I had packed with my belongings, scanned the rooms. When I didn't see anyone, I slipped into the kitchen, moving to the back wall where we stored the rice and kimchee, and canned goods when we had them.

When I first moved in, I had to lean deep into the jar to scoop out a handful of rice. The tall ceramic urn hadn't even been half-full. Every time I laid on my back, every time I went down on my knees under the honeymoon booth, I had earned another cup of this rice.

My hip bumped the rice jar, knocking the lid to the floor with an alarming clatter. Snapping my head toward the door, I squinted to see into the darkened apartment. I couldn't see anything. I didn't hear anything. So I pushed my hand into the jar, enjoying the caress of rice past my elbow.

I swirled my hand, searching for the money, letting the rice spill over the jar's lip in an elegant, tittering shower. Raising onto my toes, I plunged in deeper, up to the armpit, until my fingertips grazed the bottom of the jar. I wiggled my fingers, sifting through polished grain.

I had begun to think I was stupid, that of course Lobetto would keep moving his stash, that he probably had several hiding places. And then I felt the rough slip of twine slide through the polished rice. Pinching the string between my fingers, telling myself that it could be nothing more than a stray bit of binding, I pulled.

When I yanked the drawstring bag free, dumping cupfuls of rice onto the floor, I didn't waste time counting the money. The bag was packed to bulging, heavy in my hands. I knew by the weight that it would be enough to pay Myu Myu's way into America.

Clutching the bag to my chest, I rushed out through the kitchen. And almost ran smack into Lobetto's mother, who was standing in the dark. I dropped my arms, trying to angle the bag behind my back. "What are you doing standing around in the dark?" I blustered. I figured that if she had seen me take the money from the rice jar, she would yell, or try to wrestle it away from me.

I waited, trying to make out her expression in the shadows. "You're leaving," she finally said. "Lobetto won't like that."

I nodded, then realized that she probably couldn't see my

face either. "I suppose," I croaked in answer to both comments. I planned to knock her over and run if she tried to stop me.

"You taking the child?" Her voice rippled low, unreadable.

"I am." My head nodded again, reflexively, stupidly.

"It's better that way," Lobetto's mother said. "Lobetto would probably start working her soon."

The breath caught in my throat. "She can't even walk yet," I gasped.

"Some men like children." Lobetto's mother's voice was matter-of-fact. Flat. I thought of Sookie when she said the same thing.

"But," I argued, "this baby's different. She's, she's"—I choked out the words—"his daughter."

"You think so?" she mused, then said: "Not that that would change anything. I'm his mother. That's just the way it is; it's all he knows."

Fidgeting, I decided to inch out the door and flinched when she breathed into my ear as I brushed past her.

After a long exhale, she whispered: "What am I gonna tell him when he sees you're gone?"

"Tell him he owes me." I took a breath. "Tell him: a baby for a baby. A life for a life." I willed myself not to run and not to turn back.

For years after that night, I believed she must not have seen me take the money; she wouldn't have let me go without a fight. Only recently have I let myself think of the possibility that she watched me steal the money and, in remaining silent, gave me a type of gift. I don't know what to think about that, about how it changes the way I thought of her. I wish I had allowed myself to look back, to catch a last glimpse, a final clue as to her true face. But she remains shielded from my gaze, wreathed in shadows and darkness and time.

I knew Lobetto would come looking for me, not because he wanted me back—though I provided good income. But because I had stolen from him. His money and Myu Myu, his connections to America. I had to keep moving. I spent the following nights with Myu Myu on my back, walking the streets, not sleeping until late morning.

I hadn't meant to return, but I was tired, hunted, and went back home out of habit. Instinct. Half-asleep on my feet, I found myself on the road that led to my father's shop. I watched from around the corner, waited for the sun to lift above the wall of America Town. When I saw his wife shuffle down the steps and head toward Chinatown, I stumbled forward. Standing at the threshold of the shop, I almost called out the words familiar from childhood: "*Appah,* I'm home!" But I caught myself in time. Instead, like a customer, I offered a tentative "Hello?"

My father rushed into the storeroom, head bowed as he tied an apron across his waist. "Welcome, welcome," he said, a shopkeeper's good manners. When he looked up, his smile froze, then dripped downward. "Hyun Jin?" he whispered. He stumbled forward, hands out like a blind man's, then stopped before touching me. Stunned, he scanned my hair, face, clothes.

I felt dirty and shut my eyes, not wanting to see myself reflected in his. "Father," I croaked. I thought I felt his touch on my cheek, but it was so soft, I wasn't sure if I had imagined it or not. When I opened my eyes on him, his hands were at his sides. He seemed older, more stooped and gray than even a few moments ago.

"You can't be here," he said, looking wildly around the store.

"Don't worry." I spat out the bitter words. "She's not here."

"Still." Wiping his palms on his apron, he fixed his gaze at my shoulder, on Myu Myu. "Oh no, Jin Jin," he moaned. "You didn't."

"Please, *Appah,* you don't understand." I untied the baby from my back and swung her into my arms. "I'm going to America."

My father sucked in a quick breath. "You are . . . are you . . . married?" He spoke slowly, with care, as if not wanting to call me a liar.

Myu Myu gurgled, her hands waving at the bright colors in the store. His eyes still studying her, my father rummaged through the pockets of his apron and pulled out a purple candy. Myu Myu lunged for it and grabbed my father's fist. Startled, my father stilled, letting her gum the candy from his hand. A smile played at his mouth. He cupped his free hand and cradled her face. "I see a little of you in her," he murmured, then flicked a glance at me. "What of her father?"

I stuck out my chin. "I'm not married," I said. "I'm going to Hawai'i as a worker. I have a job lined up."

Frowning, my father growled, "Not bar work, I hope."

I stared at the spot where his brows furrowed, joining at a point over his nose. "So what if it is?" I shrugged as if I didn't care what he thought of me.

"No! Hyun Jin." He pulled away from the baby and stared at me. "Don't do that. Don't go. You could do so much more with yourself, with your life. You are so smart, so—"

"*Appah,* stop!" I shouted. When he cringed, I lowered my voice. "What else can I do? Are you going to take me back? Take this girl in?"

My father's jaw dropped. He sputtered, his mouth moved, but for a long moment no words came out. "I . . . I can't," he sobbed.

Feeling mean, I thrust Myu Myu at him. "Why not? It'd just be for a little while."

My father backed away, his gnarled hands held out in front of him. "Your mother will be back soon," he said.

I stepped forward. "And what will *my mother* say when she finds me—us—here?"

My father stopped, bent his head. "Please, Hyun Jin, try to understand. Don't you see your baby will never be accepted— not by my wife, not by most Koreans? Leave her to the Americans; they have places for children like her." He lifted his head, and I was startled to see tears in his eyes. "Then, maybe, you could come home . . ." His words died and I knew and he knew that that would never happen.

Bending forward, I shifted Myu to my back. "It's better that we go," I said. I felt tired, empty.

"Wait." My father touched me on the head, then rushed to the Coke display. He reached under it, his fingers tapping, feeling their way through years of dust, and pulled out a thin stack of envelopes. He patted the letters, blew the dirt from them. "Here," he offered, handing them to me. "I used to dream that we could leave, too, and make a new life, a better life for you."

Confused, I shook my head and squinted at the name scrawled in the corner of the top envelope: Lee Synang Man. Same name as the old president. For a crazy moment, I thought my father was passing me confidential political letters. Then I noticed the address underneath the name: 94-789 Waikupanaha Street, Waimanalo, Hawai'i. "What?" I scowled. "Who is this?"

My father shoved the packet to me. "Take it," he urged. "Synang Man is your uncle. He can help you, if you need it."

I folded my arms across my chest, knowing my father had no brothers. "My uncle?" I sneered, glaring at him.

His eyes skittered away from mine. "Your mother's—my wife's—brother. He went to Hawai'i just after World War Two. At first he sent letters, promising to return to take care of the store, take care of the family, take care of her. But then he stopped writing and he forgot about coming home. She never forgave him for that." He shrugged, then tried to tuck the envelopes into Myu Myu's blanket. "Still, he's family."

Twisting away from him, I knocked the letters to the ground. "Your wife is not family to me. He's not family to me. And now, you're not family to me." I kicked at the packet and walked out the door.

"Hyun Jin," my father called, and I could hear grief cracking his voice. "Jin Jin. Little Fox." But I refused to slow my step. I refused to turn around.

I had to chance a visit to Club Foxa to leave a message for Yoon; I didn't want Bar Mama to tell her my disappearance meant that I had changed my mind about leaving for America. From behind the garbage dump in the alley, I watched that back door of Foxa until closing time, when the bar was clear of GIs and the bringers who might know Lobetto. Then I rushed into the kitchen.

"Eh, Kitchen Auntie," I panted. I shook out one leg that had gone to sleep while I was in the alley.

Kitchen Auntie gave a small scream as she spun around to face me. "Why you got to scare somebody like that?" she scolded. Then she looked at me. "You look like shit. I barely recognize you."

I eyed her up and down. "Well, you look like shit, too." I sassed back. "Same as always."

Kitchen Auntie cackled. "I always liked you," she said.

"Listen," I told her. "Tell Yoon's people that I'll be at the airport on time." I dug into my jeans pocket for some coins, and pressed them into her palm.

She nodded. "Sookie said that you would be. Bar Mama thought you found a better deal with some Joe." Jiggling the coins in her palm, she added: "And Lobetto's been coming around every night, telling me to keep an eye out for you. Never thought you were so popular."

"Shit." I pushed away from her, fumbling for the door. "Listen. Do not let anyone know I was here. Just pass on the message, okay?"

Kitchen Auntie clucked her tongue. "Wait, wait, let me get something for the baby." She shuffled toward the stove. "She don't look so good either."

"She's tired, that's all," I said. But I stayed.

Kitchen Auntie busied herself with scooping leftover rice into a small plastic box. "Why would you cheat Lobetto like that?" she scolded me as she added a mound of kimchee and a few thin strips of *bulgogi*. My mouth watered at the sight of the beef that I knew would cost Kitchen Auntie some of her own pay. "Lobetto's a good boy. I've known him since before he was born, from the time his mama worked the clubs."

"I've known him almost as long," I retorted, "but I never thought he was good."

Kitchen Auntie tightened her lips, trying to flatten out a smile. "He said he wants the baby. He said he loves her." She looked for something to flavor the rice and reached for a cup of blackened sesame seeds.

"I've got to go. Now," I muttered, shifting from foot to foot. My heart beat faster than she sprinkled, urging me to run.

Kitchen Auntie held the box toward me, but when I grabbed

it, she wouldn't let go. "Hold on a minute," she said. "There's someone inside been wanting to see you."

"No!" I shouted. "Don't tell Lobetto I'm here." I grabbed the box and ran out the door.

"Wait, wait," Kitchen Auntie called after me. "It's not Lobetto."

I pretended I didn't hear her and rushed down the alleyway. I ran blindly, without thought. I imagined Lobetto about to catch me. I struggled for speed while balancing Myu Myu on my back, but I knew Lobetto was gaining on me. I could hear how close he was by the echo of his footsteps behind me. When his hand gripped my shoulder, I dropped to my knees, pressed Myu against the wall and covered my head with my hands.

And then Sookie's arms were around me. "Hyun Jin," she wheezed. "Hyun Jin, I've been worried about you. I didn't want you to blow this chance to get out of this place."

"I—I—I . . ." I gulped air that burned my lungs.

She patted my shoulders, my arms, my head, as if to make sure I was unhurt. She avoided touching the baby, who had begun to mewl weakly. "Lobetto has been crazy since you left," she said when she could breathe normally. "Is it true? You stole his America money?"

I shifted forward, my knees slipping on a stream of sludge that smelled of sewage. I stroked the baby's legs, then with shaking fingers, worked at the knot on the sling. "It's all right, baby," I crooned. "You're okay."

"Where you been?" Sookie asked.

Ignoring the question, I unwrapped Myu Myu, cradled her in my arms. "Sookie," I panted, struggling to my feet. "I've got to get out of here before Lobetto catches up to me."

"But where're you going to go?" Sookie persisted. She

tugged at my elbow to help me up. "It's not safe for you around here."

"Tell me something I don't know," I snapped, and pulled away, shielding Myu with my body.

"I'm just trying to help." She sniffed. "You stink."

I rubbed Myu Myu's back, trying to soothe her and myself. I wanted to find a safe, secret place, maybe under one of the piers, to feed her and sleep a while. My knees, dampened with sewage, cracked when I took a step.

"Hyun Jin," Sookie said, following me. "You look tired. Why don't I take you to Duk Hee's? You can sleep there for a little while. Lobetto won't expect that."

I stopped. My head felt thick, and the sun, dim though it was this early in the morning, was strong enough to burn my eyes. "Duk Hee's?" I asked. "She won't mind?"

"Come," Sookie murmured. "Rest. Eat. Sleep. You'll be safe."

Duk Hee was in one of the few cubicles that hadn't closed their curtains. Stripped to bra and panties, head drooping and legs splayed, she sprawled in front of the glass door. When she heard our footsteps, she lumbered to her feet, calling, "Last chance, good time. Last chance, good time."

"Pathetic," Sookie muttered, and pounded on the door.

Duk Hee squinted into the sun's glare, her painted face garish in the morning light. "You ladies got any smokes?" she slurred.

"Duk Hee," Sookie shouted. "Open up."

Duk Hee opened her eyes wider, frowned, and then grinned. "Sookie?" She stumbled forward to unlock her door. She hurried to her daughter, trying to gather her into her arms.

"I didn't recognize you at first. Imagine a mother not recognizing her own child!"

"Yeah, yeah, yeah," Sookie mumbled as she pushed past Duk Hee's attempt to embrace her.

Duk Hee stared at me, polite but distant, as I sidled in. I waited, part of me wanting her to fold me into her arms as well, to love me as a daughter. Part of me was relieved she didn't. "Hyun Jin." She nodded. "You look like an old lady. Old and worn out as me."

I scowled at her pasty skin, her bony chest, her graying hair, and said, "I doubt I look as bad as you."

Duk Hee coughed out a laugh. "You were always so funny."

I stumbled through the narrow space, to the back where the cot was pushed against the wall. Sookie had pulled the stained sheets off the mattress and piled them onto the floor. She jerked her head toward the bed. "Sit," she told me, and lit a cigarette.

The quick flare of the match illuminated her face and I looked more closely. Her makeup was starting to bleed away, and under it, I could see a string of bruises from her temple to the baseline of her jaw, mirroring my birthmark.

At my startled cry, quickly stifled, Sookie looked up and twisted her lips into a smile. "Told you Lobetto went crazy when you took off with his stash. He thought I knew where you went."

"I'm sorry, Sookie, I—" I stammered.

She inhaled, the end of the cigarette crackling orange, then passed it to her mother, who was fidgeting with her hand up.

Duk Hee pinched the stick with shaking fingers and took a drag. "You girls in trouble?" she asked, closing her eyes and holding in the smoke.

"Just want a place to sleep." Sookie took the cigarette back and nodded her head toward me.

Duk Hee opened her eyes, and for the first time noticed

Myu Myu. "Oh, is that? . . ." Her glance flickered to Sookie, then dropped back to the baby. "I heard," she said as she opened her arms. "Please?"

I unwrapped Myu, but instead of handing her to her grandmother, kept her close to my breast. "She's hungry," I said. I searched through the baby's wrappings and pulled out the package of rice Kitchen Auntie had prepared. After popping the lid open with my teeth, I placed a pinch of rice and beef in my mouth and chewed. When I felt the mouthful soften, I spit it back out and slipped it into Myu's mouth. While she gummed it, I prepared her next bite.

I fed Myu Myu, swallowing only a small portion for myself, then settled her against my side. She tugged at my shirt, which I lifted for her. She grunted happily as she nuzzled my chest, taking one nipple in her mouth and grabbing at the other with her hands.

"Sick," Sookie said. "Nothing is in there, right?"

I glanced up. Sookie and Duk Hee, less than a foot away from me, crouched at the side of the cot with their backs against the wall. Quietly, their hooded eyes on me, they had smoked through Sookie's pack of cigarettes, passing each stick back and forth between them. A small pile of ash and butts half-filled one of Duk Hee's plastic tea cups.

"Shut up," Duk Hee said. "Let them sleep." Her stomach rumbled and she looked down at it as if in surprise. She gave an embarrassed laugh. "I only get hungry when I smell food," she explained.

I looked at the tin. All that remained were a few specks of rice stained red with kimchee juice, and a bit of the shredded cabbage. Duk Hee was staring at the kimchee, so I tilted my head toward it. "It's not much, but you can have it, if you want."

Duk Hee pounced on the box, slurped the spicy vegetables

without chewing. When she had finished, she sat back on her haunches and fixed her catlike hunger on Myu Myu. "Maybe later," she whispered, "I can hold her."

Sookie stood, leaning over me in the narrow cubicle. Bending her face close to mine, she whispered: "Sleep then. I'll look out for you."

Feeling Myu Myu's grip on my bared nipple loosening as she slept, I closed my eyes under Sookie's watchful gaze.

When I woke, the women and Myu Myu were gone. Lobetto was the one twisting my nipples, gripping them so hard I cried out before I even opened my eyes. Pushing against his hands, I bolted upright and scanned the small space for the baby. "Sookie?" I cried. The pain in my breasts knifed through my grogginess.

"We're alone," he said, then pushed his nail into my nipples.

"Stop!" I scratched his arms until he snapped away.

"Shit!" Lobetto cursed. He stuck his bleeding hand against his lip and struck out with his other.

"Please," I gasped. "The baby." Dazed, I thought for a brief moment that Sookie and Myu Myu might be huddled under the bed. I tipped over to look under the cot.

"You think you can just leave me behind, throw me away like a piece of trash?" Lobetto jerked me back by the hair and flipped me over, pinning my body under his. "Why're you fucking up the plan?"

I tried to buck him off, yelling, "Get off, you *gomshi* oaf!" I spit out a mouthful of blood. Sookie had promised to watch over me, to protect me as I slept. But as soon as I let down my guard, she and Duk Hee took the baby and led Lobetto to me. I tried to think where Sookie would run to, but all I could imagine was her pushing Myu Myu under water, holding her there until I managed to scrape her arms away, her saying: "It's for your own good; you'll thank me later."

Lobetto cupped the side of my face, as a lover would, then squeezed my cheeks together.

"Where's my money?" he spat. Flecks of spittle hit hot against my face. "Where's the kid?"

"What money?" I said. My cheeks were pressed so tightly against my teeth, they cut and bled with each word.

"Why you gotta be like this? I took you in," he said, punctuating his words by yanking my head around. "Gave you a place to sleep, food in your stomach, clothes on your back. Those things cost—"

I clawed at his hands, arms, tried to get at his eyes. When he yelped and pulled away, I snarled, "I earned that money!"

"You 'earned' that money?" Lobetto yelled. "Is that what you said? All you did was lie down and spread your legs. How hard is that?" Prying my thighs apart, he ground his hips into mine. "All you have to do is lie there." He pulled at the buttons of my pants.

"What're you doing?" I screeched, trying to knock his hands away, to kick him off.

"You need me," he panted, struggling to pull my shorts off. "I was the one hustling, working the streets, making the deals. Without me, you're nowhere. There's no place for you. Who's the man keeping you down now? Huh? Huh?"

I yanked his hair, lifting his head, trying to look into his face. "Stop it, Lobetto! Stop!" I shouted into his ear: "I know you. I know your face, Lobetto. Look at me!"

When he opened his eyes, I saw that he was crying. He shuddered, frowning into my face, then leapt away from me.

I looked at him, hunched at the foot of the cot, then out the glass door. Bright afternoon light leaked from the sides of the drawn curtain. Through the thin rectangles I glimpsed people walking by. I knew they couldn't see me, and even if they had seen Lobetto trying to rape me, no one would have stopped him. The scene was nothing new. I myself had seen worse things in the tanks. I wondered what Duk Hee saw from her view on the cot.

"Hyun Jin?" Lobetto's voice broke, as it had when he was younger, in school, unsure of the answers. I thought he would apologize, beg for forgiveness. Instead, his voice hardened and he said, "Why do you have to push me like that?"

"What?" I shrieked, kicking him in the shoulder.

He grabbed my foot before I could kick him again, in the head. "Aai! That hurt," he whined. "You didn't have to do that." He dropped my leg when he felt it go limp and rubbed his arm.

"Go suck your mama's milk," I taunted, relieved to see the Lobetto I knew and could handle.

"Where's my kid?" he asked. He sounded tired, almost sad.

"She's not yours!" I scrambled to my knees, fists up, ready to fight. "You didn't want her. Sookie didn't want her. You guys would have killed her, just like you killed my other one!"

Lobetto shook his head. "What are you talking about?" he scowled. "What other one?"

"You don't even remember!" I hissed. "You owe me. You know you owe me. I won't let—"

"You think you can just take her?" Lobetto asked, knocking my hands down. "You think you can just waltz into America with her in your arms? You think you can play Yoon, fuck her over like that?"

I jutted my chin. "Yes."

The cot creaked as Lobetto got to his feet. He loomed over me, glaring, eyes slit and unwavering.

I flinched, but stared back.

"Fuck it. Take the baby," he said, his voice quiet, resigned. "And take the money, too. For her." He knelt in front of me and tapped my jaw closed. "I do love that kid," he whispered. "Tell her that. Tell her her father loves her. It's important." When I nodded, still stunned, he added: "And tell her one day I'll come to her. I'll meet her at . . . I don't know—Disneyland." He flashed a lopsided grin. "Every American kid should visit Tomorrowland, right?"

I think he was quoting another line from his own father's letter.

After Lobetto left, I didn't have the energy to slide from the bed to find my pants. I couldn't even lift a hand over the cot to yank the blanket over my body. I faced the door, fighting the urge to close my eyes, and focused on the narrow strip of light angling past the curtain.

It was only when I heard the door swing open that I scrambled to get up. I thought Lobetto was back, that he had changed his mind or was trying to trick me all along; I needed to be on my feet for the next confrontation. The room tilted around me, twisting my stomach. I bent over, struggling not to vomit.

"What did you do to my place?" Duk Hee complained. When I straightened, exposing the welts on my breasts, the scratches on my legs, she gasped. "What happened to you?"

Myu Myu was perched on Duk Hee's hip. I grabbed her, swayed, and sat on the cot to keep from falling. Myu Myu cried out, upset at the jostling. I nuzzled her neck, which smelled like salt and mildew. "Why did you leave me?" I winced when I heard myself whine; I had tried to yell.

"Lobetto?" Sookie asked.

"You know he was here," I hissed.

Duk Hee bent forward, lifting her hand as if to caress my face. I leaned toward her, wanting her touch, her comfort. Her palm hovered, a whisper above my birthmark. "Are you hurt?" she asked, dropping her hand.

Sookie snorted. "What do you think?" She pushed Duk Hee onto the cot next to me so she could squeeze past our legs. "We don't have much time now. He might come back," she said as she checked under the bed, through piles of trash and clothes for my shirt and pants.

Gingerly, my entire body tender, I craned my neck to peer at Sookie. "Are we even now?"

Sookie frowned. "What do you mean?"

"I mean, Lobetto knew I was here." I stared at her, then threw out: "He came for his daughter."

Sookie winced. "He told you he's the father?"

"Why didn't you?" I pretended to be nonchalant, but couldn't stop from asking, "How long were you guys . . . ?"

"A long time," Sookie admitted. She looked to her mother then glanced down, blindly picking at the clothes in her hands. "The first time we were still in primary school; his father bought me for him."

Duk Hee covered her face with her hands. "I'm sorry," she groaned. "I am so sorry."

Sookie shook her head at her mother, then spoke to me. "It was nothing. We got together sometimes, even after his father left, because then we were kind of the same."

"What? Poor little *gomshis?* Little throwaways?" I scoffed to hide my surprise at their long involvement. I had always thought that Sookie and Lobetto hated each other. "Half in one world, half in another?" I added, remembering something Lobetto had once told me.

"I never meant to hurt you," Sookie said, kneeling in front of me. "I never meant to keep secrets from you."

I laughed, a bitter retching sound. "But you have. So many secrets. So many lies." Myu Myu whimpered and burrowed under my arm.

"I never told Lobetto you were here. I—" Sookie started to say, but I pushed a hand against her mouth.

"Save it," I growled. "I don't want to hear any excuses, any more stories. I know what you did. I know how you are."

"Do you?" she asked. "Or do you know only what you think you know?" Sookie looked me in the eye, took my finger in her mouth, and bit.

16

I figured it was the guilt of betrayal that made Sookie buy the train tickets to Kimpo airport. "That's where I went when I left you," Sookie said. "I never saw Lobetto at all. I wouldn't."

I snorted. "That doesn't mean you didn't stop by the corner of Club Alley to spread the word where to find me," I said.

Sookie threw her hands into the air. "For the last time, I didn't tell anyone anything," she said. "Least of all Lobetto."

"I never thought Lobetto could do something like this,"

Duk Hee said, staring at my lips, cut and swollen. "I can't believe he would hit a woman. I thought his daddy had had more influence on him than that."

"Are you joking?" Sookie screamed at her. "Look at me. Didn't you see what he did to me?"

Duk Hee turned away, saying, "Lobetto did that? I thought it must have been Chazu." She sniffed disdainfully. "Or maybe one of the other boyfriends you stole from me."

Sookie threw her hands into the air and shouted at me. "Can you believe this old woman!" She marched over to Duk Hee, stepping so close they breathed each other's breaths. "It's your fault I'm the way I am! I was just a little girl. A little girl—" Sookie stopped, her voice becoming shaky and weak. "You should have protected me."

Duk Hee backed up. Her calves banged the back of her cot. "I did the best I could," she protested. "I tried." Sitting on the cot, she fumbled with the purse she kept tied around her neck. She pulled out a few wrinkled bills and reached for Sookie's hand. "Here, take this."

Sookie's eyes narrowed on the money, then shot to Duk Hee's face. "I thought you said you didn't have cash."

Duk Hee waved the money at Sookie. "Just take it. Doesn't matter how I got it."

Sookie grabbed her mother's fist. "Were you the one who told Lobetto?"

Duk Hee looked up. "I thought you were in trouble. I wanted to help." When Sookie flung her hand off, Duk Hee begged. "Please. I didn't know what he would do to her."

"You think money is going to make everything better?" Sookie shook her head and without glancing back, walked out of Duk Hee's cubicle.

"Sometimes that's all a person has to give," Duk Hee whispered. She stood, then moved toward me, holding her hands in front of her as if afraid I would run away. "I'm sorry, I'm sorry," she said. "I tried my best for you, too." She didn't look at me, but at Myu Myu. "He said he loved her," she murmured. "I believed him."

"I think he does," I said, my anger at her fading as I watched her watch Myu Myu.

She pushed the money at me. "Will you take this?" When I hesitated, she added, "For the girl. The baby." Duk Hee folded the money into the cup of my palm, her gaze fixed on her grandchild, then lifted her hand to Myu's curls—a brief, light touch—before she jerked herself back.

I glanced at Myu, then held her up. "Would you like to hold her?" I asked.

Duk Hee placed her face next to Myu's and inhaled deeply, breathing her in. She closed her eyes, and when she opened them, she shook her head. "Nah, no need," she said.

"Duk Hee?" I said, not sure what I meant to ask. I placed a hand on her shoulder.

"Hyun Jin!" Sookie yelled from the doorway. "Let's go." She leaned in, shuffling her feet outside, refusing to enter. Without looking up, she added, "See you, Duk Hee. I . . . I won't forget you."

I turned to say goodbye to Duk Hee. She was already lying down on her narrow cot, her back curved away from me.

At the airport, I kept thinking I saw Lobetto. A glimpse of a battered army jacket slouched over a tall, wiry frame; a flash of heavy curls hanging over a dark, gaunt face, and my breath would catch. But in the end, he never showed up. The scenes I imagined where he grabbed Myu from my arms as we were about to board the plane never came to pass. Just as my fear of being stopped by immigration officials was never realized.

It was unbelievable how easy it was to leave Korea; it came down to a small thing.

A lie, a modest nod of the head, when they asked if I was visiting. They darted looks at me, trying to hide their morbid fascination at my multicolored face. The stark asymmetry made them uncomfortable, so what they focused on was the papers and the money I handed to them.

When the plane climbed into the air, Myu Myu whimpered. She arched her back, tugged at her hair, and screamed at the roar of engine in her head. I felt it, too, the earth's pull reaching in through our ears, endeavoring to drag us back down. There was a moment of pain, then a small, audible *pop* of release; we were free.

Next to us Sookie bounced in her seat, exclaiming over the seat belt fastener, the tray table, the windows, the earphones. She plugged into the radio and began singing aloud to the music. When the stewardess rolled a cart down the aisle and offered us peanuts and soda, Sookie narrowed her eyes and asked, loud enough to drown out the music only she could hear, "How much?"

"Complimentary." The stewardess smiled slightly and plopped the bag of nuts on our laps.

"Complimentary?" Sookie echoed, sliding the earphones off her head. "Free?"

"Don't count on it," I grumbled, shifting Myu Myu's weight across knees that were going numb. "Mrs. Yoon will find a way to make us pay."

"That's why I'm going to enjoy it all," Sookie shot back.

"Coca-Cola," she said to the stewardess, peering at the drinks in the cart. "7 UP. Orange juice. And that—" she added, pointing to a slender red-and-white can.

"Bloody Mary Mix." The stewardess filled a plastic cup with ice and soda and another with thick red juice that Sookie refused to touch. Leaning over me and Myu Myu, she lined them up on Sookie's tray. When she noticed Sookie eyeing her cart again, she turned away and pushed it farther up the aisle.

I opened the bag of nuts and chewed one up. Spitting it out, I placed it on Myu's tongue. She wrinkled her face and gagged. Crushed peanuts came out in a long stream of drool, which I tried to catch in the small square of napkin the stewardess had handed out.

"Disgusting." Sookie shuddered, adjusted the earphones, and turned her face to the window.

The smell of peanuts made my stomach lurch. After fumbling with the seat belt, I managed to unbuckle myself and stumble into the aisle. With Myu Myu on my shoulder, I made my way to the back of the plane. Behind the line of people waiting for the toilet, I paused, noticing the rear exit door. I stepped up to the small window, skimming the emergency release handle with my fingers. For a moment, my hand tightened with the urge to pull down, to open up, to float into that endless dream of blue and white, suspended between heaven and earth. I exhaled, fogging the glass with a cloud of breath, and forced myself to step away.

We filed off the plane like cattle, jostled into lines for processing. Our passports stamped, we shuffled through a corridor toward a glass door. A pack of people pressed close to a doorway that opened and closed as passengers neared it. Peering in, their faces eager, anxious, they waited. A woman behind me cried out and pushed past me, through the doors that parted like water, and into the arms of someone who could have been her sister, or mother, someone who loved her. Travelers were claimed, enveloped in garlands of flowers, their bags taken by other hands.

Yoon was there to claim Sookie and me. Her eyes widened, then narrowed on the baby I carried. "What the fuck?" she squawked, pinching me in the ribs when she pretended to embrace me. But she pasted a smile on her face as we passed the airport security.

"This way." She took my arm, her nails digging into my flesh.

I gritted my teeth, forcing a smile as well.

Sookie sauntered up to the airport guard. "We so excited to visit this, the beautiful state of Hawai'i," Sookie said, rattling on in English as the guard, startled at her approach, stared at her. "I plan to feed fish at Hanauma Bay, climb Diamond Head, see Pearl Harbor. And, of course, shop, shop, shop at Ala Moana Center."

Yoon turned on Sookie. "Shut up," she said, shaking her arm. "There's no official here."

Sookie pouted. "But I wanted to give my speech. I thought I would be asked questions; all they did was stamp here, stamp there. I memorized for nothing."

Yoon shook her head and stomped away.

I looked at Sookie. She grinned and winked. We scrambled to keep up with Yoon's militant strides.

"And you," Yoon hissed at me. "I don't know what game you're playing. How could you bring that . . . that child. You don't know how much trouble they cause—food, clothing, rent, school, doctors. It'll be a big problem."

"I'll pay," I said grimly.

"I'll make sure you do."

Sliding doors opened and we stepped into sunlight, raw and bright. Bursts of color shot across my lids when I blinked. My eyes felt heavy, but I forced them open, wide as I could. I had expected to see the ocean, trees loaded with flowers, hula dancers. What I saw was gray asphalt that steamed with heat, concrete blocks and red dirt, chicken wire and tractors.

"Construction," Yoon said, leading us into a fenced parking lot. "America is always getting better." She stopped in front of a long blue car. "Nice, isn't it," she boasted. "Cadillac."

"Cad-o-lac," I repeated, liking the way the word slid across my tongue. I liked as well the seats, soft and sleek, like the fur of a cat. I never before felt material soft as a baby's skin.

We fell silent during the ride, Sookie and I looking out the windows. Myu Myu played with a button on the door that made my window whir down and up. Each time the window slid down, the blaring noise of tires blasted in with hot air. Yoon grumbled and pushed a lever on her door that paralyzed my window. Houses, fat and white as lice eggs, dotted the dry, brown hills that rose above us; below, sprawled under the archway of traffic, squatted a series of buildings with laundry strung out on the balconies.

"This is U.S.?" Sookie whispered to me. "This is Hawai'i? Looks like another America Town to me."

Yoon heard and said, "This is America, not America Town. Here, without me, you're nothing. You could disappear, you could die, and no one would know. Officially, you don't exist."

"What's new?" I said bitterly.

"What's new is me." Yoon braked at a light and looked at us over her shoulder. "Listen to me, do as I say, and we can all make a lot of money."

"If I can get a car like this," Sookie said, "I'm in."

Lips tight, Yoon smiled. "You're in already—for about fifteen hundred, American. That's the beginning of what you owe me. But don't worry," she added in supposed encouragement. "Work hard and in another ten, fifteen years, you could have what I have." She turned and pressed the gas. The Cadillac lurched forward.

After turning down several narrow lanes, we pulled to the curb alongside a squat two-story building. Its brown paint was chipped in places, revealing the concrete block walls underneath. Yoon unfolded herself from the car, adjusted her skirt, and motioned us to follow her.

Reaching the door at the end of the walkway, Yoon inserted a key in the lock and pushed. Something blocked her way. Yoon placed her shoulder against the door and pushed harder.

"Hey, hey!" a voice called from inside. "Wait just a minute, will you?"

Giving suddenly, the door swung open onto a darkened room. Yoon flicked on the light and snorted in disgust. "It's past noon," she said.

Sookie and I crowded against Yoon in the only open space in the apartment, the floor of which was covered wall to wall with futons. Most of the sleeping mats were occupied by girls. The girl who answered the door rubbed the sleep from her eyes. "Mrs. Yoon," she gasped, stretching her large T-shirt over her knees. "We didn't expect you."

"I told Lulu I was coming with two new girls," Yoon griped, eyes flicking over the sleeping bodies.

The girl said, "Lulu never came home last night." The girl spoke to Yoon, but spotting Myu Myu, couldn't stop staring. When her eyes jumped to my face she screamed: *"Aiigu!"*

Yoon pursed her lips. "She didn't go home with one of my customers, did she?"

The girl shook her head, forcing her eyes back to Yoon. "No, no. She went to see a girlfriend, and then, and then went to get doughnuts."

Yoon exhaled, long and slow, and eyed the girl. "That's . . . nice," she said. "I don't like it when one of my girls breaks my rules about socializing outside the club."

The girl bobbed her head, offered a hesitant smile.

"And I don't like it when my girls lie to me."

The girl's smile fell. She glanced around the room, then gestured to one corner, where there was a sink and a small refrigerator. "Can I make you some tea? Coffee?" she asked, keeping her head down.

"No, thanks, Chinke." Yoon wrinkled her nose. "I'll just leave the new girls with you," she said, backing out the door. "Fix up that ugly one as much as you can and bring them to the club early."

When the door shut behind us, Sookie and I followed the girl Yoon called Chinke, stepping over the bodies, to the kitchen area. Chinke poked at the girls sprawled in front of the sink and refrigerator. "Get up," she said to them, "we need this space."

"I heard," moaned one, without opening her eyes. "I just didn't want to get up and face Yoon."

"What's she thinking," the other yawned, "bringing in more girls, packing us in like Vienna sausages?" This girl sat up, quickly folding her blankets and futon, then glanced up. "I'm Minnie—holy shit. You are fucked up! Double fucked," she giggled, "your face and a baby!"

I hugged Myu to my chest, letting the curtain of my hair fall across our faces. Myu grabbed a handful of hair and twisted it in her fist. Eyes watering, I struggled to loosen her grip.

The girl next to Minnie sat up. She looked into and away from my face, too polite to comment. Instead she held up her arms and waved both hands. "Here, let me hold her," she urged. "I left two of these at home."

As I leaned past Sookie to hand over Myu Myu, Sookie looked at Chinke. "You from China?" she asked. "That why they call you Chinke?"

Chinke narrowed her small eyes. "No," she said.

"We just call her that because of her eyes." The girl laughed and, balancing Myu in her lap, pulled her eyes into thin slits.

"Shut your rubber-lip mouth, Froggie," Chinke shot back. "We call her Froggie because of her big mouth."

A girl lying on a mat in the back of the room near the bathroom called out: "No, we call her Froggie because when she drinks too much beer, she begins to belch like a love-sick bullfrog!" The girl let out a long burp.

Chinke laughed with the other girls, Froggie included, and opened a cabinet to pull out a teapot. "I bet Yoon shit when she saw the baby."

I shrugged, trying to hide my nervousness. "Yoon said it was my problem."

"My turn to hold the toy," Minnie said, stroking Myu Myu on the back.

"Just be sure it doesn't become Yoon's problem," Chinke said. "You won't like the way she deals with problems."

Sookie eyed the crowded room. "Where do we unpack?" she asked.

Froggie jumped up, leaving her sleeping mat in the middle of the kitchen space. "Here," she said, hopping over a girl behind her. "Next to Ari." She prodded Ari to scoot over. "You're going to have to get your own futon and blankets. You have cash?" She rattled on without waiting for an answer. "If not, ask Yoon. She'll add it to what you already owe her." She watched Sookie dump her bag onto Ari's futon and shook her head. "And you'll need new clothes," she sighed.

Sookie held up a floral halter top and orange short shorts. "What's wrong with my clothes?" she glowered.

Ari sat up and snorted. "Country bumpkins."

Froggie giggled, patting Sookie on the arm before she could retort. "Ari!" she scolded. "We were all like that when we first got here." To Sookie and me, she explained, "You don't want to look like cheap country girls from Waimanalo. We're *hostesses.*"

Trying to sound disinterested, I forced a yawn, then asked: "Waimanalo? Where's that?"

Ari got to her feet and stretched, arms overhead, her back an arc of muscle and grace. "Nowhere."

"It's nowhere you want to be," Froggie added, tapping her chin. "I don't even think it's on this island, is it?"

Ari snorted. "Who cares. Low-class dirt farms. That's what I ran away from in Korea."

Sookie, Myu Myu, and I dozed, resting during the next couple of hours, as the other girls got up to have a cup of tea and get ready for work. They seemed to have a schedule already in place; there weren't many arguments over the bathroom. One girl, who I later found out was Lulu, ran into the apartment after her turn had passed. She hurried to the bathroom and pounded on the locked door. "Let me in," she begged. Then, turning to the other girls in the room, asked, "Who's in there? Chinke, Chinke, let me come in, too!" After a muffled answer, Lulu cupped her hand to the door and shouted, "Shit!

Yoon was here? Thanks for covering for me about Stevenson. I owe you, I owe you! When Stevenson marries me, I'll pay you back for everything!"

"*If* Stevenson marries her," said a girl, someone I hadn't met yet, sponging herself from the sink. "As if that will ever happen."

"You're just jealous," Minnie said, "because Lulu found someone serious." She fluttered her eyes at the sink girl, waiting for her false lashes to dry.

Sookie and I sat next to Minnie, cross-legged on her sleeping mat, watching her put on her makeup. "Remember when Duk Hee put lipstick on us?" I asked. "She said that makeup would hide our true faces from American eyes."

Sookie stared at me, frowning. "No," she said. She poked a long finger into Minnie's cosmetics bag. "Can I use this?" she asked, pointing to a frosty blue shadow.

Minnie nodded, but groused, "Next time, get your own."

After I covered as much of my birthmark as I could, I lay back down, letting Myu Myu crawl over my stomach. When the girls called a taxi and began filing out the door, I got to my feet, lifting the baby to my hip.

"What are you doing?" Chinke demanded.

"What do you mean?" I asked.

"You can't bring a kid to the club," she said. "It's against the law."

"I told you: trouble," Sookie sang out as she brushed past me and out the door with Minnie.

"But, but . . ." I bit my lip, not knowing what else to say.

"Don't do that," Chinke scolded. "You'll get lipstick on your teeth."

I smiled despite the knot in my stomach, remembering that

Duk Hee had told me the same thing when Sookie and I were children playing with her makeup. "Your father eats his lips, too," she had laughed at me. "But it doesn't matter so much if a man has no lips."

"I don't know why you're smiling," Chinke complained. "This is a problem."

I stopped smiling. "I don't know what to do," I wailed. "I have to bring her."

"Wait," Chinke ordered, then stuck her head out the door. "Froggie, come here a second."

Froggie clomped to the door on pencil-spiked shoes. "What?" she said. "I'm ready to leave."

"You're a mother," said Chinke. "You know about these things."

Chinke and Froggie frowned down at Myu Myu, who had eaten a small bowl of rice and was happily gumming the collar of my dress.

"Well," she drawled, "I left mine in Itaewon." She tapped her foot, then said, "I know." She rushed into the bathroom and came out with a small green bottle.

"NyQuil?" Chinke said, squinting at the bottle.

"It works," Froggie said. "Give her a spoonful, maybe two, and she'll sleep through the night. No problem."

My hand shook as I took the bottle. "Do I have to leave her?" I rasped. "Alone?"

"What else can you do?" Froggie shrugged, and stomped outside.

Chinke patted my arm. "She'll be all right," she said, but her voice wavered.

I nodded. Twisting open the cap, I sniffed the bottle and recoiled from the fumes.

"Look," Chinke coaxed, "just do it for now, and I'll ask around, see if maybe I can find some girl who married out that can watch your kid for some extra spending money."

She lent me her futon, which I unfolded in a corner. Laying Myu Myu in the center, I forced some of the green medicine into her mouth. She cried and I rocked her until Chinke pulled me up.

"We have to go," she said. "We're already late; we'll be the last ones there."

I pushed some pillows and bags around the futon, blocking Myu Myu in. She whimpered when I stood and I squatted back down to kiss her tears. She blinked. I kissed her eyes closed and this time they stayed shut when I stood.

"Come on, come on," Chinke said, urging me up. "You can visit her during your break."

Yoon's club was only a few blocks away, but not wanting to sweat in our makeup and dresses, we took a taxicab. "They call this 'Korea-moku' Street," Chinke said as the cab stopped in front of a small corner bar.

I could see why. "Korea-moku" street was comprised of a string of dingy-looking bars and Korean restaurants. Signs announcing naked girls and *kalbi* glittered in English and Korean. Across the street, between a club called Rose and a *pornu* shop, I saw a market advertising kimchee and hair perms.

Yoon's bar was modeled on the Korean Club Foxa. "Same same, only mine's bigger. Better. American," Yoon liked to boast. Chinke led me through the curtained door and into the dark, windowless room. I recognized a song that hit the Korea Foxa just before I left—"Spinning Wheel"—and for a moment I was spinning in time and place, unsure of where I was. I panicked, my heart pumping in time to the music, looking around, expecting to see Bar Mama and Kitchen Auntie, and the uni-formed *gomshi* GIs bellying up to the stage with bills in their fists. Chinke hustled me past the bar, where she waved a greet-ing to the bartender, past the stage where Froggie was already rubbing her bared breasts against the pole, and toward the booths.

Instead of a blur of khaki uniforms, the men lounging at the bar and in the booths wore flowered shirts and jeans, T-shirts and shorts, soft-colored pullovers and slacks. In the dim and smoky light, I made out varying degrees of brown skin. Some of the men looked Korean. Or Chinese. Or Japanese. Or some combination with too much mixture of features for my eyes to focus on, to identify. Men who looked like Lobetto.

I spotted Sookie sipping a drink in a booth, squeezed against an enormously large man with pale skin, black hair, slanted eyes. He could have been Japanese or Chinese or white; it was hard to tell because his face was obscured by fat.

Chinke saw where I was looking and said something under her breath.

I shook my head, pointing to my ears. Leaning closer, I asked, "What?" I could barely hear my own voice above the music.

"I said," Chinke yelled, cupping a hand to her mouth, "your friend works fast. She's already latched on to one of our regu-lars." She shook her head and when the music stopped for a change of dancers, she explained: "Fat Danny's been looking for a girlfriend, but most of us can't stand him because he's so fat. You have to balance on that stomach mountain, bouncing up and down on a little pinkie penis—scary! I always think I'm going to slip off and crack my head."

"A shy ugly," I said, but Chinke didn't hear; she was hurrying to the last booth, where Yoon was bent over an opened notebook.

"We're here," Chinke panted.

"You're late," Yoon said without looking up. She scribbled something in her book. "You both owe me forty-five minutes." She snapped her book shut and stood.

"It's almost my time on stage," Chinke said, backing away. "I'm going to go now, get ready . . ."

Yoon ignored Chinke. "I hope you're not late because of that *tweggi* bastard," she sneered.

I bit my lip to silence my retort. Eyes narrowed, I shook my head.

"That's good," Yoon drawled. "I brought you here. I can send you back."

"Yes," I said through gritted teeth.

Yoon stared at me for a few more minutes, then, apparently satisfied, she nodded and jerked her head, beckoning me to follow. We walked past the restrooms and the out-of-order video game, to two doors. "These are the backrooms," she said, "where we take any customers asking for special attention."

"How much?" I asked.

"You broke the first rule," Yoon said. "Never be the first to mention money. If he asks, you say, 'You tell me' and play hard to get until they name the right price."

"Which is?" I prompted.

Yoon pursed her lips. "You need manners," she said. "Tell them they can use the rooms for fifty dollars for half an hour. That's rent to me," she stressed. "Anything extra between you and the customer is between you and the customer."

The first night, I wasn't able to get anyone into the backroom. "Too bad," said Minnie. "That's where the real money is—make them order champagne, *pupus,* stretch out the time with eating and drinking, rack up the commission before you even get on your back."

Sookie had better luck. Fat Danny couldn't stop looking at her, and she stared at him as if he was the most fascinating man she had ever met. At the beginning of the night, I had tried to join them, but Sookie glared at me. "He's mine," she said. Her voice was light, and she laughed as if she were teasing both me and him, but her eyes were hard and I knew that she was warning me off.

Fat Danny had chuckled, his jowls slapping his neck. "Who's your friend, Sookie?" he asked, his English spiced with an accent I came to identify as local to Hawai'i. "You know, there's plenny of me for go around."

Sookie introduced us, and we taught him a few Korean folk songs that we sang in high, girlish voices. He told us a few jokes that I didn't understand, but laughed at anyway. And then I left. I knew Sookie wasn't joking when she had marked him as her own.

I worked the way I always worked, the way Lobetto and Sookie had taught me; I cruised the room, targeting the men who were alone and nursing their drinks. I got them to laugh at my mangled English, giggling over my own stumbling tongue. I let my hands wander, stroking their muscles—or lack of muscles—telling them they were big men but treating them like babies. I even cut up their meat for them, popping the tiny morsels into their mouths. And all the time, I encouraged them to drink, knowing that each beer or vodka tonic or tequila lessened my debt by a few pennies.

After a few hours, when Yoon disappeared into one of the

backrooms with a regular, I left the booths and cornered Chinke in the bathroom. "I'm taking my break," I told her. "How do I get home?"

Chinke's eyes drooped so that they were almost closed. "Don't be stupid," she said, slurring her words slightly; she had spent the last hours bouncing quarters and drinking.

"Come on, Chinke," I said.

She shrugged, then swayed to the sink to fix her makeup. She opened her eyes wide, and with exaggerated care applied her lipstick.

"Chinke," I growled.

"All right, all right." She dug through her purse for a napkin, blotted her mouth, then sketched a quick map on the flip side of the napkin.

I rushed back to the apartment, taking off my shoes to jog most of the way, and found Myu Myu motionless, curled into herself, butt in the air. I tiptoed into the room, bent over her inert form, and waited for her breath. She snuffled, exhaling a long breath, and I released my own. Once I knew she was still alive, that she hadn't been killed off by the NyQuil, I backed away and silently shut the door behind me.

In my scramble to get back to the club before Yoon noticed and penalized me for my absence, I left the map next to the baby. After several minutes of walking, I looked around and realized I didn't know where I was. I slowed, continuing for several blocks—past girls dressed like I was, girls who hooted at me, glared at me, warned me away from their sections of the street—and came to the ocean. I circled back, trying not to panic. I couldn't even remember the name of Yoon's club. I backtracked, turning circles, until I finally recognized a Korean market near Yoon's bar.

"Where were you?" Sookie screeched when I ran in. "The place is closing—are you trying to get us both in trouble?"

"I got lost," I panted, bending down to adjust the straps on my shoes.

Sookie held up her hand. "Don't tell me," she said. "You went back to check on that kid." She shook her head. "I told you she'd mess you up."

I glared at her. "And I told you, I'd deal with it."

"So deal with it," Sookie said.

Chinke hurried over. "Yoon's been asking about you," she warned. "Don't tell her I know where you went, okay?"

Though I expected her to, Yoon never asked where I was. She just glared at me, opened her notebook and scribbled something next to my name.

Despite warnings from the other girls, I continued to use my breaks to check on Myu Myu. Most nights, the NyQuil kept her in deep sleep, and I was able to get back to the club before Yoon started docking my time. Twice, however, Myu Myu was awake and crying so loud I could hear her from the sidewalk outside the apartment building. I comforted her as best as I could, pacing the room while marking the minutes on the clock, then gave her another dose of NyQuil. After a few weeks, I had to start the night with a double dose of NyQuil, though some nights not even that much of the drug would be enough to keep her from crawling around and crying for my return.

One night when I went to check on her, I didn't hear crying as I unlocked the door. At first I was relieved, thinking that Myu Myu had slept since I left her. As I walked toward our corner of the room, however, I heard gagging. I rushed over, stumbling on the pillows I used to confine her. Myu Myu was tangled in the blanket, facedown in the futon and choking. I flipped her over. Eyes rolling up into her head, her body spasmed, limbs clenched and jerking. She heaved, bile bubbling from her throat, suffocating in her own vomit. I cleared out her mouth, placed her over my knees and slapped her back. She coughed, then after a brief moment of quiet, cried. I held her against me, cheek to cheek, crooning.

I refused to leave Myu Myu behind again that night, and brought her with me when I returned to Foxa Hawai'i. Carrying her in a cardboard box cushioned with my clothes, I tried to smuggle her into the kitchen. But Yoon was waiting for me.

"Where have you been?" she screeched.

I ducked my head. "I'm sorry, Mrs. Yoon. This won't happen again."

"Damn right it won't!" She pulled me into one of the backrooms. "Don't think I don't know. You've been disappearing every night! You're working the streets for extra money, aren't you?"

I jiggled the box, hoping Myu would remain quiet despite Yoon's yelling. "No, no, that's not it," I whispered.

"I don't like liars and I don't like cheaters," Yoon screamed, flecking spittle into my face. "You're both. In Korea, I thought you were something special. Here, when you do show up for work, you dance like a robot, nothing like you did in Foxa Korea."

"Half the things I did in Korea are against the law in America," I retorted. But I realized that that might be the only difference; though I was three thousand miles away from Korea, I was still trapped in America Town.

"Phah!" Yoon spat. "Only if you get caught." She eyed the box I carried, distracted from her tirade. "What is that?"

"Just some clothes," I stammered, trying to back away from her.

"This bar is not one storage closet," she scolded, yanking my arm so that I almost dropped the box. "And don't you dare walk away from me. I'm not—"

Startled by the sudden violent motion of her cradle, Myu Myu cried out.

"Don't tell me you brought that fucking *tweggi* to my club! How dare you!" Yoon yelled. "What did I tell you about handling this problem?"

Myu Myu pushed the top of the carton, popping her head out. She whimpered, grasping at my chest.

"I'll handle it," I said.

"Now you've made it my problem." Yoon shoved me toward the door. "And that's it. I've had it with you. Get out. Get out of my club."

I clucked to Myu Myu as Yoon propelled us from the backroom. The other girls and their customers looked up, gawking at me carrying a baby in a box. I caught Sookie's eyes—black and empty, unreadable in the dark—only for a moment before she turned her back on me. "I'll get a baby-sitter for her, Mrs.—"

"Don't bother," Yoon said, shaking her head. "You're not coming back here. You can pay off your debt to me from Korea."

17

I hid in the parking lot, behind the Dumpsters, waiting for closing time. Chinke, Froggie, and Lulu hopped in a taxi after the last of the customers stumbled out the door. Almost an hour later, Sookie walked out with Yoon. "I didn't know what she was up to," Sookie said. "I told her that baby was going to drag her down. I begged her to leave it behind."

Yoon fussed with the lock on the door. "Mmmmmm," she mumbled. Sookie nodded. "I'm a hard worker. You'll see."

Yoon stomped off, walking past the trash bins to get to her car.

I hunched deeper into the shadows, peeking into the box to make sure Myu Myu was still asleep.

Sookie waved as Yoon pulled out of her parking space. Yoon stared out her window without bothering to glance in Sookie's direction. Sookie dropped her hand, her smile fading. "Bitch," she said. She wrapped her arms around her waist and looked out at the street. After a few minutes she smiled, once again raising her hand.

This was what I was waiting for.

The car Sookie waved forward wasn't Yoon's blue sedan, but a white wagon of some sort. Squashed in the driver's seat, his bulk pressed against the wheel so snugly that he had to suck in his stomach to turn into the space next to Sookie, was Fat Danny.

Balancing the box, I leaped forward and almost fell because my legs had fallen asleep. "Sookie," I gasped, stomping the feeling back into my feet.

Sookie whirled around, her mouth opening when she saw me. She gulped air like a fish. "What are you doing here?" she hissed.

"I need you to take me somewhere."

"The only place you're going is Korea." She narrowed her eyes. "You are on your own."

Electricity ran up and down my legs; I had to fight a desperate laugh. I made my voice mean. "If you don't want to end up back in America Town with me, you better help me now."

"Sookie?" Fat Danny leaned his bulk toward the passenger-door window. "You ready?" He grinned when he saw me, waved his hand. The meat under his elbow quivered.

Sookie ignored him. "What are you talking about, Hyun Jin? You can't make me do anything."

I smiled at Fat Danny. "Hello, Danio!" I sang out. "You give me ride tonight?" To Sookie, I asked: "What would Yoon say when she finds out you've been going home with Fat Danny almost every night, cheating her out of her commission?"

"Get in the back," Sookie ordered, opening the back door.

I slid Myu Myu into the rear seat and jumped in. The warm vinyl stuck to my skin even though the windows were down and the night air was cool.

Fat Danny nodded at me. His glasses slid down his nose, revealing the deep indentations where they had rested under his eyes. He pushed them back up with a chunky middle finger. "Sure, sure, Hunni," he said. "Where you like go?"

"Just drive," Sookie snapped. "Get us out of here."

Fat Danny fumbled with the transmission. "Did I come at a bad time?" he asked. "I did like you said, waited for Yoon's blue Caddy for drive away . . ."

"You did good," Sookie assured him, patting his thigh. "That was good thinking. You are so smart."

I rolled my eyes at Sookie's verbal and physical stroking and lifted Myu Myu from the box. She was wet through her clothes and had soaked the contents of the carton as well. Myu Myu's fingers clenched; she clung to me even in sleep.

Sookie turned around and glared at me. "Where are we going?"

"Give me a minute," I said. "Let me think." I rummaged through the box for a dry scrap of cloth, and cleaning Myu as well as I could as she sat on my lap, changed her diaper. When she stirred, I stuck a finger in her mouth until she settled back into sleep.

"Why didn't you use your brain before this moment?" Sookie threw her hands into the air. "I don't get how you're supposed to be so smart. Was it smart to bring the kid to Yoon's place? To America? Even into this world?"

"Talk English," grumbled Fat Danny, interrupting. The rolls on the back of his neck glistened with sweat. I remembered what Froggie had told me about him: she said that she hated going into the backroom with him because of the folds of fat she had to lift just to find his penis; the creases smelled, she said, like the wax you cleaned out of your ears.

"Okay, okay. Hyun Jin say thank you for driving her to—" Sookie broke off, raising her brows at me. Before I could answer, she said, "To the airport. She say, Danio really one nice guy. Handsome, too," she added, giggling. "I say that, not her."

"Airport?" I yelped. "You're doing Yoon's dirty work—sending me back to Korea? Now—just like that?"

Fat Danny glanced at me through the rearview mirror. "You're welcome," he said, smiling. His jowls jiggled with the car's engine. Even from the backseat, I could see the large, glistening pores on his nose, ripe with black oil.

Sookie said, "I never told you you had to go back to Korea. But you do need to leave Hawai'i. Now. Before you drag us both down."

"But—" I gaped. "What about Yoon?"

Sookie grinned, reminding me of her younger self. "I'll tell Yoon you ran." She shrugged. "What could I do? You always were faster than me."

"English," scolded Fat Danny. "Speak English."

I shut my mouth and Sookie squared her body to the front, refusing to look at me. At the airport, Fat Danny missed the departure ramp, so we had to circle around again. Sookie betrayed her impatience with a cluck of her tongue.

"Terrible signs," Fat Danny muttered, then asked: "What airline?"

"Stop," Sookie said. She tapped him on the arm and pointed out the window.

"But if you tell me what airline," he said, "I can take her right—"

"No need." Sookie cut him off. When the car edged the curb, she jumped out, then flung my door open. "Get out," she said in Korean. "I tell her," she added in English for Fat Danny, "'we're here.'"

I shook my head. "I'm not ready," I said, shaken by the danger of possibilities. "Where am I supposed to go? What am I supposed to do?"

Fat Danny turned his head as much as he was able and looked at me from the sides of his small piggy eyes. "We stay at the wrong airline terminal?" He frowned at Sookie, his eyes shrinking even more into the flesh surrounding the sockets. "I told you for ask what airline she flying." He tilted his head back at me. "United? American? TWA?"

"Danio," she sighed. "Can you get that box for Hyun Jin? Please? Thank you." She tapped her foot as she watched Fat Danny strain to push himself free of the front seat. He panted as he grabbed hold of the door frame. Grunting, he hoisted himself onto his feet and paused to press at the sweat along his hairline.

Suddenly, Sookie swooped in and grabbed Myu Myu from my lap. Myu wailed, gripping my shirt and tangling a fist into my hair. I scooted out quickly. "Good," Sookie said. "Now disappear. This is the only chance you're going to get."

"What about you?" I asked. "Come with me."

She grimaced at Fat Danny, who was tugging the carton of clothes from the back. "I'm better off here, taking my chance on him. He can pay my way out from under Yoon. Then maybe I'll start my own bar. I've seen enough to know how it all works."

"Yeah?" I nodded. "I can help."

She stared at me, her face blank, her expression flat. "No."

I studied Myu Myu, dangling from Sookie's arms. With both of them looking at me, I realized for the first time that they had the same eyes. "I don't want to leave you," I whispered.

Sookie gazed at Myu Myu, cupping her cheek in the same way she told me she had touched me when I was born. Then she thrust the baby into my arms so quickly I almost dropped her. "How much cash you got?"

Picturing the wad of bills rolled in the money purse at my waist, I said, "Two hundred. Maybe."

"Fat Danny," Sookie yelled, leaning into the front seat. "Pass my purse." Fat Danny grunted as he tipped over the front seat to nudge Sookie's purse toward her. Bent over, the bulk of his body wedged in the door frame, Fat Danny wheezed and sucked in his breath when he tried to back out.

"Never mind." Sookie rolled her eyes as she reached into the car and plucked up her handbag. She pulled out a roll of money and handed it to me. "Here's another hundred. You should have enough for a ticket to the mainland. I heard L.A.'s good. Lots of Koreans there. Lots of work."

Suspicious, I glared at her. "Is this a trap?" I said.

"What?" Sookie said. She pushed the money on me. "Just take it. Cut us both free."

I stared at her, slowly reaching for the money. "What's in it for you?" I asked. "You never gave me anything in your life."

Sookie snorted. "You don't think I ever gave you anything?" she said. She looked at Myu Myu and then at me.

"Myu doesn't count," I said quickly. "Because you didn't want her in the first place."

"I saw you come into this world, Hyun Jin," Sookie said, "with my handprint on you." She held her hand up, as if to touch my face, but it stilled inches from my cheek and then dropped. "And I knew you were mine. I would have done anything for you."

"Right," I said, scoffing.

"It's true," Sookie said, and I almost believed her. "Maybe you never realized what I was willing to give because you were too busy trying to think of what you could take."

"Where you want it?" Fat Danny huffed, and without waiting for an answer, he dropped the box at my feet. "Could you hurry it up?" He lumbered toward the car, shoved his body behind the wheel, and turned up the air conditioner. Even though he positioned the jets on his purpling face, most of the cold air flew out the open doors.

"We just saying goodbye," Sookie said, trying to placate him.

"Then say it in English," Fat Danny wheezed, trying to suck in the cooling air. "Li' this: Good. Bye."

"Wait." I grabbed Sookie as she bent toward the door. "That's it?" I said, twisting her arm. "You can't leave me like this. I won't let you."

"Je-ez Louise!" Fat Danny griped. "What she want now?"

Sookie wrenched away and slid into the seat, but kept the car door open. "Fat Danny," she said. She used English, but I know she spoke to me. "When I was little girl, my mama tell me one fox story. This fox had good life in—what you call it? plenty trees, grass, wild animals—we call *sup*. But this little fox not happy. She jealous—jealous of the humans in the village. She all the time cry: 'I want warm house and clothes and shoes on feet.'"

Fat Danny groaned. "Sookie," he pleaded. "Let's go. I no feel too good." He tugged at his collar, stained with a ring of sweat. He closed his eyes.

She reached behind her without looking, patted him on the thigh, and continued her story. "Little Fox decide she will turn herself human. So she make like a human girl and sat in road until somebody find her. One farmer, he find and take her home and love her like daughter. The fox girl try to live like people, but she have secret: animal hunger.

"One night, she cannot stand it. She eat the farmer's pig and chickens and still she hungry. She eat his goat. Still she hungry. She have to eat the farmer. 'But I loved you,' cried the farmer. The fox, she cry, too, and say, 'But I'm hungry.'"

"What kine story is that?" complained Fat Danny. "Never even have one happy ending."

Sookie slammed the door shut as I jumped out of the way. She rolled down the window. "Fat Danny," she said, "only Americans believe in happy endings."

I stared at Sookie. "I don't get it. What does that story have to do with anything? What does that have to do with you leaving me?"

"Do you feel sorry for the fox, Hyun Jin?" she asked.

"I don't know," I said, irritated. "Sure. If that's the right answer, I'll feel sorry for her. Maybe that fox girl had a family to feed or something."

Sookie shook her head. "The people still get eaten," she said. "I'm changing the ending before I get eaten."

"Huh?" I said.

She smiled thinly. "You're the fox, Hyun Jin. Making yourself what you're not to get more than you need. In the end, you'll destroy yourself and everyone around you."

I gasped. "You're a bitch, Sookie, and you always were."

Her lips flattened and she looked out the front window. "The problem with you, Hyun Jin," she said, "is that you cannot see people as they really are. You've always thought I was like you."

"Aren't you, Sookie?" I asked, and I truly didn't know. "You're my sister."

Fat Danny frowned, looking from Sookie to me. "Watchu saying?" He tapped Sookie's shoulder with a beefy paw. "What did she say?"

"Nothing," Sookie snapped. "She just say, 'Goodbye.' Go."

She turned a crank and her window rolled up, closing her in, and for a brief moment, I saw our faces pressed together, merged in a trick of light and reflection.

Then Fat Danny stepped on the gas pedal and the car jerked forward. I watched the back of Sookie's head, waiting for a last look, a final acknowledgment. There wasn't any.

Juggling Myu Myu on one hip, I lifted my box of clothes and walked through the glass doors to the ticket counter. I scanned the list of cities, wondering how far into the forest three hundred dollars would take me.

The ticket agent looked at me blankly. "Where?" she asked again.

I took a deep breath, concentrating on my pronunciation. "Wai-Ma-Na-Lo."

"Waimanalo," she repeated, tilting her head so that the over-size orchid above her ear appeared about to topple her over. "Not Waimea? Not Wailuku?"

I shook my head, and gesturing to the pad and pencil behind her desk, I wrote the address from memory: 94-729 Waiku-panaha Street, Waimanalo, Hawai'i, U.S.A.

"Ma'am," the ticket lady said, "you don't need an airplane ticket to go there."

Glaring, I snapped, "I can't fly there myself."

"No need." She smiled and pointed out the door. "Take a taxi. No *hu-hu.*"

"Hungh," I grumped, sounding like Lobetto when he thought I was acting like an idiot. I snuggled Myu into the cardboard box, then lugged the thing to the taxi station.

The taxidriver whistled between his teeth when I showed him the address. "Long drive, this." He eyed me. "About forty dollars long."

Lips pressed into a thin line, I nodded.

"Okay, then." The driver jumped out of his seat and popped open the trunk. "Let me get that box for you."

"Wait!" I set the box down, opened the lid, and lifted Myu to my shoulder. "Okay, then," I said, repeating his words.

"That's one baby in there," the driver said. He shook his head, gaping at me, then threw the box into the trunk.

Before starting up the car, the driver opened his glove compartment and pulled out a mapbook. "W-w-w," he murmured. "Wai-wai-wai." He flipped through the pages, using his fingers to sight the longitudinal lines of the grid. "Got it!" he announced, and pulled away from the curb.

I knew this was the same route that Yoon took on the day she picked Sookie and me up from the airport; there was only one major road into town from the airport. But the trip was different in the dark. I couldn't see the ramshackle houses on the hillside, the strings of laundry hanging to dry from squat, gray apartments, the broken pavement and tenement housing under the freeway.

Instead, I hurtled through a darkness punctuated by the occasional exclamation of a street lamp, across an unknown landscape. The driver took us up a cliff, the road winding around the mountain's lush hair of verdant green, then into and through the hole in its belly. "This the Like Like," the driver intoned, his voice hollow. The shrieking spin of the taxi's wheels echoed through the long tube of the tunnel.

When we emerged on the other side, I let go of the breath I hadn't been aware I was holding. Below me stretched the curve of the ocean, white-capped waves glinting in the light from the thin smile of the moon sitting low on the horizon. We drove down the mountain toward the water, the road narrowing from four lanes to two, then, finally, as we cut inland, to one that snaked deeper into the brush, weaving through vine-covered poles. We encountered a closed-for-business Jack-in-the-Box— the giant dome of its white-headed clown seeming to pop up on the corner out of nowhere—then continued on, past a few paddocks fencing in a couple of bony horses or two or three wiry goats, past small wooden homes more than partially engulfed by the wild growing things.

At a sign that read ROCKY ROAD EGG FARM, the taxi driver turned a corner and stopped. "This here Waikupanaha Street."

I nodded, trying not to breathe in the thick stench of manure. My eyes watered and I gasped, "Keep going, but slow." I stared out the window, straining to spot anything—post, building, mailbox—with numbers.

The driver eased the car into a slow crawl up the street. He turned on the radio and it wailed, "She's a ho-o-o-onky tonk woman! Gimme, gimme, gimme some honky—" before he clicked it off with a grunt. "I just don't get this kind of music nowadays," he complained. "I mean, is that supposed to be a love song?"

"Stop!" I yelled. "This is it!"

The driver braked hard and though we were traveling only about ten miles per hour, it was fast enough to send me sliding off the seat at the sudden stop. Myu Myu squawked, smashed between my chest and the front seat. "Sorry, sorry," muttered the cabbie. He squinted out the window. "You sure you want out here?"

I followed his gaze. The numbers 94-729 were painted on a wooden board and fastened to a chain-link fence. "I think so," I said, then more firmly: "Yes." I pulled Myu to my face, kissing her forehead, then opened the car door.

The driver set my box down underneath the address sign, then helped me out. "You got everything?" he asked as I handed him two twenties. "Sure you can manage?"

I nodded, already bending to settle Myu Myu into the box. She whimpered, and I jiggled the box. She rolled onto her back. I shifted my arms, adjusting to her moving weight, and left the lid of the box open so she could see my face. "It's going to be all right," I told her. "We're going to hide out here for a while."

Listening to the song of the crickets, which filled my ears in tandem with the beating rhythm of my heart, I followed the fence until I found the gate. Balancing the box against one knee, I lifted the latch and started up the gravel road. There was just enough morning light to make out the long, looming shadows of black-screened hothouses on either side of the path. I edged close enough to one of them to peer through the mesh into a jungled world. Plants in baskets hung from the ceiling, their twisting, groping tendrils long enough to sweep the floor. Palms grew up from the ground, leafy fingers scratching at the sides and tops of the hothouse. And on the rows of tables that filled the enclosure, hundreds of potted plants in various stages of infancy stretched their heads, limbs straining, toward the shadowed sky.

"Hallooo!" The greeting was almost immediately drowned out by the baying of dogs. Three large mongrels bounded forward, barking as they circled me. A smaller dog with long, matted fur ran toward my ankles, teeth bared and nipping.

I wrapped my arms around the box, keeping my body between it and the dogs as much as I could. Myu Myu whimpered at their noise and burrowed under my clothes. I kept my eyes on the dogs, afraid to turn my back to them.

"Shoo, shoo! Comet, Cupid, go on, you mangy mutts." A flannel-sleeved arm swung at the dogs. They dodged the blows but slunk away. "Can I help you?"

I looked up into a craggy face, weathered by the sun despite the large straw hat perched above it. "Yes, I . . . uh." I frowned into the person's face, unsure if this was a man or a woman, unsure of how I should address him or her.

The person smiled, revealing bright blue front teeth, and stuck out a gloved hand. "I'm Geraldine, the big boss. You can call me Gerry." The fingers of the glove were also stained blue. "Oh, excuse me." Geraldine, the-big-boss-Gerry, stuck the glove into her mouth and tugged it off. Grinning around her glove, she offered her bared hand.

"My name Hyun Jin," I told her, touching her palm. "I looking for my uncle. Synang Man Lee. He here?" I glanced around the nursery, almost expecting him to appear, summoned by the commotion.

Gerry frowned. "Singhand, Sigmund, whatever, Lee? No one here by that name."

"I don't understand," I stammered, my knees buckling. The

box tilted as inside Myu Myu slid from one corner to the other. "I got, my father got a letter from him. Synang Man Lee. This address."

"Lee. Lee. Lee." Woman slapped her glove across the thighs of her baggy jeans. "Korean guy?" When I nodded, she shouted, "Oh! Down the street a ways, at 789, there's one Lee, a FOB from Korea. Ziggy Lee."

I laughed, embarrassed at remembering the address wrong and dizzy with relief. I turned to walk back down the path, already constructing what I would tell him: how my mother always talked about him, her favorite cousin; how she sobbed when I left her, making me promise to look him up; how she knew that he would look after me and my child.

Then Gerry called out, "But he's not there anymore. Good riddance, I say. Handsome buggah, but turned into one *pakalolo* head, him and his friends."

"Not there?" I repeated. The woman's face swayed in front of me, back and forth like one of the palms in her hothouses.

"Went to California about five, maybe six, years ago. San Francisco, I think," she said. Her words, like the crickets' chirping, sounded both far away and right in my head at the same time. "Strange guy. Whoever heard of a Oriental trying for find hisself? Thought that was for those *haole* hippies."

The box slipped out of my hands, crashed to the ground with a thump. Myu Myu tumbled out, skidding across gravel, screaming—the high-pitched keening of a wounded animal. The dogs charged forward, frenzied and howling, that little hairy one chasing its own tail and yip-yip-yipping; Gerry shouted, an ongoing siren: "Oh my God! Comet, Cupid, get away! Oh my God! Back, Blitzen! It's a baby! No, Vixen! Oh my God! A baby!" And then it was as if those long-limbed vines in the hothouses burst through the seams, whipped around my head, and yanked. Eyes rolling up into my head, I dropped to all fours, ear pressed to earth, and heard the world singing like the crickets, with that in-and-out beat of the tides, of the blood in our veins, of the panting of the fox. Then everything stopped, went dead, and I knew that it was all over. I had nowhere else to go. I was run to the ground.

We play a game, Myu Myu and I. I wrap a scarf around her eyes—"No peeking!" I scold as she giggles—and place a map of the United States under her fingers. She wiggles her fingers and laughs as if she is tickling herself.

"Myu Myu, point!" I tell her.

From under the cloth, she bites her lip, then pouts. "My name is not Myu Myu."

I scramble, trying to remember her name of the week. "Macy?"

The girl who is not Myu Myu today shakes her head.

"Malia?"

She shakes her head again, then sighs. "I am Maya," she says reproachfully, as if she is deeply hurt by my careless memory but forgives me anyway. Then she sends her hands skittering over the map. The whirlwind settles on a bile-colored square. She peeks under the blindfold.

"What'd you land on this time?" Gerry calls out from the sink where she is peeling and mashing fresh stems of aloe into a poultice for my hands. The skin between my fingers has started to flake off again, exposing the vulnerable pink of fresh meat.

"You gotta wear gloves," Gerry is forever scolding me when it comes time to tend the dieffenbachia. But the rubber gloves make my hands feel like paws, the fingers too thick and clumsy to pluck the wilted leaves from the healthy plant.

Maya taps the map. "Read it! Read it!" she demands. "Where are we going?"

"New Jer-sey," I sound out and shrug. Saturday we will visit the Waimanalo Book Mobile, poring over its current selection of travel guides and encyclopedias, requesting the books—if any—that feature this state. Gerry will read aloud to us, and we will learn about the state's population, its capital city, its flower, and its bird. By week's end, we will have toured the "hot spots," the museums and the zoos, the arboretums and the occasional Mystery Mansion or dead author's home. By week's end, Myu Myu will have gotten to know that piece of America, will have made it her own, and will have moved on to a new name.

"Hmmmmm," says Gerry. "Never been to Jersey before." After five years of this weekly game, Myu Myu has yet to land on a place where Gerry has visited.

The girl sticks her tongue between her lips and blows what she calls a "cherry." "Have you ever been *anywhere,* Tutu

Gerry?" Because she giggles as she says this, and because Gerry is elbow-deep in cactus sap, Maya gets away with her impertinence.

"Las Vegas," Gerry snaps back. "I could tell you stories about that place." She side-eyes Myu, then presses her lips together primly. "When you're older."

"Myu Myu," I growl, warning her. Though Gerry says she's made us family, *hanai*-ing Myu as her granddaughter, I still worry that she might turn on us, throwing us out of this apartment she constructed at the back of hothouse number three. True to herself, Myu ignores me, humming as she studies the map.

Each time we sit at the kitchen table to play this game, I prepare myself for the possibility that the place of the week will be Maryland, where Myu Myu's grandfather lives. Or Los Angeles, where her father dreams of one day seeing her with stars at their feet and flocks of elephants flying overhead. I tell myself that when she points to these places, it will be my signal to begin to tell her about the place she was born in and the people she was born to. But I am afraid to bring those secrets to life. Right now, we are still hidden, underground and safe.

Slipping the scarf down around her neck, Myu Myu suddenly looks serious. She stares at my face, her forehead wrinkled in concentration. I try to turn away, thinking she will see me as the rest of the world does: ugly.

Myu Myu cups my chin in her hands to keep me still. "Your face is a map, Mama," she announces, breathless, solemn. "Your head is the world!" Then, blinking, she explodes with laughter, spraying me with spittle. "I pick to go . . . there." She waggles her fingers and points to a black pit on my temple.

Relieved, I tickle her. "Well, then your face is a map, too," I say. And I am struck by the obvious truth of my words. Her face *is* a map—an inheritance marked by all who were once most important in my life. I have caught familiar but fractured reflections of Lobetto and Sookie, Duk Hee and even my father. They have traversed time and distance, blood and habit, to reside within the landscape of this child's body.

"No, silly," she answers, smoothing her hands over her cheeks. "I'm clean."

"You think so?" I tease, grabbing her arms. "Then what's this?" I lean over the table and lick at a patch of imaginary dirt on her cheek. "And this?" I say, as, slurping drool, I move to her chin.

"Gross!" she squeals, wrestling away from me. She leaps to her feet, her breath coming in staccato gasps, as she tries to decide whether to run away or attack.

And for a quick moment, it's Sookie I see—sloe-eyed and wild-haired—her presence evoked by the power of my memories. "Sookie?" I whisper, feeling shaky, needing to hear her name. I close my eyes, and when I open them, I see my baby again, hovering over me, her face crinkled with worry. Like the fox spirit—the hunter and guardian of knowledge—this child possesses the gift of transformation.

When I smile up at her, she clucks her tongue. "I told you," she says, "my name is Maya."

"Maya, Mary, Mushu, whoever you are today, here." Gerry plops a bowl of her homemade gel onto the table. "Put that on your mama."

When I hold my hands out, Myu puckers her lips and dips a delicate finger into the aloe. Dabbing at my shredded palms, she rubs a rough patch, and a thin ribbon of translucent skin peels away from my hand. "Ewww," she grimaces. But she raises my fingers to her lips. "Does it hurt?" she asks, and kisses each one.

I suck in my breath, from the pain of it, from the joy of it. Inhaling, breathing her in, I know with absolute clarity that the best of Sookie, of Duk Hee, of Lobetto, of me—everything we could have hoped for and wished to be—is here and has always been here under the skin, in the bone and in the blood, in this jewel of a girl who holds the world in her hand and sees it, loves it, as her own.

—